"Kis-Lev has created the ki...
superficial, silly, or a plot sideli...
real than anything else. It will m

"Wonderful... A wry, sharply observed tale of both heroism and coming-of-age-story during one of the darkest times in humanity."

—Nadia Joels, *The Bookreview Club*

"Compulsively readable... Kis-Lev establishes himself as a distinctively contemporary literary voice. His dialogue resounds, and his humor gives texture to the prose."

—Dr. John Vitals, author and speaker

"Biting, brilliant exploration of a female friendship from the eyes of a sensitive man. And though *The Two Marias* focuses on young women, readers need be neither young nor female in order to enjoy it..."

—Alison Kahn, *Peace For The Future*

"Riveting... More than an exploration of friendship, this novel is about what happens when the things we take for granted slip away and we are forced to test our inner strength."

—Joan Kelvin, author *The Secret Inside*

"The Two Marias is a slim, sometimes piercing novel... Kis-Lev's hyperaware voice lends the story poignancy and shades of relatability."

—Laila Hoja, *The Book Reviewer*

"Set in WWII war-torn Europe, young Helena and Maria struggle to do what is right, in a world where cruelty is the norm. Never boring... this book is a pageturner."

—Joel Springfield, speaker and author

"The novel's depiction of the dynamics of friendship—how there's often affection and admiration mixed with disappointment and frustration—is uniquely authentic."

—Dan Klein, *The Last Opinion*

"Kis-Lev's prose reads like the voice of the charmingly blunt friend you wish you had; his observations are sensitive and insightful."

—Gillian T. Harold, Harold Books

"Comedy and pathos are braided together with extraordinary skill in a haunting novel... riveting intensity and originality"

—*Daily Preacher*

"Clever and suspenseful... Kis-Lev has his finger on the old-school girlfriends' zeitgeist... and this riveting tale will make older readers fondly recall the days when kids got in trouble for passing (print) notes in class."

—Maria Velázquez, coach and trainer

"Kis-Lev captures the complexities, naiveté and angst of teenage girls so well my stomach was in knots. What had happened to Helena Goldstein, the Jewish girl in Nazi Germany? You'll find yourself staying up all night to find out."

—Aven K. Lint, author and speaker

"I couldn't believe this was based on a true story. I cried and laughed. Kis-Lev does a fine job of building suspense and creating characters, notably Maria and Helena, whom the target audience—both adults and older teens—will care about and empathize with."

—Maria von Klaus, *Der Tage*

"Fast-paced and suspenseful... a page-turning story of friendship mixed with a bit of a thriller. Shines a light on the power of true friendship in times of external challenges."

—Jo Levi, *The Reviewer*

"A tale of elaborate mystery intertwined with the tenderness of a mother's love, *The Two Marias* exudes warmth at every turn... Gripping and uplifting, it is a true pageturner."

—Mira Hudson, *The Life of Mira*

"*The Two Marias* is interested—almost single-mindedly so—in the friendship between Maria and her friend Helena, two young women who are in the process of discovering that life as an adult in war-torn Europe is vastly different than it was as teenagers in the 1930s. *The Two Marias* is refreshing in part because it's hugely uninterested in the surrounding characters and focuses on the main two characters, which you are bound to fall in love with…"

—Jane Silva, author and columnist

"Kis-Lev is a gifted documentarian… The novel is filled with keenly observed details, especially about the role that outside events plays in his characters' lives."

—Daniel J. Okla, The Jewish Daily

"There is a sentimental delight in reading *The Two Marias* and its roller coaster ride of friendship facing existential threats. In the end, Kis-Lev draws a vivid and convincing portrait of a true friendship."

—Bill J. Harry, Harry Books

"A sharp, funny and uplifting exploration of a 70 years-old story about true female friendship."

—Janice Kline, speaker and author

"I couldn't believe this was written by a man… It is admirably, readably realistic—he knows these girls and the world they live in in the most profound way… Kis-Lev nails the complex blend of love, loyalty, and courage that binds female friends."

—Jill Abrahamson, "The Weekly Bite"

"*The Two Marias* is a moving, focused, very funny novel, told with a calming amount of perspective by a trustworthy, precise voice. It is intimate and insightful regarding two decades of life (early teens to twenties), and on the topics of endurance (both emotional and physical) in Nazi Occupied Poland."

—Loreta Smith, Smith Press

"Truth-teller Jonathan Kis-Lev hurls his heart and his mind into this touching, bittersweet tale of the strongest friendship you'll ever read about, based on a true and riveting story."

—Cloe Dutton, author, entrepreneur, Dutton Wear

"Kis-Lev traces the lives of his subjects with unswerving candor and compassion… In his telling, neither evil nor good is banal; and if the latter doesn't always triumph, it certainly inspires."

—Damien Tate, author and artist

"As chronicled… with unblinking accuracy, their agonies are appalling to contemplate, their stories of survival and friendship under duress enthralling to hear."

—Michelle Hannover, speaker

"Haunting account of bravery, friendship, and endurance."

—Nicholas Hill, founder, Hill Solutions LTD

"Compelling… Kis-Lev weaves into his suspenseful, detailed narrative myriad moments of friendship, challenges, and valor."

—Danielle Grable, *The Danielle Show*

"Heightened by electrifying and staggering detail, Kis-Lev's riveting story stands as a luminous testament to the indomitable will to survive and the unbreakable bonds of friendship."

—Drake Eakin, Eakin Bloomberg

"Even history's darkest moments can be illuminated by spectacular courage, such as courage that Righteous Among the Nations Medal Recipient, Maria Bozek-Nowak, displayed toward her childhood friend Helena Goldstein… The author has created a detailed account, sensitively rendered… of human triumph."

—Meg Mariner

"The first complete account of these extraordinary women and, incredibly, over 70 years later we are still learning new and

riveting truths about the courage of people during WWII…
An important new perspective… Careful research and
sensitive retelling."

—Abraham Miseler, author, *Thinking Different*

"As Kis-Lev delves deeply into the two women's fight for
survival, his narrative seamlessly comes together in order to
share a significant part of history whose time has come to be
heard."

—Steve Gilbert, The Writer's Life

"A miraculous story about friendship and the will to overcome
extraordinary heartache and loss. A small wonder of a book."

—Michal Sender, The Sender Report

"A book so simple, so seemingly effortless, that it's almost
perfect."

— Joanna Berlinger, author, *The Night's Sorrow*

"The whole work is seamless, compelling, and memorable—
impossible to put down; difficult to forget."

— Hue Night, author, *The Corner of My Heart*

"Humorous, heartwarming, often nostalgic, *The Two Marias*
captures the spirit of true friendship, one that will bring both
laughter and tears to your eyes. Guaranteed."

—Alisa Bloomberg, *The Reviewer*

"Fabulous… It is seldom that I read a book that continuously
draws me through it with interest. Though I avoid books
about the Holocaust out of discomfort for the empathy I have
for Holocaust victims, I was impressed with this uplifting and
inspiring story."

—Dennis Clark, *This Week*

Published in the United States by Goldsmith Press LLC.

Editor: Tania von-Ljeshk
Cover photograph: Scott Durham
Profile photograph: Doug Ellis Photography
Cover design: Slava "Inkjet" Noh

THE TWO MARIAS

A True Tale About a True Friendship

Jonathan Kis-Lev

Dedicated to the memory of the
Goldstein and Bozek families

THIS EDITION INCLUDES:

PART ONE:
THE TWO MARIAS: THE NOVEL

Based on a true story

Maria stood in the train station.

It was finally spring.

The war was now over. How long she had been waiting for this moment?

Her hands fidgeted with her purse. She bit her lip. She missed her friend so intensely.

And now she was finally coming. Maria sighed, "The poor girl…"

Who could have imagined things would turn out this way?

Taking a deep breath, she bit her lip again. She shook her head disapprovingly at herself. "You should stop this," she thought, "don't bite your lip that way. It's not ladylike!"

She folded her hands together. "Oh God, bring her here already!"

At the same time, on the train approaching the border into the country, a young woman wearing a green dress sat quietly by the window, her thoughts wandering.

It was over.

The war was over.

And now, she could finally return to her beloved city. To her beloved city square, to the famous fountain in front of the city hall. To the many doves there. To the sound of the trams moving slowly on the old streets. To the theatre. To the ballet.

But more than anything, she missed her friend.

The train stopped at the border.

She sat up as border police officers passed in the aisle. She smiled at the officer and handed him her identification papers. Before the war, she knew nothing about these things. One ID was fine. But nowadays, one had to carry multiple forms of identification.

The officer looked at the photo and then at her, "Maria?"

She nodded.

"Date of birth?"

"January 22nd," she said calmly, "1920."

"And what was the purpose of your stay abroad?"

"The war," she murmured.

The officer said nothing and proceeded to look at her birth certificate, her baptism certificate, and her high school graduation diploma. He then nodded and handed them back to her.

She nodded back and put the documents in her file, and tucked it into the front of her suitcase; these very documents saved her so many times in the past three years.

But soon she wouldn't need them any more.

Soon she could return to herself. Her *real* self.

She gazed at the views of the countryside through the window. In a few hours, she'd be there. Her beloved city.

She would see her best friend again. Her savior.

She smiled to herself, gazing at the fields outside. To think, she did not want to be seated next to Maria in class in the first place! How different things could have turned out.

"Helena!"

The harsh tone of Mrs. Schlesinger startled Helena from her daydreams. "Yes, Mrs. Schlesinger!"

"You are going to sit near Maria," Mrs. Schlesinger said and pointed at the desk in the front of the class.

Helena dreaded this day. For the past two weeks, since the school year began, she sat next to Gisele, who was funny, witty and beautiful. The two of them sat at the back of the classroom near the window, where Helena could stare out at the sky. She loved looking outside, especially during boring science lessons, and math lessons, and all that nonsense.

She sighed, took her textbooks, and walked to the front of the class, sitting down next to the shy girl,

Maria.

Maria stared down at the desk, smiling sheepishly at Helena without looking at her. Trying to smile back, Helena's face formed a grimace, her eyebrows frowning. She sighed. This would be like sitting in a graveyard, she thought.

Mrs. Schlesinger continued to assign new seating arrangements for the students, as she had promised on the first day of the school year. Helena looked around the class. She was devastated. She tried her best to make a good impression, hoping the severe-looking Mrs. Schlesinger wouldn't separate her and Gisele. She had known Gisele since elementary school. Gisele was fun, and funny too.

But now Gisele looked forlorn as a new girl, Sofia, was placed in Helena's old seat.

Helena sighed a little too loud. Mrs. Schlesinger gave her a fierce look. Helena lowered her eyes at once.

When Mrs. Schlesinger finished arranging the classroom, the class was quiet. Helena shook her head. Mrs. Schlesinger didn't have a clue what she was doing.

During the break Helena tried to change things. She went to Mrs. Schlesinger in the teacher's room. Mrs. Schlesinger gave her one quick look and said, "Not a chance, Helena!"

"But Mrs. Schlesinger!" Helena pleaded.

"These are the new seating assignments! You would be wise to learn some manners and discipline from Maria!"

Helena tried, "But... *please*, Mrs. Schlesinger!"

But the teacher turned her back to her. The conversation was over.

Feeling desperate, Helena went to Gisele, who was waiting at their favorite spot - the bench in the school yard they had claimed as their own over the past two weeks.

Gisele was also depressed. Her desk was now four rows apart from Helena.

"Perhaps," Helena said, "we could get your parents and my parents to speak to Mrs. Schlesinger?"

Gisele shook her head, "It won't work."

They were silent.

Then Helena said, "What do you know of that girl she put me with?"

"Who? *Maria?*" Gisele asked, "I guess she's... well... I don't really know, I never noticed her before..."

"Exactly," Helena sighed.

Weeks passed and Helena noticed how difficult it was to look out of the window from her new position. Mrs. Schlesinger would tap on her shoulder, or worse, call out her name to get her attention. She was all too *visible*. All too in the *front* of the class, along with all the bookworms. She *hated* it.

To make matters worse, the mute classmate sharing her desk, the Maria girl, was *always* listening and taking notes. She continually nodded but never said a word. She never raised her hand, though Helena noticed she always wrote the correct answers in her exercise book as if testing herself before the answer was revealed.

It drove Helena crazy. One day, after the bell rang, before heading into the yard with Gisele and the others, she asked Maria, "Why don't you raise your hand?"

"Excuse me?" Maria mumbled, looking down.

"Mr. Kissinger asked the square root question and you knew the answer!"

"No I… didn't…"

"Liar," Helena said, "I saw you writing it in your notebook!"

Maria's face reddened. No one ever called her a liar!

But Helena raised her eyebrows knowingly and left the classroom.

Maria stayed frozen in her chair. She was stunned. She gulped and opened the biology book. She wanted to go over her homework and make sure she had done everything correctly.

It was an unlikely friendship. They didn't have anything in common. Helena was perhaps the most popular. Maria was perhaps the least.

During one particular literature lesson, Mrs. Schlesinger asked who would like to read the poem. Helena—happy about the class *finally* becoming interesting—volunteered.

Mrs. Schlesinger asked her to stand in front of the class, and Helena jumped off her seat, grabbed the book and began reading excitedly:

"Stars circle round thy head," she raised her hand above, and then lowered it, "and at thy feet surges the sea, upon whose hurrying waves," she raised her hand again drawing a large arch, "a rainbow glides before thee, cleaving the clouds!"

Maria sat up, mesmerized. All the students were.

"Whate'er thou look'st upon is thine!" Helena continued, "Coasts, ships, men, mountains, cities, all belong to thee!" She shouted, "Master of Heaven as earth, it seems as naught," her voice suddenly turned into a whisper, "could equal thee in glory…!"

She grinned, bowed, and went back to her seat. Everyone cheered.

"Well done," smiled Mrs. Schlesinger.

Later when the bell rang, Maria said to Helena, "That was beautiful."

Helena was somewhat startled by her mute classmate speaking to her. "Uh? Oh, thank you…"

"Have you…" Maria continued, as Helena's eyes grew bigger, noticing this was now the *second* sentence initiated by the mute, "Have you…" Maria searched for words, "You demonstrated so beautifully, Helena, the *sea* and the *waves*… Have you ever *been* to the sea?"

Helena bellowed, "Why, of course! Every summer!" She looked at Maria, "Don't tell me you *haven't*…?"

Maria looked down. Helena was puzzled. What else was there to do in the summer *but* go to a summer house by the sea?

Gisele tapped her on the shoulder. "Are we going or what?"

When they were in the yard, Helena whispered,

"Could you believe it, Gisele? I think Maria has never been to the sea!"

Gisele shrugged her shoulders.

"But," Helena exclaimed, "not going to the sea? What else can she do each summer?"

Gisele smiled, "Not everyone goes to a summer house, Helena!"

"But *you* do!" Helena exclaimed.

"Yes, but not *everyone*." She lowered her voice. "Maria's father works for the railroad, and I heard that her mother works in some factory, you see? They don't have much money…"

Helena's eyes grew bigger, "But she's so… *dignified*… and *smart*…*!*"

"Well," Gisele shook her head, "that's because she's a bookworm. But," she whispered, "she's very poor. Haven't you seen how her lunch is always only bread and a boiled egg, nothing else?"

Helena was baffled.

Gisele laughed, "Close your mouth. You'll swallow a fly."

The following lesson was biology. Helena didn't care about chromosomes and genes. She wrote in her notebook, "Have you NEVER been to the sea? Seriously??"

She slid her notebook over to Maria.

Maria glanced at the notebook and quickly looked back at Mr. Kissinger. She gently pushed Helena's notebook away.

Helena was stunned. Did that girl just push her notebook away? Did she just refuse to *talk* to her? That couldn't be! She took her pen and drew a big question mark in the center of her notebook, then slid it again toward Maria.

Maria gulped. She bit her lip. She didn't want to miss a word from Mr. Kissinger's lecture. But, she had to admit, she already knew everything he was saying. He was just repeating what was in the textbook. She had read it. She knew it.

"No," she wrote on her own notebook. She slowly moved it for Helena to see. Her heart beat faster. She felt like she was committing a crime.

"SERIOUSLY?" Helena wrote in capital letters. "What do you do in the SUMMER???"

Maria bit her lip. She kept looking at Mr. Kissinger, her heart pounding, and wrote, in her small handwriting, "babysitting." She *wanted* to write, "I take care of my young brother and sister," but it would have taken too much time.

Helena was puzzled and whispered, "Really…?"

"Helena and Maria!" Mr. Kissinger exclaimed, "To the principal's office! Right now!"

A murmur passed through the class. Maria's eyes widened. Had he just called her name?

Mr. Kissinger wrote them a small note and handed it to Helena with gusto, "Go!"

Helena stood up, her chin held high, and walked

out of the class.

Maria, wide-eyed, looked at Mr. Kissinger in utter horror.

He raised his eyebrows, "You heard me!"

Maria's legs felt heavy, her knees buckling. She got up and slowly walked out of class. This had *never* happened to her. Never!

The school's secretary told the two girls to sit and wait in the hallway.

Maria thought of her mother. What would she think? How would she respond?

She began to weep.

Helena put her arm around Maria's shoulder, "Hey! Don't cry, it will be fine…!"

Maria's shoulder quivered as she buried her face in her hands.

"Wait…" Helena said slowly, "is this your first time?"

Maria nodded her head vigorously.

"Oh…" Helena said, "don't worry about it, they just write something in a book, and it's all fine. We'll be back in class in a moment."

Maria shook her head, "I shouldn't… I shouldn't have…."

Helena thought of something to say to distract the poor girl from crying. "Do you," she finally said, "really *babysit?*"

Maria nodded and wiped her tears, "My two younger siblings…"

"No!" Helena's eyes shone. "You have *two* younger siblings? I always wanted to have younger siblings! Girls? Boys?"

Maria sniffled, "A boy, Eddie, and a girl, Sashinka—I mean—Sasha…"

"Wow!" Helena jumped off her seat, "A boy *and* a girl! Wow! Which one do you like best?"

Maria tilted her head, "I don't know…"

"Sure you do!"

Maria smiled through her teary eyes, "I guess… Eddie can be really annoying at times. But I can speak to him… Sasha is too young, but she's as sweet as a candy!"

Helena sat down and sighed, "I wish I had little siblings."

Maria looked at her, "You don't have any…?"

"Oh, I do have two brothers, but they're older. The eldest, Solomon, he has a girlfriend now. Her name's Hannah!"

Maria nodded.

"And my other brother, Reuben, he'd do anything for me. They both spoil me to bits."

"Really?" Maria whispered, "You must feel so lucky."

"Lucky? Hell no! I wish I had little ones. I would *play* with them, and *dance* with them, and *sing* with them..."

The principal's secretary called their names. She looked at them disapprovingly, "The principal is busy..."

Taking a big breath, Helena said excitedly: "Mrs. Burtman, I just asked Maria about the chromosome because there was something I didn't understand, you see, and I didn't want to stop Mr. Kissinger's flow, because when he begins talking, he never stops, you see, and so I asked Maria and she just tried to explain it to me, and when he called our names, I *tried* to explain to him that Maria was just explaining to me about the chromosome, but he would have none of it, and it's too bad, you see, because had he *asked*, he'd see that not everyone understands what he says, in *fact*..."

"Alright, alright," Mrs. Burtman sighed, and signed the slip of paper. She looked at Helena, and then at Maria, "Don't do this again! Now hurry back to class!"

Helena grinned, "Thank you so much, Mrs. Burtman. You won't regret it!"

Helena grabbed Maria's hand, and they ran down the hall. Then, out of sight of the principal's office, Helena began climbing the stairs to the third floor.

"But," Maria asked, bewildered, "aren't we going back to—"

Helena smiled, "No! There are only a few more minutes before the class ends. We'll go to my favorite spot…"

"But," Maria gasped, looking nervously around, "I… What will Mr. Kissinger…—"

"Mr. Kissinger wouldn't like us coming back now and interrupting his speech, right?"

Maria stammered, "Bu… But…"

"And you know," Helena continued, "how the other kids would whisper and get all excited when we come back, and Mr. Kissinger, well, this will upset him!"

"I… I…"

"Come on already!"

Once they reached the top floor, Helena opened a large window, stretched her leg over the ledge, and climbed onto the roof. She reached for Maria's hand.

Maria pulled her hand back, "I'm not… I can't…!"

"Of course you can. Give me your hand!"

Maria gulped and looked at the empty hallway around her.

Helena pressed, "Give me your hand!"

Maria gave her hand to Helena, placed her leg on the ledge, and then stretched her other leg out. The view was frightening. She could see the whole schoolyard below, as well as the street and the top of the trees. She gasped. The roof tile under her foot groaned. She looked at Helena, "Are you sure it's…—"

"Positive," Helena smiled. She squatted on the roof tiles and moved away from the window. "Here," she whispered, "if we squeeze here, no one can see us from the corridor!"

Maria squeezed into the small place. "How did you find this place?"

"In my old school," Helena said, "I knew *all* the spots. My favorite one was in the theatre's dressing room... Oh, it was truly magical!"

Maria smiled. The view was both frightening and exciting. A wrong move could cause them to tumble down. But the view was breathtaking. She had never been so high in her life.

"...And when this school year started," Helena continued, "the first thing I did was to look for quiet spots..."

Maria was surprised, "But I thought you always like to be around the other pupils."

Helena shrugged her shoulders, "I'd much rather be around good books. Or poems. Or plays!"

Maria's eyes widened. "I thought you only... that you only like to be with everyone around you..."

Helena shrugged her shoulders again, "Yes and no."

Maria nodded. She liked that answer. Yes and no.

They sat quietly.

Maria wanted to ask about Helena's brothers. And which books she liked reading. And what her favorite subject was. She liked it when Helena talked. But now she was quiet. They looked at the buildings in the horizon from the view of the roof. Each of them hugged her knees to her chest. Then Helena sighed. Maria did the same. She wanted to be as carefree as Helena.

A few minutes later, Helena said, "I think we should go back."

Maria nodded. They crawled slowly to the window, climbed inside and closed the window behind them. They hurried downstairs and entered their class just as the bell rang. The children turned to look at them, excited. Mr. Kissinger frowned. Grabbing his bag, he took the note from Helena's hand, giving them both a glare, and stormed out of the classroom.

"Helena, how was it?" one of the children asked. "What did the principal say?" asked another. "Did he suspend you?"

Soon a small circle formed around Helena and Maria. Helena related the events as Maria looked at the floor, embarrassed yet exhilarated by the attention.

But then she noticed the homework assignment written on the blackboard and returned to the desk to write the homework down.

Helena looked at her and exclaimed, "Oh, stop it! Let's go!"

Maria's eyes widened. "But, the homework...!"

Helena shook her head. She glanced over to Gisele and Isabella who were waiting near the door. She whispered into Maria's ear, "It's not as if you didn't read the whole book already!"

Maria shrugged. Helena grabbed her hand. "Come!"

Soon after the incident with Mr. Kissinger, there was a day when Helena was ill and did not come to school. Maria felt like the class was dead without Helena's presence. She sent a note with Gisele, wishing Helena a quick recovery.

Two days later, when Helena returned, she hugged Maria. "Thank you for your note!"

Maria enjoyed being hugged like this. She was not accustomed to embraces. She was discovering Helena was always like that: hugging, giggling, dramatic. She always saw opportunities, solutions, and ways of turning a dull moment truly magical.

In class they sometimes wrote to one another in

their notebooks. Maria never liked it, but sometimes it did help making a boring lesson a little livelier.

During breaks she always joined Helena and the girls. Doing her best to imitate the other girls by nodding and laughing, she hid the fact she didn't enjoy all the conversations. The ones about the boys embarrassed her. But she tried.

One morning, when they were returning to class after break, Helena pulled Maria closer, "I have a ballet performance!"

"A ballet performance?"

"Yeah, nothing too big. But I would love for you to come and watch!"

"I... when is it?"

"Tomorrow at five!"

"But... I... I can't..." Maria sighed, "I have to be with my siblings. My parents only return home at seven... Oh, I wish I could, Helena!"

"But Maria!" Helena exclaimed, "This is a big performance for me. You *must* come!"

"But... What will I do with Eddie and Sasha?"

"Bring them with you! The performance is free to attend!"

"I'm... I'm... not sure if my mother will let me."

"Sure she will!" They entered class and sat down. "Just don't pose it as a question, Maria. Announce it to her!"

Maria shook her head, "I can't. I'm not like *you!*"

"Of course you are! Tell your mother that you can either go for the performance *and* stay for the dinner afterwards, or just come for the performance and skip the dinner."

"I…" Maria shifted uncomfortably, "she wouldn't let me, Helena!"

"Maria, Maria, Maria…" Helena smiled. "Trust me. Tell her the same way I've told you. Give her these two options, and she'll pick the one that is least bad for her. If you ask her if you can go or not, of course she'll say no!" Helena dropped her voice to a whisper as Mrs. Schlesinger walked into the class, "But if you ask her if you could stay for the dinner or not, she'll have to allow you to go to the performance at the very least!"

The following day, Maria exclaimed to Helena, "You're a magician!"

"She said yes?!"

"She did!"

"Marvelous! A few others from the class will come too. I'm so excited that you'll be there!"

Holding her young brother with one hand, and her toddler sister with the other, Maria climbed on the tram. Though it was only four o'clock, it was already getting dark. All of them, bundled into their coats, sat down. She lifted Sasha onto her lap so that she could see outside. It was exciting.

They disembarked near the theatre. On entering the theatre's foyer, Maria spotted Gisele, Isabella, Sofia, and a few others from school.

"Goodness, Maria!" Gisele exclaimed, "you brought your siblings with you!"

"I…" Maria said, trying to look for the right words, "I had to be with—"

Isabella exclaimed, "It's such a brilliant idea! I should have brought my little sister. She would have loved it!"

Gisele nodded, "So considerate of you to bring them…"

Soon Maria became the center of attention as the other girls exclaimed, "They are *so* cute!"

A woman approached Maria, "You must be Maria, darling. I'm Helena's mother."

"Oh, pleased to meet you, Mrs. Goldstein!"

"Oh, darling, you are so kind. I'm so glad you could come! Helena said she was excited about you coming!"

"Did she…?"

At that moment, Maria was interrupted by a spoon tapping on glass as one of the mothers asked everyone to enter the auditorium.

The performance was dazzling. Maria loved every moment of it, as did Eddie and Sasha. Biting her lip nervously, Maria tensed as Helena did some turns—she was afraid Helena would fall—but her friend finished them triumphantly, raising her arms up high and giving her stunning smile.

After the performance, everyone waited for the dancers to come out while they talked with their ballet teacher. Maria looked at the big clock. It was six thirty. She promised her mother she'd be home before seven. She decided to wait for only five more minutes as she rocked tired Sasha in her arms.

After five minutes passed, Maria helped Eddie and Sasha with their coats and hats. She quietly left without saying a word and headed towards the tram station.

Sasha cried, "But you said we would meet Helena!"

"Oh Sashinka, we'll see her next time."

"But I wanted to see her now," Sasha cried.

They suddenly heard a voice behind them, "Maria!"

Helena ran out of the theatre still wearing her tutu.

"Helena!" Maria exclaimed. She stuttered, "You're… You're not dressed, you'll get sick!"

"I just wanted," Helena said, panting, "to say hello to you all. You must be Eddie, right?"

Eddie nodded.

"And you," Helena said to Sasha, "must be the one and only: Princess Alexandra!"

Sasha smiled, shyly burying her face in Maria's neck.

Maria saw Helena shivering, "Go now, Helena!"

"Okay," Helena said, "but I wanted to thank you so much for coming. It means the world to me!"

Maria smiled. "Go!"

Later, on the tram back home, Maria suddenly realized she had not said anything to Helena about her performance. She sighed and said to herself, 'Ignorant fool!' She should have at least said *something*, about how stunning Helena was, how poised, how majestic, how beautiful!

At home, after she endured her mother's scolding for being late and after dinner was over and her siblings were in bed, Maria sat in the kitchen and wrote Helena a note. She decorated it with flowers and wrote:

> *"To Helena, thank you for a brilliant performance. It was truly magical! Maria"*

She smiled to herself. Helena always used the words, "Truly magical."

Sometime before the end of the school year Maria got sick. She did not go to school, which was unlike her.

Helena asked everyone but no one knew why Maria was not at school. Helena then decided that if Maria didn't come to school the following day either, she'd visit her.

The following day Maria did not come. Helena, who was always rather worry-free, began to fret. She asked the other girls where Maria lived. No one knew the address exactly, only that she lived near the rail station heading east.

Helena went to the school's secretary. "Mrs. Burtman, I have to find out Maria Bozek's address!"

Armed with the address in hand, Helena skipped school. She shook her head as she left, knowing she'd miss Mr. Kissinger and his boring amoeba and cell formation lectures. But she knew that without Maria's interest in the lesson, she'd be even more lost than usual.

She took the tram to the eastern part of town and found the street. It was dreary, filled with plain-looking houses. She walked down the street lined with small houses, looking at the numbers. Then she stopped and looked at her slip of paper – this was it.

Helena knocked on the door.

There was no answer.

She knocked again.

Nothing.

She felt aggravated. She knocked forcefully on the door, shouting, "Maria? Maria, it's me, Helena!"

Maria's puzzled voice came from the other side of the door, "*Helena…?*"

"Yes! Open up!"

The door opened instantly. Maria gasped, "What on earth are you—"

Helena embraced her, "I thought something happened to you! You never miss a day, and now you missed two!"

Maria smiled. She looked pale.

"My god," Helena exclaimed, "you don't look well." She followed Maria down the hallway and into the living room. The house was dark. "Let's open the curtains... How are you feeling?"

"I'm... I'm fine..."

"Well you certainly don't look fine!"

Maria lay on one of the three long sofas, her hand holding her belly.

Helena clapped her hands, "No, let's go to your room. I'll take care of you! Do you want some tea?"

Maria shook her head, "No, thank you."

"I will take it as a yes!" Helena said, walking into the tiny kitchen. She filled a kettle with water and turned on the gas. She called to Maria, "In a moment you'll have some tea..."

Maria murmured a quiet, "Thank you..."

Helena came to the living room and sat down on the opposite sofa, "But why are you lying here, let's go to your room..."

Maria tried smiling, "This... is where we sleep. That's Eddie's bed," she pointed at where Helena was sitting, "and this is my bed. And that's Sashinka's."

"Oh," Helena said, and felt terribly stupid, "I... *knew* that..."

She felt awkward, "I guess I meant..." she shook her head, "How are you feeling?"

"I'm fine, I'm... fine..."

Helena moved and sat on Maria's bed. "Here, let me see. Do you have a fever?"

Maria shook her head.

"No," Helena concluded, "you don't have a fever. Does your throat hurt? Here, open your mouth…"

Maria laughed, "I'm not going to open… *I'm fine!*"

Helena smiled. "Is it your belly?"

Maria shrugged her shoulders, "I guess."

"I knew it! You ate something bad…"

"No, it's not that…"

"Then what is it?"

Maria shrugged again.

Helena sighed. The sound of the boiling kettle broke the silence. "Well, we'll make you some tea and you'll feel just like new!"

She removed the whistling kettle from the stove and made two cups of tea. She looked around the small kitchen, crammed with the sink, an oven and a stove, and a small table with five chairs around it. She shouted, "It is certainly cozy here! What a lovely kitchen!"

Maria grimaced.

Helena brought two cups of tea, placing them on the small living room table. She noticed a blanket on the floor, covering a towel. The room looked messy. She got up and began folding some of the clothes thrown around and opened the curtains.

Maria sighed.

When Helena came to the blanket thrown on the

floor, Maria grabbed to it, "No, please don't…"

Helena saw the towel underneath it, "Oh my God!" she exclaimed, "Dearest Maria!"

Maria covered her face with her hands.

"Dearest Maria!" Helena said again, "You're a woman now! Congratulations!" she jumped around the room, "I can't believe it, I'm so happy for you!"

Maria's face reddened, "Shhh…" she whispered, "you want to shout it to the whole street?!"

"Why not! What a blessing! You are now a w-o-m-a-n!" Helena collapsed dramatically onto the bed, "My mother would be so *happy* for you! What a celebration!"

Maria stared at her. Was Helena *out of her mind?* What was there to *celebrate?*

"Tell me, tell me," Helena begged, "how does it *feel…?*"

Maria sighed, "It… hurts… my belly…"

"Of course!" Helena exclaimed, "That's because one day you could have a *baby*, and now your cycle is… um… disappointed for not having a baby, so it goes away!" Helena sat up and sipped her tea, as joyful as ever.

Maria looked at her, puzzled.

Helena looked at her face, "Your mother told you about the whole…"

Maria shook her head.

Helena's eyes grew larger, "Didn't your mother …"

Maria shrugged.

"What?!" Helena exclaimed, spilling some tea, "Are you telling me your mother didn't tell you what was *going on?* Wait," she hesitated, "Maria, does she… know…?"

Maria shrugged, "She just thinks I have some tummy ache…"

"This is…" Helena jumped up, "ex… exasperating!" She walked around the room, "Maria! She needs to *know*, and you must get yourself a… menstrual apron, for these days every month…! I can't believe your *mama* didn't tell you!"

Maria stared at the carpet.

"Well," Helena said, sitting down again, "my mother gave me this talk two years ago! But as for me… it hasn't come yet… Oh… I wish it'd come. She told me we'll go shopping together and celebrate…"

Helena looked at Maria, who was biting her lip. She decided she must explain to her the little she knew. She stood up, mimicking her own mother, "I guess I must tell you what every woman should know."

Maria buried her face in her hands, "No, please don't!"

"Now-now," Helena said, trying to remember her mother's words, "there's nothing to be *ashamed* of. This means that your body has *ripened* and is ready for the *art of reproduction*…! Which only means that for *now*, for many years, until you are an old woman, you'll be… um… *visited* by this… a… splendid visitor! Sometimes it will hurt…" she nodded, reciting her mother's explanation, "but you will get used to it! It is a blessing from God as it means that you have finally come of age!"

Maria blushed and shook her head disapprovingly, her eyes closed.

"Now," Helena said, "we'll have to tell your mother, and make sure she gets you some menstrual aprons, or one of those pads, you know…"

"I'm…" Maria whispered, "I'm not going to wear *that!*"

"Sure you will! What are you going to do, sit around the house once every month for the rest of your *life?*"

Maria shrugged and covered her face in her hands again, "I don't know!"

"Well, Gisele already got hers, and so did Isabella!"

Maria peered between her fingers, "Impossible!"

Helena smiled and nodded.

Maria's eyes widened in surprise, "Gisele?! Isabella?!"

Helena nodded, "I've been praying to get mine soon, but the doctor has said it will take more time…"

"You… spoke about it with your doctor?"

"Yes, she's a *wonderful* doctor. My mother took me to her. And she said that it will take some time. Look," Helena whispered, "you already have some real breasts budding, and I don't even…—"

Maria now covered her face in her pillow. Helena reached over and pulled it away, "Now-now, we must be able to talk about this like ladies!"

Maria reddened, "I can't… believe… we're *talking* about *this!*"

"Well believe it! Sooner or later we'll *have* to! You've seen the funny little hairs under Roman's nose, and Alexander's voice change…We have our share too!"

At that moment the door opened. A rough woman's voice was heard, "Why isn't the door locked! Maria, I told you a thousand times…"

"Mama," Maria exclaimed, "I have a guest!"

A tough-looking woman appeared through the small corridor and looked at Helena. "Who are you?"

Helena reached her hand cordially, "Helena Goldstein, Madam!" she bowed, "And you must be Mrs. Bozek. I'm most honored to meet you!"

Mrs. Bozek looked at her suspiciously, "You're the dancer."

Helena looked at Maria and grinned, "Aspiring dancer, Madam. *And* actress, and singer too!"

Mrs. Bozek muttered something under her breath. She looked at Maria, "How is your tummy? Could you collect Sasha from kindergarten?"

Maria tried to say something, but her voice broke.

Helena jumped, sensing the complicated situation,

"I…"

Maria and her mother both stared at Helena. She took the plunge and said, "Congratulations, Mrs. Bozek!"

She reached and shook the mother's hands firmly, "I believe that your daughter has received it."

"Received what?"

Maria mumbled, "*Oh God…*"

"Well," Helena said, "Mrs. Bozek," she exclaimed, "she has received it. It-it. *It!*"

Mrs. Bozek's eyes suddenly widened. "Oh!"

Helena smiled at her, her big smile, anticipating.

"Oh," Mrs. Bozek said again and frowned, "well… That's quite *early…*"

"No, it isn't!" Helena said and sat down, "A few girls in our class have already received it... My mother keeps waiting for me to receive it, Mrs. Bozek…—"

"Does she?" Mrs. Bozek said, looking at her daughter, and sighed. She looked around the room and began folding the few clothes. "Well," she groaned, "what else would she say, that mother of yours?"

"Well," Helena said, looking puzzled at Mrs. Bozek and Maria, who was hiding her face in her hands, "she'd say… '*Congratulations*' and she'd get me the needed… *equipment…* to… *deal* with… the *situation…*"

Mrs. Bozek groaned, "I see," and quickly disappeared into the kitchen.

Helena leaned toward Maria and whispered, "*Should I go…?*"

Maria's eyes widened, "No! Please don't! I'm so glad you are here!"

They heard Mrs. Bozek's voice from the kitchen, "Well," she shouted and paused, "I better go and collect Sasha before I am too late." She passed by the living room, "Do lock the door, Maria, I beg you!"

"I will, Mama," Maria murmured.

The door closed.

Helena motioned for Maria to keep lying down. She hurried to the door and locked it. She sighed to herself. Wow, what a mother. She didn't say a thing!

When she entered the living room again she put on a big smile, "Well, we *must* celebrate, Maria!"

Maria sighed. "Right now I can't imagine doing anything…"

"Oh please, Maria! It can't be all *that* bad!"

Maria frowned. "It doesn't feel… right."

Helena breathed in. "Well, I guess… that in due time you will start liking it, no?"

"I doubt it."

Helena wanted to say something to cheer her friend up. "Well, you have certainly been missed in school."

Maria snorted, "No one probably noticed I…—"

"Of course everyone noticed!"

"You are very kind to me, Helena."

"Well," Helena searched for words, "Mr. Kissinger looked for your approving eyes… And he stared at me with constant disappointment!"

Maria laughed, "I don't give him 'approving eyes'…"

"Of course you do," Helena laughed, "you are the only one actually *listening* to him. He only speaks to you!"

"No he doesn't! Roman listens as well!"

"Well, maybe Roman too, but that's it!"

They smiled.

Silence ensued. This was a little odd. Sure, they were friends. But they weren't *good* friends. Helena tried to think, what would she speak about with Gisele?

She knew the answer. Gisele was mostly into talking about boys. But Maria always seemed so… shy about this kind of thing.

Finally, Maria spoke. "What… what did you study, with Mrs. Schlesinger?"

"Right!" Helena jumped up, "We learned 'Captain, O Captain.' Do you want me to recite it to you?"

Maria smiled and nodded.

"O Captain!" Helena exclaimed, "My Captain! Our fearful trip is done, the ship has weather'd every rack, the prize we sought is won… The port is near," she put her hand to her ear, "…the bells I hear, the people all exulting, while follow eyes the steady keel, the vessel grim and daring…"

She grabbed to her chest, "But O heart! Heart! Heart!"

Maria laughed, "Three 'hearts'?!"

Helena nodded excitedly, "But O heart! Heart! Heart! O the bleeding drops of red, where on the deck my Captain lies," she fell down on the sofa, "Fallen… cold… and dead."

Maria clapped, "Terrific!"

Helena smiled, "Then there's something about 'Rise up' and 'hear the bells', but I don't remember it…"

"But you memorized the whole first stanza!"

"Yeah," Helena shrugged, "I also memorized the end, 'From fearful trip the victor ship comes in with object won; Exult O shores, and ring O bells! But I," Helena got up again, "with mournful tread… Walk the deck my Captain lies… fallen… cold… and dead…"

"Bravo!" Maria laughed.

There was a knock on the door.

Helena said, "I'll get it."

Maria jumped, "No, please, don't!" and ran to the door. She unlocked it. "Mama! Sashinka!"

Mrs. Bozek handed Maria her young sister. "Now I must go back to work."

Helena, in the living room, heard the conversation

at the door. 'Say something,' she prayed, 'you are her *mother* for God's sake, *say* something!'

"I will see you at seven, Maria. Make sure Eddie does his homework."

"Yes Mama."

The door closed.

"Now Sashinka," Maria leaned down and said, "I have a surprise for you in the living room! Guess who is here?!"

A few days later, during Mr. Kissinger's class, Helena wrote to Maria in her notebook: "I want to take you out on Sunday."

She gently rotated her notebook for Maria to see.

Maria wrote back in her own notebook, "Can't." She pushed her notebook towards Helena but then quickly took it back and wrote: "Sorry."

Helena penciled her usual large question mark, drawing and thickening its curved line several times.

Maria bit her lip. She kept listening to Mr. Kissinger's words. By now they were both more trained. And Mr. Kissinger, too, seemed more relaxed. Perhaps he had lost hope.

Maria wrote in her small handwriting, "Will be with

my family. Sorry…"

Helena wrote, "You need to…" and then drew balloons and fireworks. "My mom said she'll take us both shopping!"

Maria pursed her lips and sighed. It sounded so good and so much fun.

Helena wrote, "Sunday! Surely you don't have to babysit on *SUNDAYS!*"

"No," Maria wrote, "but my mother won't like it…"

Helena had anticipated this. She appreciated Maria's honesty. "Tell her," she wrote, while nodding a little too enthusiastically at Mr. Kissinger's speech about plasma and red blood cells, "that you have to HELP me with the MATH EXAM next Tuesday."

Maria read and gulped.

"Either that," Helena wrote, "or you could come and sleep over at my house on Monday. This way she will let you go."

Maria shook her head and frowned.

Mr. Kissinger looked at the two of them, and they both quickly lowered their heads.

When the danger passed and Mr. Kissinger was scribbling on the blackboard, Maria wrote, "Let me see."

"I see it as a YES." Helena wrote, and then embellished the "YES".

That Sunday Helena's mother took them both shopping. Maria tried to resist Mrs. Goldstein's offer to buy her a dress. But Mrs. Goldstein said plainly, "Don't insult me, young lady! When someone offers to give you something nice you simply say, 'Thank you very much.' And that's it."

Maria nodded, her heart pounding, "Thank you very much Mrs. Goldstein."

"You are most welcome!" Mrs. Goldstein said cheerfully.

The dress looked stunning and was incomparable to anything Maria had ever worn. It was expensive, too. Helena smiled at her. "It compliments your eyes, Maria!"

Maria was more embarrassed than ever.

Then they proceeded to a local pharmacy. Maria loved looking at all the bottles and jars spread across the counter. But when she heard Mrs. Goldstein asking the man for a menstrual apron and twenty pads, she immediately pulled Helena out of the store. Helena exclaimed to her mother, "We'll wait for you outside, Mama!"

"Good, I'll be there in a moment."

Outside, Maria covered her face in her hands, "Oh dear, this is so embarrassing!"

"No, it isn't, Maria!"

Mrs. Goldstein exited the pharmacy smiling and handed Maria the bag.

Maria whispered, "Thank you Mrs. Goldstein, very

much."

Mrs. Goldstein smiled. Helena jumped, "Soon it will be my turn, right mama?"

"Everything in its due time, darling."

As the school year came to an end, Helena made Maria promise to write to her at the Goldstein family's summer house. She also made Gisele and the others agree to do the same.

But Helena was surprised a few days after they arrived at the summer house, when the family's servant handed her father his letters and then said, "And this, young Miss Goldstein, is for you."

Her eyes grew wide as she received the letter in her hands. She recognized Maria's handwriting. "Oh my!" she exclaimed, "I received a letter! I received a *letter!*" She ran to the balcony, "Solomon! Reuben! I received a letter!"

"Who from?" Reuben shouted at her as she ran back into the house.

"My friend Maria!"

Lying on her bed, she carefully opened the letter. Whilst she had wished for Gisele and Isabella and Sofia to have written, it was Maria who had sent the first letter.

"Dearest Helena,"

Helena read slowly, her chest rising up and down,

> "It's been three days since the beginning of the summer break, and I think of you often. Yesterday I sang to Sashinka and Eddie the song you taught me, of the Queen of the Night... It was great. I couldn't quite sing it like you, but we had lots of fun in the living room, while I dressed up in black, trying to hit those soprano notes of yours..."

Helena grinned and leaned her back against the wall.

> "The city feels empty. Especially without you. I think of you and your brothers having fun at the sea, and, while I refrain from being jealous, I must admit that I wish I could be with you and see the sea as well...
>
> Sashinka prepared some food with me today in the kitchen, and we had lots of fun. Eddie is with his new Karl May book, reading and pretending to be an American cowboy. He's so funny...
>
> Promise me you'll look into the math assignment early on, and not leave it for the

end of the summer. I found that for me, bit by bit every day is the best. Don't put it off!

Tell me about the sea, shore, and the sand... In fact, everything else too!

I hope I wrote well (surely not as artistically as you!).

Fondly yours,

Maria Bozek."

Helena stood up, then sat down, then lay down and smiled. She read the letter again, lavishing each word. This letter was for *her*. For her *only!*

She quickly pulled out her notebook from the desk drawer and sat back on the bed. She turned to the middle pages, where she could pull out some paper without damaging the notebook. She wrote:

"Dearest Maria!"

She then embellished the writing with cursive twirls, adding a few stars next to the line,

"It was such a pleasant surprise to receive your kind letter. I feel glad to hear you like The Queen of the Night. I'm sure Mozart would have been most pleased to hear it!

Mind you, I don't sing it very well either. I do hope to one day after enough training! My singing teacher said that one famous singer, when she finished that whole aria of ten minutes, collapsed on stage! And she also said that Mozart designed it that way! To "pull out your soul!""

I disagree though, dearest Maria. I think he designed it to evoke emotion. If that requires writing the most complicated of arias, then he was willing to do so. But not to make the singer faint! If anything, he might have wanted the audience to faint!"

Helena looked at the letter. She frowned. It was so boring.

She decided to start anew. She pulled out another piece of paper from the notebook.

"Dearest Maria,"

This time she didn't invest as much time in the twirls. She felt a little guilty about that. But then she concentrated and wrote:

"Your letter finds me well."

Good. She liked the sound of it. She went on.

"It was splendid to read of your adventures with Sashinka and Eddie. You have such a lovely family. The fact that you could sing to them is incredible. Whenever I sing to Reuben or Solomon, they most often roll their eyes.

Solomon thinks of Hannah all the time.

And Reuben, too, I bet you, is thinking of some girl as well. I've seen how eager he was to go to the beach and look at all the women there. I told him he should close his mouth so that he won't drool. But he didn't like my comment!"

Helena smiled and sighed. She continued writing.

"I like it here. I especially like that my father is around more. Back in the city he is busy all the time. Here he reads the newspaper. Sure, don't be mistaken, he did bring with him quite a few folders from the office. But he's also available. Somewhat.

My mother is the happiest. And so am I."

Helena wanted to write more. But she didn't know what to write. This was odd. In the books, whenever she read about such correspondence between friends, she thought that had *she* been partaking in such correspondence, she would fill pages and pages.

She thought of writing about a boy she saw on the beach, who reminded her of Alexander.

But it wasn't proper. Not for a letter at least. Besides, Maria wasn't that kind of girl.

She thought of writing about a novel she was reading. But she thought that would be boring.

She thought of writing about how much she missed everyone in class. But the truth was that she didn't *really* miss anyone. Not yet.

And so, she spent two more days trying to figure out what to write. This became her obsession. She even skipped lunch one day trying to think of what to write in her room.

Two days later, her mother finally said, "Helena darling, just send the letter as it is. Don't worry about it any more."

"But Mama, it's only one page!"

"Better short and concise than long and melodramatic, darling."

Helena grimaced. This task had become overly difficult. If she had needed to write a long fairy-tale about two siblings separated in some mysterious circumstances, she would have completed it in a couple of hours! But this whole *letter thing* was not as easy as she had expected.

Finally, she took the piece of paper, which had accompanied her to the beach, every meal and even to bed, and wrote on it,

> "P.S.
> I searched for what else to write. I wish I knew what to add! But I see that each day makes the letter older and also further away from you, dearest Maria. So I will let the letter go as it is. This does NOT show my utter appreciation for your kindness to have addressed me here. Please do so again as soon as you receive this letter! I hope that by then I will know what to write to you next time!
>
> Until then, faithfully yours,
>
> Helena Goldstein."

She added her swirly new signature, on which she had worked for hours and hours during Mr. Kissinger's lessons. It was perfect. Almost.

Maria waited to open the letter until evening. She wanted to have time alone, and to read it when she could concentrate and be able to respond right away. She sat in the kitchen and excitedly opened the precious letter.

"Dearest Maria,"

She loved seeing Helena's handwriting. It had been ten days since the end of the school year, and there were still fifty-two days ahead.

She always loved school, as she loved learning. But now she also missed school for other reasons, such as seeing her neighbor's beautiful handwriting as she was practicing her twirling signature again and again in her notebook.

She smiled to herself and looked at the signature.

She didn't want to hurry. She saw it was only one page, and wanted to linger on each word. She remembered how she had once asked Helena, "How many times do you intend to write that signature of yours?"

Helena was not taken aback. "Why, until it's perfect, of course! I'll have to sign it thousands of times, you understand? So I must practice!"

Maria loved that answer. It was so Helena.

As she loved the twirling and the little stars next to her own name. "Dear Maria." The way Helena wrote her name made her feel special.

> "Your letter finds me well. It was splendid to read of your adventures with Sashinka and Eddie. You have such a lovely family. The fact that you could sing to them is incredible. Whenever I sing to Reuben or Solomon, they most often roll their eyes."

Maria laughed quietly, wishing not to wake up her siblings. From her parents' bedroom she heard her father snoring. This was now time for *herself* to read this letter, this treat she'd been awaiting the whole day. She read the last sentence again, enjoying every word.

> "…whenever I sing to Reuben or Solomon, they most often roll their eyes.
>
> Solomon all the time thinks of Hannah.
>
> And Reuben, too, I bet you, is thinking of some girl as well. I've seen how eager he was to go to the beach and look at all the women

there. I told him he should close his mouth so that he won't drool. But he didn't like my comment!"

Maria shook her head, "Helena Helena…!"

"I like it here. I especially like that my Father is around more. Back in the city he is busy all the time. Here he reads the newspaper. Sure, don't be mistaken, he did bring with him quite a few folders from the office. But he's also available. Somewhat."

Maria smiled. That's good.

"My mother is the happiest. And so am I."

Maria touched the paper with her finger, over the small stars separating the next paragraph.

"P.S.
I searched for what else to write. I wish I knew what to add! But I see that each day makes the letter older and also further away from you, dearest Maria. So I will let the letter go as it is. This does NOT show my utter appreciation for your kindness to have addressed me here. Please do so again as soon as you receive this letter! I hope that by then I will know what to write to you next time!

Until then, faithfully yours,

Helena Goldstein."

Maria bit her lip. This was wonderful. Just wonderful! She took paper and her favorite pen. It was late already, but this was important.

She wanted to write back. Now.

But instead, she found herself copying Helena's beautiful signature. Trying, unsuccessfully, to get that twirl, especially around the "H" and the "G". She sighed. She knew she needed to begin writing soon.

"I received another letter! I received another letter!"

Everyone was amused. Helena ran around the house, told her brothers, the servant downstairs and the maids upstairs. She thought of running to the beach and screaming it out loud. But... that, she knew, would be a waste of time.

So she ran into her room, slammed the door, indicating she had some *real* work to do. Staring and sighing at the math assignment could wait.

She lay on her stomach on the bed, and eagerly opened the letter.

"Dearest Helena,

I just now read your letter and I intend on going first thing tomorrow with Eddie and Sashinka to the post office. They will enjoy it.

It's now been ten days since the beginning of summer break, and I dread thinking of the rest. This break is too long. I wish they would have broken it into smaller breaks throughout the year. Also, this would be so much better for the students as the flow of our education would not stop so abruptly."

Helena shook her head. This was so typical of Maria. "The flow of our education." *Maria Maria!*

"The city feels a little dull. I realize many people have gone out of town for the summer. Father spoke of busy days at the train station, but now it has eased. At the post office there is no line anymore. Nor is there a line at the grocery store. Also, the vendors seem less enthusiastic to work. It's a pity. Everything happens so slowly.

Sashinka is excited about being the eldest in kindergarten next year. I promised to sew her a bag embroidered with her initials. I hope this will keep me busy for several days. But I desperately think of what to do.

I did take some books from the library. I was the only one in the youth section, can you imagine?"

Helena laughed and exclaimed at the letter, "Of course, Maria!"

"Eddie finished his Karl May book, which makes me happy. We'll borrow a new book for him soon, maybe tomorrow. In the meantime all he talks about is Indian chiefs and cowboys, and speaks in tongues and explains it is Indian... he can be so funny...

Do tell me about the sea, and the waves, and the sound of the seagulls. I would love to explore sea life, see sea stars and seahorses... Do you notice the tides? Does it really change according to the moon? Tell me, please, do not spare your thoughts.

Yours fondly,

Maria Bozek.

P.S.

What do you think of my new signature? Not as beautiful as yours, but I like it better than my old one!"

Helena turned over onto her back and smiled. What a beautiful letter! She looked at it again. Two full pages. She must be able to respond with *at least* that length. She looked at the small handwriting and at the funny looking signature. "Oh, Maria!" she laughed.

Helena had never before wanted to return to school as much as she did that year.

"I have a surprise for you!" she whispered into Maria's ear as they hugged when seeing each other for the first time after the long summer.

"And I for you!" Maria whispered back, her eyes shining.

During the long break between classes they ran up to the third floor and quietly climbed out the window onto the roof, each holding a small bag in her hand.

Helena looked at the view. "It's so good to be here again!"

Maria nodded. There was so much she wanted to

say.

"I've missed the city," Helena continued, "and I even missed the school!"

Maria smiled.

"Here," Helena said and handed Maria a small brown bag, "I got these for you. But..." she hesitated, "please don't tell Gisele or Isabella or anyone because I didn't—"

"I promise."

Helena then took the brown bag back, "Guess what it is!"

Maria shrugged her shoulders, "I don't know."

"Guess!"

Maria searched for the right answer.

Helena pressed, "Just guess!"

"Helena! I don't know!"

Helena shook the bag in front of Maria's face. It sounded like small stones.

Still, Maria wouldn't guess.

Helena shook her head and handed Maria the gift. "So open it!"

Maria opened the small bag and exclaimed "Helena!"

Seashells in various golden colors filled the bag. She touched them, caressing the different shapes and sizes. She held them to her nose. "They smell like the sea!"

Helena laughed, "Of course they do!"

Maria inspected them, turning each one, looking at it from every angle. "Wow, Helena, it's *exactly*… it means so *much* to me…"

"Did you see the small bag inside?"

"Small bag?"

Inside the brown bag there was a tiny paper bag.

Helena's smile grew bigger, "Open it!"

Maria opened it. It was a fossil of a…

"No!"

"Yes!"

"No! Is this the tail of a… *seahorse?*"

"Yes Maria! Reuben found it! He said it must be from a tiny seahorse."

"Oh Helena!" Maria said and embraced Helena. "This is…"

"Magical, right?"

"Yes!"

Helena smiled. The schoolyard was busy with students. Gisele and the others would be wondering where she was.

Maria bit her lip. She had also brought Helena a present, but it was nothing in comparison… She sighed, "Helena, I'm afraid this does not match your generous gift…"

Helena tut-tutted, "Don't be silly!"

Maria handed the small brown bag to Helena.

Helena opened it. Inside she saw a small handmade purse. "Oh my!" she exclaimed, "It's beautiful! And it has my initials!"

Maria looked down, "I tried to capture your swirling signature..."

"I love it! This is so much better than my gift!"

Maria shook her head, "Yours is much better. All I did was to sew this together...—"

"Yeah, but you *made* it, Maria. I just *found* these..." She hugged Maria. "Thank you so much!"

The school bell rang.

They crawled carefully back to the window and climbed inside, closing it behind them and running to class. Each girl hid her precious bag in her hand, protecting it.

She was 25 years old now, but she looked older. She'd been through so much these past few years. The war. Escaping.

The train, now in her beloved homeland, chugged its way through fields and forests. The announcements in the train were now made in her own language. She missed her language.

She sighed. Somehow she felt safer now, in her own country.

She opened her valise, which held her only possessions in this world: some clothes, a few letters, a journal and the little, old, time-worn brown bag; She reached and pulled it out. It had been folded and unfolded hundreds of times over the years.

She thought of getting rid of it. It was too revealing of her true identity. It could have proved disastrous. It could have cost her her life.

But she kept it.

Carefully opening the brown bag, she took out the tiny purse.

She had not allowed herself to cry for so many years. But now her eyes stung and the tears filled them as her fingers caressed the embroidered letters.

"H. G."

Not long after the new school year began, Helena invited Maria to come to the synagogue with her. "It's a special day for us, I think you'd like it."

Maria asked her parents; whilst her mother did not want her gone for too long, her father insisted that she should go.

Helena was in heaven when she heard the good news. "We'll have so much fun together! It's always so boring for me alone…"

Maria was excited. "Do I need to bring anything?"

"No, just come dressed in white."

"In white?"

Helena nodded.

As they approached the building, Maria was amazed to see everyone was wearing white: men, women and even the children.

They climbed the stairs following Mrs. Goldstein to the second floor of the large synagogue. Helena whispered to Maria, "We call it the Day of Atonement. We need to atone and ask for forgiveness for our sins, I think...."

They sat down on the wooden benches, looking at the grandeur below; Maria liked the stained glass windows. The place looked like a church, but... whiter. Especially with all the people wearing white.

Helena whispered to her, "It goes on like this for hours, sitting, standing. It can be very boring..."

But Maria found none of it boring. The men downstairs were moving and nodding their heads incessantly. And many women upstairs, around Maria, did so as well. She watched with fascination how the women moved their lip rapidly, as if under a trance.

But what moved her most of all was when people began crying, really crying, when the lead man (Helena called him the 'cantor') started singing with a deep voice, looking up to the ceiling, and the entire synagogue shook with the power of his voice.

Even Helena's mother had tears in her eyes.

Maria couldn't stop herself from asking Helena, whispering ever so quietly, "What is he *saying?*"

Helena grimaced, "I'm not quite sure... I'm not

sure anyone here understands really..."

The following day, Helena did not attend school. It was a day of fasting for her. Nearly half the class did not go to school that day. And a few teachers were missing too.

But the day after, the whole class returned, and life continued as usual. Mr. Kissinger spoke monotonously while most students didn't follow. Mrs. Schlesinger was in love with the current poet they were studying. And the new history teacher spoke about the Great War with fervor.

Winter approached, and the streets were decorated for Christmas; in the schoolyard Roman boasted to the girls about how he and his father had gone to the forest and cut down a *huge* tree to place in their house for the Holidays.

When he was gone, Helena lamented to Gisele, "I wish we could celebrate Christmas as well."

Maria, seated next to them reading a book, tilted her head and listened.

Gisele shrugged, "But they don't get to light the candelabrum and eat our great food…"

"Yeah, I know," Helena lamented, "but, you know, Christmas is so festive…."

Maria's eyes widened. She thought it was

impossible for someone not to celebrate Christmas. It was the best thing about the winter!

Two days later, during history lesson, Maria wrote down: "Do you want to come and celebrate Christmas at my house?"

Helena squinted at the note, her eyes growing large with disbelief. She quickly wrote "Really???"

Maria smiled and wrote, "YES!"

Helena's eyes glittered. "But," she wrote, "your parents…???"

"My mother invited you," Maria wrote.

"That can't be!!!" Helena wrote back.

Maria smiled. "But it's true!"

Helena grinned too. She couldn't believe it.

Maria ran to the door, "I'll get it!"

Mrs. Bozek hurried to the door from the kitchen, and shouted at her husband sitting in the living room, "Come now!"

Maria opened the door and exclaimed, "Helena!"

Helena stood at the door, wearing her new fur coat and carrying a suitcase. Mr. Goldstein was standing behind her in the snowy street.

Eddie and Sashinka hassled to join and hid behind

their parents.

Mrs. Bozek quickly said, "Well, come in already Helena, don't stand there outside!"

Helena walked in.

Mr. Goldstein raised his hand, "Thank you. Merry Christmas!"

Maria's father raised his hand as well, "Happy holidays! Why don't you come in for a moment, have something warm to drink? Make a toast?"

Mr. Goldstein waved his hand, pointing in the direction of the tram. "My wife..."

The other man gestured knowingly, 'Of course!' and nodded his head.

Helena's father tipped his hat and walked away.

Mr. Bozek closed the door and headed back to the living room. Mrs. Bozek was already back in the kitchen. Helena and Maria remained at the entrance, jumping in each other's arms. "I can't believe I'm here!"

"I can't believe you're here!"

"Girls," Mrs. Bozek shouted, "enough with that. Maria, take Helena's coat already!"

"Yes, Mama!"

Helena whispered, "It's okay," and took her coat off, placing it on the hanger.

Maria whispered, "What's with the suitcase?"

Helena's eyes glittered, "Well, my night clothes and

all, but also," she whispered, "presents for Eddie and Sashinka!"

Maria shook her head, "You shouldn't have!"

"I wanted to!"

Eddie and Sashinka were now in the living room, playing; Helena entered and gasped, "Wow! What a beautiful tree! And what a huge table! Where are the beds?"

Maria's mother came out of the kitchen, beaming. "Beautiful, right?"

Helena nodded, and Eddie and Sashinka hurried to show her the decorations they had made for the tree.

Helena smiled, "Wow, you made that Eddie? The star?"

Maria smiled at her.

Helena then looked at the large table with chairs and plates already set up. A white tablecloth covered the table, but there seemed to be hay all around. They must still need to do some final cleaning, she thought.

Maria looked at her with joy and whispered, "The table – it's made of two beds put together!"

"No!" Helena motioned with her mouth.

"Yes! My father put a big wooden board over the two beds, see?" She moved the large tablecloth.

"Brilliant!" Helena whispered. She smiled at Mr. Bozek, who was reading the newspaper.

Mrs. Bozek shouted from the kitchen, "Maria, I

need you!"

Maria walked to the kitchen, and Helena followed her, saying, "I can help too!"

Mrs. Bozek waved her hand, "You are our guest! Now go to the living room and leave us alone. I need to concentrate!"

Maria smiled at Helena. Helena smiled back and went to the living room to play with the younger children.

A few minutes later the grandparents arrived. Helena was introduced to them. They were Mrs. Bozek's parents, and were much younger than Helena's grandparents. They sat in the living room and the grandfather began to have a long conversation with Mr. Bozek; the two laughed together amiably. The grandmother tried to help in the kitchen but was soon shooed away by Mrs. Bozek, "Mother, don't disturb me," she exclaimed.

The grandmother then came to the living room and played for a while with the grandchildren.

Soon, the doorbell rang again. This time it was Mr. Bozek's parents. They looked much older. Helena thought that, in fact, the grandfather looked quite ancient.

The small living room was packed. Helena tried to fit in, but really hoped Maria would come out of the kitchen.

Eddie was running to the window every minute or so, exclaiming, "I don't see it yet, Papa! I don't see it yet!"

Mr. Bozek kept talking with his father in law. The other grandfather soon fell asleep on his wife's shoulder.

Then, Eddie exclaimed from near the window, "I see it Papa! The first star!"

Mr. Bozek walked to the window. "Indeed."

As if waiting for that moment, Mrs. Bozek ran out of the kitchen, snatching off her apron, "Very good. Now sit down everybody! I don't want the food to get cold!"

Everyone sat down quickly.

Silence ensued.

Mrs. Bozek elbowed her husband, who looked at his father and coughed, "Papa!"

The old and feeble grandfather seemed to be awoken from a daze, "Yes?"

"The prayer, Papa!"

"Why, of course," said the puzzled grandfather, and the children burst into laughter. Mrs. Bozek silenced them at once.

The old grandfather joined his hands with his wife and the other grandfather, and soon everyone was holding hands. Helena held Maria and Eddie's hands. She found it quite weird. They each held their hands very tightly.

The old grandfather said a prayer, and they all said "Amen" and crossed themselves. Helena did not, hoping no one had noticed.

Then Eddie exclaimed with excitement, "The Christmas wafer!"

The old grandfather took the large piece of unleavened wafer at the center of the table, and broke it into two pieces. He looked at his wife and said, "Merry Christmas!"

He then turned to the other grandfather and said, "Merry Christmas." He handed them the broken pieces of wafer, and soon they began passing and breaking the wafers to others, blessing everyone with Merry Christmas and other wishes.

Maria handed her a small piece of wafer and smiled, shyly, "Merry Christmas, Helena!"

Helena smiled back, "Merry Christmas, Maria!"

Helena also received a small piece from Eddie, and to her surprise everyone kept chopping their pieces of wafer and them passing from one to the other, exclaiming "Good year!" and "Health and prosperity!"

Then everyone ate their wafers and crumbs. Helena thought it was so peculiar!

Maria's mother left the table, and Maria hurried to follow her. Helena noticed there was something tilting under her plate—no, under the tablecloth—and quietly sneaked her hand below the tablecloth to remove some... hay?

"Father," Eddie said, "she's removing the hay!"

Helena's face reddened at once. Was she not supposed to...—

Maria, serving the first bowls of red beetroot soup, smiled and whispered, "It's tradition to place hay under the table and under the tablecloth."

Helena mumbled, "Of… of course…" She was determined not to move or do anything else that would attract attention.

But the old grandmother smiled at her from across the table, "It's to remember that Jesus was born and put in a *manger*, you see?"

Helena mumbled, "Of course…"

Luckily, Maria's father changed the subject, "Tell us, Eddie, what have you been studying in school…"

When the soup was served, Maria sat down and noticed Helena's red face. She smiled, "Is everything okay?"

Helena whispered, placing her hands on her hot cheeks, "Why? Do I look redder than the soup?"

Maria grinned and said reassuringly, "It's so great to have you here!"

The evening continued with more and more food. The tiny kitchen kept producing dishes heaped with rollmops, cabbage rolls, cooked mushrooms, dumplings filled with cheese and potatoes, stewed sauerkraut, salad and fish.

Mrs. Bozek looked at Helena, "There is no meat here, only fish, so eat!"

Helena looked at her, puzzled.

"I went to the market," Mrs. Bozek said, "and asked what you *cannot* eat, but I understood fish always works, right?"

Helena nodded.

"Well, eat everything then!"

Maria, feeling a little guilty, whispered to Helena, "It's our tradition that you have to eat all twelve dishes."

Hearing her, Mr. Bozek added, "Because of the twelve months of the year. It's for you to have a good year!"

"Fool," Mrs. Bozek retorted, "it's because of the twelve *apostles!*"

"Well I heard it was the twelve months of the year!"

"Who," Maria jumped, "who... wants *kompot?*"

Everyone cheered, and so Maria hurried to fetch the pitchers of the sweet beverage from the kitchen. Helena, seeing that Mrs. Bozek was sitting, got up to help Maria, and looked at Mrs. Bozek worriedly, fearing she would scold her. But she was busy eating and talking to the grandmother.

In the small kitchen, Maria smiled at Helena, "Is everything okay?"

Helena, still red and quite embarrassed, said a little too eagerly, "Yes! It's so... *lively!*"

Maria smiled, took one pitcher and pointed at a second, and Helena carried it and followed her to the living room.

They poured kompot for everyone; when Helena poured some kompot for Mrs. Bozek, she was surprised to see Maria's mother looking at her and nodding, "You're a good girl, Helena."

This made Helena feel much better. But it would not last for long.

After all the poppy seed cakes were eaten, the dried apples and plums were finished, and all the small sweets were tasted, Helena helped Mrs. Bozek and Maria take the dishes to the kitchen. All the while, Eddie kept nagging, "Now, Papa? *Now?*"

Mr. Bozek did not respond, and kept talking to his father-in-law. Eventually he said to Eddie, "When your mama says!"

When the table was finally clean Mrs. Bozek said, "We can now move to the tree."

Eddie and Sashinka cheered. Everyone carried their chairs, and Mr. Bozek, with the help of his father-in-law, pushed the table-made-of-beds to the corner of the room.

Helena hurried to her suitcase. She opened it and excitedly took the two large packages out. She placed them under the tree along with the other presents, and asked Maria, who came and sat down, "Is it okay where I put them?"

Maria smiled and nodded.

The old grandfather once again fell asleep on the

old grandmother's shoulder. Eddie and Sashinka were ecstatic. Mrs. Bozek sat near the tree, and Mr. Bozek stood behind her, massaging her shoulders; this was a little embarrassing for Helena to watch.

Mrs. Bozek then cleared her throat, "First, Sashinka will open her present."

Little Sasha eagerly took her gift from under the tree, and tore the wrapping paper apart.

Maria smiled at Helena.

Sashinka discovered a white dress, perfect for her size. "Mama, Papa!" She exclaimed.

Maria said to her, "Now kiss Mama and Papa!"

Sasha kissed them. Mrs. Bozek said, "It's from your grandparents too. Go kiss them too!"

After Sashinka finished the round of kisses, Eddie shouted, "Now it's my turn!"

Mrs. Bozek said, "Now you Eddie."

He opened his gift. It was a small train, made out of wood, painted in red. He thanked his parents, kissed them, and then kissed the grandparents.

Then came Maria's turn. She opened her package. "New notebooks!" she exclaimed.

Helena smiled. She was a little disappointed for Maria.

"Look inside," Mrs. Bozek said proudly, "with a set of pens! Like those you like!"

"Mama! Thank you!" Maria kissed her mother,

"Papa!" she kissed him as well. She went around and kissed the four grandparents. She then said excitedly, "But... there are two more packages! Let's guess who they are for?"

Sasha and Eddie began screaming, "Me! Me!"

Maria looked at Helena, who whispered, "The red for Sasha, the blue for Eddie."

"Go ahead Sashinka," Maria said and pointed at the large red gift.

Sashinka opened it eagerly. It was a beautiful doll, with a dress and a brown hair, braided into two braids. Sashinka couldn't hold her excitement, "Is this for me? Really? Really?!"

She jumped around and ran with the doll. Maria laughed, "Now kiss Helena!"

Helena leaned down as Sashinka kissed her shyly. Helena looked at Mrs. Bozek, who did not seem overly pleased for some reason.

Then Eddie exclaimed, "My turn, my turn!"

He waited for his mother's nodding approval, and then opened the large package. "Wow!!!" he screamed. "A train! A mechanical train!"

Helena smiled. Then, her smile disappeared instantly as Eddie screamed, "This is so much better than the wooden one!"

Mrs. Bozek got up at once, "Come, Maria! We need to clean the dishes!"

It all happened very fast. Maria gave Helena a sorry

look, and she disappeared. There was a long silence in the living room, as if Helena had done something awful. The only one speaking was Eddie, who was moving the train around, looking at its intricate wheels, rocking levers and the various springs.

Mr. Bozek was the first to speak. "Well! Let's... sing a little!" He got up and brought out a guitar. He began singing, and the grandparents joined him.

Helena knew the song, and in different circumstances would have begun singing with her beautiful soprano. But now she stared down at the floor and tried to smile at the excited two kids with their gifts.

She wanted so badly to go and see Maria in the kitchen, help her, speak to her, hear from her that it was just her imagination and that she hadn't done something unforgivable....

But Maria was gone. Mr. Bozek tried cheering the atmosphere, but Helena felt stupid. Stupid, stupid, stupid! She shouldn't have brought such expensive gifts! Tears welled in her eyes, and she got up and ran to the back door. She exited the house and entered the small bathroom hut in the backyard.

She stood there, in the cold and smelly toilet, for what seemed like forever, cursing herself, crying, wanting to go home so badly.

"Helena? Helena is everything okay?"

Helena heard Maria's voice, wiped her tears and shouted over the door of the bathroom hut, "Sure..."

"Helena, did you *cry?*"

"*No…!*"

"Helena, open the door for me!"

Helena opened the door. Maria looked at her puffy face. She stretched her hands to hug her, "Come here!"

Helena embraced her. "I feel like a *fool.* I didn't mean to…"

"Enough with that, all is well! Did you see how Eddie liked your gift—"

"But your mama…"

"My mother can sometimes be… You'll see, tomorrow she'll be hailing your generous gifts…!"

"No she won't!"

Maria grabbed Helena's arms, "Listen to me, Helena! You are *so* kind, you've been *so* kind. You should be *proud* of yourself for being so… *generous…!* Helena!"

Helena sniffled and nodded.

"Now," Maria said, "in a moment we'll go inside where it's warm, and you'll join us for the singing… I want the little ones to hear you sing! And then we'll go to the midnight mass. Have you ever gone to the midnight mass?"

Helena shook her head 'no' and wiped her cheeks again.

Maria smiled, "You'll *love* it!" She hugged Helena

again, "I am so happy you are here!"

"You *are?*" Helena murmured, "Didn't I embarrass you…?"

From inside the house they heard singing. Maria said, "Of course not! And I'm so happy you are here with us! Now come, let's go inside."

Helena nodded. All she wanted was to go *home*. But she was a big girl now. What would Reuben and Solomon say if she suddenly returned home?

'No', she thought to herself. She was strong. She would stay.

She would even have fun.

Maria looked at her. "Ready?"

Helena nodded.

They walked inside.

Spring came. And in Helena's house everyone was preparing for the big Passover dinner.

Helena made sure that everyone in the household wouldn't say or do anything embarrassing during the big dinner. She was so excited about Maria coming and sleeping over for the first time. But she was also nervous.

Memories from her uncomfortable visit at Maria's during Christmas made her extra cautious about her friend's visit. Helena knew that her uncle, Bernie, could be rather foolish and inappropriate, and so she asked her mother to speak to him in advance. She wanted no embarrassments. No chagrins. No exasperating moments. She wanted Maria to feel like a part of the family. Welcomed.

Maria fit in perfectly. She was pleasant, cordial, and smiled politely to everyone: Helena's parents, her two brothers, four grandparents, uncle and aunt and two cousins.

Everyone seemed to like her. Helena was so pleased. As the long and arduous ceremony continued, she prayed that it would soon finish without any incidents.

But then it came.

Helena watched it happen. She saw uncle Bernie as he looked at Maria a little too intently.

He snorted at her loudly, "Aren't you *afraid*, little girl, that we will *cook* you tonight and drink your *blood?*"

Mrs. Goldstein exclaimed, "Bernie!"

His wife, aunt Goldie, buried her face in her hands, "Bernie!"

Helena was *mortified*.

But Maria didn't miss a bit, "No, sir. And Helena had already warned me about you!"

Everyone laughed, and Helena, who had caught her breath, now exhaled deeply. Mrs. Goldstein said, "Well done, Helena, for warning Maria. And well done, Maria, for listening. My brother Bernie can be rather nonsensical!"

Uncle Bernie smiled lovingly and nodded.

This was not it, though. When the ceremony was

about to end, Helena's grandfather stood and began an emotional speech, which Helena found quite embarrassing, about the "enemies of the people", and how in each generation someone comes to "kill us all". He exclaimed, "And now we should not be afraid of this lunatic…!"

Maria looked at Helena and whispered, "Who is he talking about?"

Helena shrugged and whispered, "I think he's talking about this man, a nationalist, who was just elected somewhere… My father and brothers have been arguing about him… but I'm not sure…"

The grandfather continued for what seemed like eternity to Helena, passionately talking in his hoarse voice about how "this *lunatic* won't succeed where *Pharaoh* failed!" and how all would be well, "…as long as we put the *family* above all!"

Mrs. Goldstein hurried to use his dramatic pause and chimed, "Well said, Dad. They tried to kill us, we survived, now let's eat!"

Everyone clapped as the grandfather finally sat down. Helena whispered, "Phew! What a speech!"

Maria grinned. She actually enjoyed the passionate speech. She whispered to Helena, "My grandpa, had he needed to give this speech, would have probably fallen asleep in the middle!"

They smiled at each other.

Maria loved all the various foods. But more so, she

loved how after the dinner they were all looking for the hidden flatbread, which the grandmother hid somewhere around the house. Helena and Maria looked for it like mad, and so did Reuben, Solomon and the two cousins.

From the library, Maria called to Helena, who was searching the pantry; "Helena, is it wrapped in a white towel?"

"Yes! Did you...?"

Maria came with the towel wrapped flatbread, "I'm not sure...?"

"Everyone!" Helena jumped, "Maria found the hidden Afikoman!" Helena ran to the living room where everyone was resting after the meal, "Maria found the Afikoman!"

The grandfather leaned forward and exclaimed, "Very well!"

Maria looked at everyone staring at her.

Helena clapped her hands, "You get to ask for a *prize!*"

Maria reddened, "A prize? I don't..."

Everyone looked at her.

Maria looked down, "I don't..." she shrugged her shoulders, "Just *being* here is a prize..."

Everyone clapped, "Well said!"

The grandmother exclaimed, "Helena! What a good friend you've got!"

Helena beamed.

Helena's grandfather said, "But that won't do. You need to choose something, anything!"

Mrs. Goldstein hurried to say, "Leave her alone. It's okay, darling," she said to Maria, "you can decide later. Now, everyone, let's sing some of the oldies... Bernie...?"

It took three weeks of pleading.

"But mama!" Maria cried, "It's not charity!"

"Even if it's not, I'm not going to let you go away for a whole week! What will I do with Eddie and Sashinka?"

"Mrs. Szymborska said she'd help with them!"

"Well, you know what I think of Mrs. Szymborska!"

"Mom," Maria cried, "I really want to go, I've never been to the sea!"

"So what?! I've never been either, and do you see me crying?"

At school, Helena gave Maria *all* the methods. Whenever Maria gave up, Helena came up with a new plan. Maria would memorize it, but she didn't have much faith in any of Helena's weird ideas.

"Mama," Maria tried again, "I promised Helena I'd help her with the *summer math assignment*. Last year she couldn't do it, and she asked me to—"

"Isn't her father an accountant? He can help her!"

"But we also told Mr. Kissinger we'd do the summer Biology experiment at the sea, with barnacles and seaweed. He already approved the experiment for us!"

"Oh leave me alone Maria will you!"

Helena kept searching for more ideas. Finally, she decided to involve her mother.

Mrs. Goldstein came one day to pick Helena up from Maria's. "Mrs. Bozek," she said in the living room, "can I have a moment with you?"

"I'm here, am I not?" Mrs. Bozek said.

Mrs. Goldstein smiled to Helena, who, along with Maria, took Eddie and Sasha to play outside.

Helena's heart beat fast. "You'll see," she told Maria outside as they were throwing the ball among the four of them, "my mother will make it happen."

Thirty minutes later Mrs. Goldstein came out of the house, smiling. "She'll think about it," she said to Helena. "Now say goodbye to Maria and the kids and let's hurry, we don't want to be late for the ballet."

It was unclear what was said in the living room, but, miraculously enough, it worked. On July first, boarding the train for the full-day journey toward the country's seaside, was—in addition to the usual yearly quintet of Mr. and Mrs. Goldstein and their three children—also the daughter's best friend: Maria Bozek.

Maria's father, who worked at that very train station, climbed on the train to bid them all farewell, wearing his engineer's uniform. Mr. Goldstein reassured him, "Don't worry, Mr. Bozek, Maria will be safe with us."

"It's not me who's worried. It's her mother. As for me," Mr. Bozek said and winked at Maria, "I'm just jealous!"

Maria laughed. Helena hurried to say, "Perhaps next time the whole family could come?"

Mr. Bozek smiled, "Whatever God wills." He looked at Mr. and Mrs. Goldstein and tipped his hat at them, "Have a pleasant journey!"

He then got off the train, and tapped the train's conductor on the back, "Take care of them, my daughter is there!"

Maria looked eagerly through the window. "I can't believe we'll spend four full days together!"

Helena jumped, "Right?! Oh, I have to take you to the deserted house on the hilltop, if it's still there. Oh, and to the ice-cream parlor, you'll love it…"

"But we must leave time for the biology assignment," Maria added.

"Right." Helena smiled. "Plenty of time!"

It's hard to point out a person's happiest times in life; most of the moments blend together. But those four days on the beach were, for both Maria and Helena, some of the most memorable moments in their lifetime: how Mrs. Goldstein bought the two of them matching bathing suits and Helena cheered ("Don't you just love the belt, Maria?"); how they ran up the hill to the deserted house and hid and scared one another (given Helena's many times there with her brothers, she was already a pro); how they ate ice-cream trying *all* the different flavors (until they got sick); how they sunbathed on the beach for hours (and Helena cursed each cloud that hid the sun); how Maria tried learning a few ballet moves from Helena (without much success, but with tons of laughter); how they gossiped on the beach about Reuben and Solomon ("I can't *believe* you think Reuben is handsome!"); how they giggled into the night, chattering about Alexander, Roman, and the other boys in class (rating them according to new categories they came up with); how they took pictures with Reuben's new camera and made funny poses (which Helena masterfully directed) and how they took the biology sampling of barnacles' level of acidity and alkalinity in the tide pools (that is, *Maria* took the sampling while Helena mostly chattered).

When the four days were over, they cried in each other's arms at the train station.

Solomon was with them, making the trip back in order to help in his father's accounting firm for a few weeks or, according to Helena, to spend time with his darling Hannah. He was also to escort young Maria to the doorstep of her house, as Mrs. Goldstein promised Mrs. Bozek.

Helena cried to Maria, "Promise you'll write to me as soon as you enter your house!"

"I promise. Promise you'll look into the math assignment, a little each day!"

"I promise."

They hugged and whispered, "Friends forever."

"Forever!"

Solomon coughed. "Shall we?"

Helena nodded.

Maria climbed with him unto the train, "I'll write as soon as I get home! Please thank your parents again!"

Helena walked on the platform, following them as they took their seats. They waved goodbye to each other on both sides of the window. The conductor blew the whistle. The doors closed.

Helena motioned with her lips, "I'll miss you!"

"I'll miss you too!"

The train began moving. They waved to each other. Helena kept waving on the platform as the train left, leaving a trail of smoke above the platform as it slowly disappeared in the horizon.

The years passed.

An older Maria and an older Helena now sat at the front of the class.

Over the years their friendship had only grown stronger.

Maria often spent holiday evenings with Helena's family, learning of their intricate traditions, deeds, and unique humor. Helena, too, didn't miss an opportunity to be with the Bozeks. She learned to develop thick skin with Mrs. Bozek, learning that ultimately the matron only had good intentions. When they held hands before each meal, she prayed with them too. When they crossed their chests, she looked down and waited for them to finish.

But apart from such minute differences, they were

like sisters.

They had their ups and downs, too, like sisters.

Helena was very much interested in boys, while Maria was always more reticent about the subject. Helena sometimes scolded Maria, explaining to her that life "Isn't all about books and exams!"

But Maria didn't spare Helena from her reprimands either, explaining to her, as if she were a child, that she must "Invest time in studying," and that "Grades do matter!"

Peculiarly enough, they slowly became more similar. Helena began to find some pleasure in numbers, especially when it came to money. Maria began to enjoy social circumstances; she was still very quiet, but some of the freedom she learned from Helena began showing up in her.

The other students referred to them as "Helena and Maria." Helena's name did come *first*, but Maria's name was never forgotten. They were invited together to parties. They were always seated together when going to a café or a performance.

They sometimes even completed each other's sentences, bursting into laughter and leaving everyone else a little envious of their close bond.

However, while their relationship seemed unbreakable, the safe world around them began to crack.

The army recruited many young men, trying to

prepare for a severe blow from the growing army-nation across borders.

But the military, as much as it tried, soon lost to a brutal attack. Now, the new occupying army was beginning to change things.

It started with laws that at first seem trivial, such as not allowing people of a certain heritage to wear fur, for example.

Then, large businesses, some of which were owned by members of Helena's extended family, were confiscated and nationalized.

Helena and Maria were not too worried. They were excited to finish school and begin university together, making sure they were both going to the same place. They fretted for months about what to study.

Helena thought of following the footsteps of her brothers.

"But Helena," Maria retorted, "*accounting?* Seriously? I cannot see you possibly...—"

"Look," Helena sighed, "it's a good profession. It's a *stable* profession..."

"You sound just like Mr. Goldstein!"

Helena tried to smile, "Well, I guess, there's acting in it *too*, you see? With large clients one must know how to present and convince... And being a *woman* accountant is quite a big thing, Maria, there aren't many, and I can change that..."

Maria sighed. "I'm not sure you'll be happy..."

"Well," Helena said, calculating her words, "it is a *needed* profession. And now with the *war* and with things changing like that…"

Maria understood that reasoning. The Goldsteins had moved from their large house into a smaller apartment, trying to save money and assets as much as possible. She could understand Helena, to an extent.

"And you?" Helena asked, "Are you sure about Pharmaceutical sciences?"

Maria's eyes glowed, "It's the closest thing to being a doctor, you know, and I hope to help people that way…"

Helena smiled, "One day you'll invent the cure for some big disease, and you'll be world famous!"

Maria laughed, "If anyone will be famous out of the two of us, it'll be you!"

The atmosphere at university was different than in high school. Sure, it was larger. But that was not it. There were some people who were adamant that Helena and people of her heritage should not be admitted into universities.

Maria argued with one of the new friends on campus, "Of course they should be admitted! And to *all* universities!"

"Are you one of *them* or what?" the friend retorted, "Besides, there isn't enough space in all of the academies for all of those who seek higher education, so it's only reasonable…"

Maria tried arguing, but she slowly saw how the army's radio, the pamphlets and the posters were being successful in changing people's thoughts.

People changed. Even people from her old class.

One day she met her old friend Alexander on the street. She hadn't seen him for over a year. They spoke for several minutes. He then asked, "Are you still a friend of Helena?"

"Of course! Why shouldn't I be?"

Alexander looked around. "Well, it's not very *wise*, you know…"

At home, Maria shared her frustration with her parents and siblings. Eddie was now in high school, and Sasha was soon finishing elementary school. Maria complained all the time, "I just can't understand people's idiocy!"

But things were tense at home as well; her mother was laid off from her work in the factory, as the occupying army was bringing its "own" people, and unemployment among factory workers was high due to the occupation of this new workforce. The occupying country's economy was booming, but Maria's beloved country was now carrying the burden.

Her mother ceaselessly looked for employment, but to no avail. In the meantime, she was cleaning houses when she could, although the demand for cleaning ladies and maids was not high.

They were all now dependent on Maria's father's

income. The occupying army had fired many of the train workers. There was danger of Mr. Bozek being fired as well.

At the dinner table, Maria was exasperated. "I just can't stand seeing how people fall into this talk of hatred…"

Eddie, who was usually quiet by the dinner table, said, "But there is *some* truth to it, isn't there? What about that corrupt Minister? He was one of *them.*"

Mr. Bozek suddenly slammed his fist on the table. They were all startled. "I will not," he muttered through his teeth, "let you… speak this way… in my household!"

Eddie looked down.

Mrs. Bozek went to the stove to get more potatoes.

"Father," said Maria, "there's no need to—"

"What do you even know, Eddie," Mr. Bozek stood up, pushing his plate, "what do you even know about that Minister, huh? Don't believe everything you hear, son. I think it was a set up!"

Eddie sighed, "But Father, they found…"

"I'll have none of it!"

"Now-now," Mrs. Bozek said, "we should all finish eating. Sashinka, how was school? You had an exam, didn't you?"

"Yes, Mama. It went well."

"Good," Mrs. Bozek said and tried to smile.

Silence ensued. All eyes were fixed on the plates.

One morning, as Maria left the house to university, she saw large posters stuck to walls everywhere. Reading them, her heart sank.

She hurried to the Accounting studies Faculty to find Helena. But she wasn't there. No one had seen her.

Maria uncharacteristically decided to skip university. She took the tram to the Goldstein's apartment.

As she climbed the stairs, she heard noise behind the door. They were talking and arguing. She rang the bell.

Silence ensued inside.

"It's me!" Maria called, "Maria, for Helena!"

"Maria!" Mrs. Goldstein opened the door.

Maria looked at them. Helena was there, along with Mr. Goldstein, Reuben, Solomon, and Solomon's fiancée, Hannah. Helena came over and hugged her. Her eyes were worried.

"Have you all," Maria asked, "seen the signs?"

They nodded.

Helena sighed and walked over to the sofa. Maria followed her and sat down next to her, holding her hand.

Mr. Goldstein looked tired. Maria realized how old he had become. He looked at his wife. "I'm not leaving my parents! If your brother wants to go, let him go."

Mrs. Goldstein fidgeted with her hands. "Bernie says nothing good will come out of it. And that the war won't be over any time soon. The occupying army, he said, is only advancing..."

Maria murmured, "My father says the same."

Everyone looked at her. She nodded, "He's been saying how the army is only sending more and more soldiers and equipment on the tracks all the time, advancing East and South."

Mr. Goldstein sighed. "This too shall pass."

Maria looked worriedly at Helena, whose eyes looked somewhat hollow. "You all," Maria said slowly, "should not move into the enclosure. I don't feel good about it."

Solomon walked around the room. "Me neither. Father, it's insane! Now this enclosure, then what?"

Mr. Goldstein sighed. "Bernie says he's unable to procure any permits for my parents or," his voice grew stronger as he looked at Mrs. Goldstein, "or for your parents. I'm not leaving *anyone* behind! We are together in this!"

Solomon stormed out of the room. Hannah got up and joined him.

Maria realized she had walked into a sensitive situation. What would she have done had she been in their position?

Soon after the Goldsteins moved into the enclosed neighborhood the whole area was surrounded by a tall fence. Maria tried to convince the soldiers at the entrance, several times, with various pretenses, to let her in. But they never did.

Nor was she able to give a letter to anyone. All of the residents of the enclosure were now to wear an armband indicating their lower status. And if they were caught outside the enclosure or near the fence speaking to anybody, the punishment was death without trial.

"I can't stand it!" Maria said one evening at the dinner table.

The family dinners had become quieter. Mr. Bozek became more agitated, and no one wanted to make him upset.

Maria continued, "I must know how Helena is doing. It's springtime, that's when they celebrate Passover…"

Quiet ensued.

Then Eddie spoke, "I heard of a boy from school who manages to get things across."

Maria looked at him, "Do you? Eddie! Why didn't you tell me?!"

"I just found out today," Eddie said sheepishly, "He has a friend from the enclosure, who works outside. He has a permit, and he sneaks things in."

Maria stood up, "I'm going to write her a letter right now."

Mrs. Bozek said, "Right now you'll finish your dinner…—"

Mr. Bozek put his hand on his wife's hand.

Maria went to the living room and began writing.

The response Maria received three days later was laconic.

"Dearest M.

Your letter brought a ray of light into my day.

I think of our days on the beach often. Also,

of the fun we had.

I wish I could see you soon. I hope the war will be over soon.

H."

Maria read it again and again, not understanding. Why was Helena not writing *more?* This was so odd! Was there some sort of code in her words?

She read the short letter again and again. She was puzzled. Did she do anything that might have offended Helena? Why was Helena so brief?

Was she in a danger? Was she upset with her?

These thoughts tortured her. She found it hard to concentrate in university. All of the chemistry lessons blurred together. She found none of it important. None of it made sense.

One day, while she was in class, she heard shouting in the distance, and some gun shots.

What was going on?!

Two days later, Eddie brought home a letter.

"Dearest Maria,"

Maria looked at the short letter, her hands trembling.

"They took my father, and many of the men in the enclosure, to a work camp. The soldiers didn't say where it is.

My mother is going crazy with worry.

Could you please find out where this camp is?
I was wondering whether your Father could
find out somehow at the train station…? I
hope it's not too much to ask. It will mean the
world for me to know where the work camp
is.

I hope I have not offended you in any way.
You are always in my heart.

H."

The following evening Maria's father did not return
home for dinner.

Maria was upset, "Why is he so late? He promised
he'd find out and tell me. Where is he?"

"Hush now," Mrs. Bozek said. Her husband was
over an hour late. "We'll begin eating. Eddie, do you
want to lead the prayer?"

Then they all ate quietly. Maria jumped out of her
seat at each noise, hoping it was her father at the door.
She needed to know where that camp was so she
could write Helena and have it sent to her first thing
in the morning with Eddie's friend. The thought of
Mrs. Goldstein's pain bothered her tremendously.

She waited and waited.

At eleven o'clock at night the key was finally heard in
the door.

Maria, studying her pharmaceutical textbooks in the

kitchen, jumped to the door.

She was disgusted. Her father smelled like alcohol. "Father!" she scolded him, whispering as to not to wake up Eddie and Sasha, "I've been waiting for you!"

"Move aside...!"

Her father barely made his way into the house. He was very drunk. Maria had never seen him that way.

Mrs. Bozek stood at the end of the hall. He walked toward her and fell into her arms. She took him into their bedroom and closed the door.

Maria was shocked. What was going on? She knocked on her parent's door.

"Leave me alone...!" her father groaned from the bedroom.

Maria opened the door and closed it behind her.

Her mother looked at her, worried.

Maria swallowed her saliva. Her father was laying on his back on the bed. His eyes were staring at the ceiling.

"Father! I've asked you to find out...—"

"Can't you," he muttered, "just leave me alone?!"

Maria's chin began quivering. Her mother looked at her, her eyes wide open, saying nothing.

"Father?" Maria said, "what did you...?"

Her father shrieked. He began crying.

She had never seen him cry before.

"The trains," he muttered, "they go into the forests full, but they…"

Silence followed.

He stared at the ceiling. "They… come back empty."

The years had passed. The train proceeded quickly toward her beloved city. She watched as the landscape changed in front of her.

Home.

It was home. She remembered these views from her childhood.

She did not want to think about what had happened.

She sighed. Could one just erase certain events from one's mind?

She remembered how she and Maria, so many years before, sat on the beach, writing things in the sand. Then the sea would come and wash them away.

Could she just magically erase some of her

memories?

She wanted to so badly.

She looked at the views. Spring was here. Things were blooming.

Blooming. As if Mother Nature was unaware of these past years of the war. As if she didn't hear what happened. As if nothing had happened.

She looked at the forest through her window. She remembered how she and Maria used to run through the trees.

Would she ever be able to be so carefree again?

After the transport that took Helena's father away, there was another.

Eddie's friend no longer had his acquaintance that could smuggle letters in and out.

Maria asked around. But it was dangerous to ask around.

You never knew who was listening, who could report.

Friends became enemies. Enemies disguised themselves as friends.

One day at university she spotted Roman. She remembered that towards the end of high school he used to date one girl; she was one of *them*, wasn't she? Perhaps he could pass a letter to Helena?

Maria took Roman aside, trying to read his eyes. Was he now brainwashed as well?

How could she ask him?

He looked back at her. "How have you been doing, Maria?"

She looked at his eyes. "Roman, can I trust you?"

He smiled. "You'll have to trust yourself first."

"Do you…" she hesitated, "How is that girlfriend of yours?"

He looked around nervously. "Shall we go into a quieter place?"

They walked the campus and went into the empty auditorium, then climbed upstairs to the mezzanine. Roman looked around as they were walking to make sure no one was following them.

"She's safe," he said.

"Who? Helena?" Maria gasped.

"No, my girlfriend, Rebecca. I found her a hiding place."

"In your village?"

"No, are you crazy? It's too dangerous. In a far away, small farm, at my old uncle's."

Maria's chest began pounding. "Could you do the same for Helena?"

Roman wetted his lip. "You two are still… friends?"

"We'll always be friends, Roman! And you are her friend too. I need your help."

"They've taken many," Roman said and looked away, "I think it might be too late. They're liquidating the enclosure."

Maria's heart pounded fast. She knew what would happen to her if she was caught having this conversation. She knew what would happen to Roman as well. She appreciated him trusting her. "I think," she whispered, "I... *know*, that she's still there, Roman! I... *feel* her...!"

Roman smiled, "Well, let me see. I have a contact who gets in and out of the enclosure. I'll ask him to find out if she's still there."

"Oh Roman!" Maria shrieked, "It will mean the world to me!"

Roman spotted Maria on campus. His eyes signaled her to follow him.

It had been three days since their last conversation. He now had some information.

Maria followed him through the university into the Biology building, and into one of the labs. There was a door to a storage room. He had the keys. He opened the door and then quickly closed it behind them.

"The good news is," he whispered, looking at Maria's wide eyes, "that she's alive."

Maria shrieked, "I knew it." She crossed her chest, "Thank you, God. Thank you!"

"The other good news is," he sighed, "that she is working outside the enclosure."

"Outside?! Does she…?"

Roman nodded. "Each morning she is taken out with some other women to a factory owned by the occupying army… Then they all go back in the evening. So… I guess that's good."

She looked at him. "Go on."

He sighed and looked away, "The bad news is," he continued nervously, "that they took her mother and one of her brothers."

"No."

Roman nodded.

Maria covered her face with her hands.

Roman sighed. "And… she's basically alone. She told my friend's friend, who met her yesterday, that we shouldn't bother about her."

"That we shouldn't *what?!*"

"Bother about her. That she'll soon join her family, wherever they are."

Maria clenched her fist. "We need to get her out!"

Roman sighed, "It's not that simple."

They heard a noise from behind the door. Steps. The steps came closer. Maria's heart stopped. Then the steps continued away.

She waited until the steps disappeared.

Roman whispered, "Even if we somehow manage to smuggle her out, we need to get her documents… It's very expensive, and quite risky…"

"I'm done with risky," Maria said. "I cannot live this way anymore!"

Roman was quiet.

Maria looked at him. "How much?"

"A forged ID costs twenty thousand."

"Twenty thousand?!" Maria's eyes grew wide, "How can *anyone* come up with *twenty thousand?!*"

"You'd be surprised," Roman said.

Maria bit her lip. She shook her head.

Roman sighed, "I hate to tell you this, but even if we get that ID, and fill up a fake name and number, one must still have several other documents, matching documents, which are even harder to get…"

Maria shook her head. She began crying.

Roman sighed, "They took Gisele too, and her whole family."

Maria's eyes widened, "Has the world gone *mad?!* This is hell on earth!"

"You're…" Roman whispered, "a believer, right?"

Maria nodded.

"So you'll have to pray. I pray all the time."

Maria nodded.

"Twenty thousand?" Maria's father exclaimed, "How on earth…?!"

Maria sat on her parent's bed, her eyes red. She

whispered, trying not to disturb Eddie and Sasha in the living room. "And he said that even if we *get* that sum, it's not easy to find someone to sell one, and then there are other documents one must get as well…"

Mrs. Bozek pouted her lips, "The other day a damned soldier stopped me. He looked at my ID and then said, 'Insufficient verification!'"

Mrs. Bozek shook her head, "He examined everything I had – my birth certificate, city registration, high school diploma, everything, as if I was a criminal!"

Maria looked at them. "I have a thousand of my own money. I borrowed another five hundred from a friend, and another three hundred from another friend…"

Mr. Bozek's eyes grew larger, "I don't want you going around asking for money. It will get people talking."

Maria's chin quivered, "I don't care, Papa! They took Helena's whole family! And Gisele is gone too…"

She began crying.

Mr. Bozek said, "I can only come up with five hundred myself," he opened the closet and moved a box aside, opening a small hidden place in the wall. "That's all I have, Marinka. We've exhausted everything…"

Mrs. Bozek fidgeted with her fingers. "Not

everything."

She took off her wedding ring. "This used to be worth some fifteen thousand, maybe more…—"

"Mama! Are you sure…—"

Mrs. Bozek pursed her lip in determination, and handed Maria the ring. "Now go and fetch the poor girl, do whatever you need to do."

Maria nodded. Mr. Bozek crossed himself. They all did.

"Dearest H.

I miss you terribly. It seems like I am able to procure you an empty ID. Please do your utmost efforts to get me a suitable photo of yours. I anticipate it will be ready by tomorrow, or at the latest the day after. Please don't lose hope. Yours, always,

M."

"Dearest M.,

I do appreciate your efforts. As not to offend you, I've attached the photo you asked for. But I beg you not to do anything foolish. They've hung a girl who tried to get her fiancé out. It's too dangerous. I'm fine here. I hope to soon join my family.

Yours, H."

"Dearest H.

Please give anything of value to the boy carrying this letter. Leave nothing in the enclosure of value. In one of the coming days, when the ID is prepared and stamped with your photo, I will come to take you, possibly in the morning when you are on your way to work. Please be prepared.

Hang on.

M."

Maria climbed the stairs of a building not too far away from the entrance to the enclosure. The small windows of the stairway were dirty. She climbed to the third floor and looked down from the small window.

From there she could see the entrance. Four soldiers with rifles stood there, talking.

She memorized the names mounted on the doors of the second and first floors. This was in case someone living in the building would ask her what she was doing there, and then she could say she came to visit someone...

She shook her head. It was a weak story. But it was the best she could come up with.

Outside the sun was just breaking over the skyline.

Maria looked at her clock. A quarter past six.

She waited.

Thirty minutes later she finally saw something. On the horizon, in the main street of the enclosure, a group of people appeared. They marched towards the gate. Their armbands were visible even from this distance.

They looked horribly thin.

She still could not see their faces, but it seemed like all of them were men.

Those damned armbands, she thought. They were as bright as anything.

The soldiers opened the gate, and then led the group of men out. Then the gate closed behind them. Maria gasped at the number of soldiers escorting the group. Seven soldiers, no, eight soldiers with rifles.

Maria's heart beat fast. It was going to be more difficult than she had thought.

As the group passed by the building she was watching from, she looked at their faces. Helena was not there.

Few minutes of silence continued. Maria saw a few people walking on the street outside the enclosure's gate. The city was slowly waking up.

Her legs hurt from standing so long, on her tip-toes, looking out the window.

Then she saw them. A group of women marching on the horizon, down the main street of the enclosure.

She bit her lip.

Her heart pounded. The soldiers opened the gate. The group of women was led by only one soldier. As they came out, though, Maria noticed another soldier walking behind them. She looked carefully at every face. All the women looked so gaunt. She hadn't seen Helena in over a year and a half. She worried that she would not recognize her best friend.

Finally, she realized that Helena was not in the group. Tears came to her eyes as she thought that perhaps she had come too late - perhaps they had already taken Helena.

Her heart pounded. No. Please don't, God. Please, God, please. Please.

Just then, she saw another group of women led by a soldier, emerging in the distance, walking down the street inside the enclosure. She looked at her pocket watch. It was now three minutes before seven.

Then she saw her.

She gasped.

Was it indeed her?

The soldiers opened the gate, and the one at the head of the group led the row marching toward the building. Maria nodded to herself. That's Helena!

She ran down the stairs.

She exited the building. She saw the group of

women walking on the sidewalk across the street. She walked quickly, trying not to attract attention to herself. Roman had told her the ID should be ready yesterday. Her heart pounded. She needed to be prepared.

She walked on the other side of the street. The women looked so feeble, their armbands so bright. They were walking tightly together, almost as if they were holding each other up.

The soldier at the back of the group looked at her. She looked away. Damn! She needed to be more careful.

She hoped her face didn't reveal her intentions. She wanted so badly to get a closer glimpse of Helena. But she knew it was not wise. The soldier leading the front turned right to the large street with the tram in its center.

Maria waited for the soldier at the back of the group to turn as well, and then she walked behind them, keeping a great distance.

More people filled the streets, hurrying to work. She kept her eyes on the group as they walked. Then she gasped. The group disappeared into one of the buildings.

She cursed to herself.

This route was impossible. It was too short.

She walked to that building. The occupying army's banner stretched over it. A soldier stood at the front. She continued walking.

She crossed the street and made her way back. This route was impossible. They only walked out of the enclosure, down the street, and then turned right at the central street, straight toward their factory.

Her face revealed her frustration. With a soldier at the front and a soldier at the back, this was just... impossible. How could she take Helena away?

She traced her steps back. She turned left at the corner back to the street leading to the enclosure.

She then made her way from her "lookout" building down the street, experiencing the walk as if she was one of them. She looked at the shops on the way, trying not to attract attention to herself from passersby.

That was when she then saw a narrow passage between two buildings.

She walked down the passage, away from the street. Could they escape from here?

She was disappointed to see it was a dead end, leading to the back of one of the buildings. It was too dangerous. Even if she ran with Helena here, they'd still have to go back out to the street.

She was exasperated.

She was mad at Roman. "What do you mean it 'isn't ready'?!"

Roman looked offended. "I told you, Maria, that I'll do whatever I can, but the person handling the ID has many…"

"I don't care!" Maria exclaimed.

"Shhh" Roman whispered. The lab in the Biology building was deserted, but you still never knew who was lurking nearby.

The air in the small storage room was stuffy.

"You said," Maria whispered, "that it would take a day or two, not a week!"

"I'm going to him every day, and…"

"I want to go and see this man! I gave my mother's wedding ring for it, and I'm not going to…—"

"Maria," he whispered, "this is a matter for grown ups, not of…—"

"I'm twenty-three and so are you, Roman," she whispered, her eyes shining, "and you'll be taking me to see him today!"

Roman sighed, "I promised him I'd keep his work a secret…"

"Roman! It's Helena! It's Helena I'm talking about…" Maria bit her lip, trying not to cry, "It's our *Helena!* 'Stars circle round thy head, and at thy feet surges the sea, upon whose hurrying waves…'" her eyes watered, she put her chin out, "It's our Helena!"

Roman nodded.

Maria grabbed his coat, "It's our Helena, Roman! They could be butchering her right now, and you and I will have to live with the blood on our hands…!"

Roman's eyes watered. "I'll take you to him this afternoon."

Maria shook her head, "You'll take me to him now."

The man opened the door slightly, with the door chain still on. "Who are you?!"

Roman looked at him, surprised, "I'm… I was here yesterday and the day before…"

"I don't know you!" the man said and looked at

Maria, "The people I know don't bring spies with them!"

Maria looked at the man behind the door with her fiery eyes. "I'm not a spy," she muttered, "and unless you want me to become one, you'll open the door right now."

The door slammed in their faces.

Roman shook his head. "Maria…!"

Maria raised her chin up.

Suddenly they heard the door's chain jingle. Roman's eyes grew bigger. The door opened slightly. The man motioned to them to come in, quickly. They walked in.

The man looked down the stairway and closed the door, securing it with three locks. "No one followed you here?"

Roman shook his head, "No, I looked."

The man sighed, "Now, why do you bring me this trouble!"

Roman was about to say something, but Maria interrupted. "Sir, I'm the one who gathered the remaining money of my family, including my mother's…—"

"Spare me your words, girl, I hear these stories all the time…"

Maria was taken aback, "You'll hear me until I'm done!"

The man's eyes grew bigger, as did Roman's. Maria

muttered through her teeth, "Now you're either going to get me that ID right away, or I will open that window there and scream to the whole street what you are doing here."

The man shook his head. He sighed, "I have IDs from three weeks ago waiting, I'm only one man…"

"I'll help you if you need," Maria said, "But we're not leaving this place until I have that ID!"

He stared at her, puzzled.

She looked at him, her eyes fiery. "My best friend's life is on the line. Now, shall we get to it, or do you need more drama?"

The man suddenly smiled. He looked baffled. He went to his bookcase, moved some books around, and pulled the whole bookcase away from the wall. It revealed a small desk with a pile of IDs on it. Maria felt her heart beat as she saw them.

The man shuffled through the pile. "Now, what was her name again…?"

"Helena," Maria said and came closer, "Helena Goldstein."

He looked through the photos. "Is this her?"

Maria looked over his shoulder. It was her Helena. "Yes!"

He took a breath and placed the photo next to him. He took an empty ID and a black pen. "Shall I just invent a name," the man said, "or do you…"

"Invent?!" Maria cried, "don't you have some list

of… names…?"

He shrugged. "I invent the names. Then people forge documents accordingly elsewhere…"

Maria bit her lip. She eyed Roman, who looked rather helpless, and asked him, "What name did you give your girlfriend?"

"I didn't. Rebecca is in hiding. If she were to be found, then…"

"And can Helena also…?"

Roman shook his head. "My uncle already said he's too afraid of having just one…—"

"I see." Maria breathed heavily.

The man looked at her, "I'm sorry, but I don't have the whole day."

"Give her my name. Maria Bozek."

The man looked at her, raised his eyebrows, and turned to look at Roman.

Roman gulped. "Maria, that's… too dangerous… If they find out…—"

"What else do you propose!" Maria shrieked, "You two are constantly telling me what *not* to do, but you offer no help!"

"But… Maria…" Roman mumbled, "your family. They can kill them all…"

The man looked at her, "The punishment for giving someone your ID is death without sentence…"

Maria reached for her purse. "This way I could give

her my birth certificate, and high school diploma," she sighed, "and the baptismal certificate…" she took her ID out and put it on the man's desk. "Copy it."

The man shrugged again, "They are very clever… They match the registry…"

Maria spoke quietly. "Please copy it."

The man looked at Roman again and shook his head, "I'm afraid you don't know what you're…"

Maria shouted at him, "Copy it now I say!"

The sun was just rising. Only a few shops had opened. Maria was waiting, hiding in the narrow passage between the two buildings. Roman was near the tram station down the street. He had warned her. "We need a better plan," he said, "possibly someone from within the enclosure could somehow smuggle her out at night..."

But Maria would have none of it. These were all ideas, empty ideas, without a concrete way of implementation. Options for the future. Vague thoughts. She felt her time running out.

Roman insisted, "But the risk! You can't just grab her like that on the street!"

"That's exactly what I'll do."

"But they'll shoot you. You'll kill yourself and her!"

"Roman," Maria shook her head, "where is Gisele? Where are Helena's brothers? Her parents? Where are they all?"

"They were taken…"

"Taken where, Roman?"

Roman was silent.

"Wake up, Roman! We've all been blinded! We cannot continue waiting! Every minute we waste might be Helena's last…!"

"But, Maria…"

"All I need is for you to speak to your uncle. I can't take her home. It's too visible, too dangerous, everyone knows her. We'll get Helena to your uncle's farm. Then I'll figure it out. Just for a day."

Roman sighed. He wanted so badly to say 'no', but he knew he couldn't. He knew he could never forgive himself if he refused to cooperate, and if Helena would then… "But," he said, "I'm taking no part in your crazy abduction! It's doomed to fail, Maria! I can convince my uncle to hide her in his barn for one night, maybe. But I'm not going to endanger her and you by cooperating…—"

"That's fine," Maria said, "I've done my homework."

Now her heart pounded. She was doubting her plan. Had she, indeed, done her homework?

She put her hands on two fur scarves. She thought

they would help Helena look more dignified, and disguise that poor dress she had seen her with two days earlier.

She took a deep breath in. The fur will do *something*, she thought. She needed to get Helena quickly to the tram for a short ride to the train station, where they'd get her out of the city and to the farm. Then they'd plan what to do next.

She saw a few people passing in the street. It was six thirty in the morning. She pretended to look at the names on the mail boxes, fearing one of the neighbors might come out of their home.

Yes, she thought, the scarf would do something. One of the earliest stipulations of the occupying army was for all 'enemies' not to wear fur. The fur scarf could make Helena, now, look less like she's one of *them*.

But Maria knew she'd also have to get rid of the horrific armband instantly.

She suddenly heard the steps, marching down the street. She bit her lip. It was the men. She knew. She saw the first soldier marching down the pavement, so close to her. She saw the men with their armbands, bent over in weakness, walking, surrounded by other soldiers with their rifles.

She pressed her back against the wall, not wanting them to see her.

She closed her eyes and nodded to herself. This was the best plan. The best plan. Here, between these buildings, right near the corner. The lead soldier would be in the front, he wouldn't see. And the soldier at the back of the row would still be around the corner; he wouldn't see either, right?

She breathed heavily. God, she prayed, make the other women in the line say nothing. God, good God, make it work. Make it work.

She kept praying in her heart, now moving away from the wall as to not seem odd. She stared at the mailboxes. She then heard it. Another group. The steps were distinct. She looked out to the street. She saw some people passing by, probably on their way to work. Then she saw the soldier coming. She gasped and pressed her body against the wall. She saw the women with the armbands walking. She looked carefully, walking closer, just in case Helena might have somehow gotten into this group. She looked at their faces intently. Being in such close proximity to them, Maria suddenly thought how instead of grabbing Helena, she should reach and hug her, then carry her into the passage. In case one of the soldiers noticed, she could then explain she just… passed by… and suddenly saw her old friend. Hugging a person is not a crime, right?

Her heart beat heavily. What a lame story. They'd probably shoot her. She had already heard similar stories. The soldiers were merciless.

The women's row ended, followed by a soldier with his rifle. Soon, Maria thought. She prayed again.

She thought she heard the steps of the other group coming down the street. She tried listening. No. Not yet.

Any moment now.

Then she heard the steps. The soldier appeared on the pavement, walking quickly. Then the first woman. Not Helena. Then the next, not Helena either. That's not Helena. That's not Helena. That's not Helena…

Her heart nearly burst out her chest.

That's not Helena. That's not Helena. That's Helena. "Helena!" she exclaimed jumping over the thin woman. Helena's eyes grew bigger, anticipating a bullet shooting at her at any moment. Maria grabbed her and ran with her into the narrow passage, then she pressed herself against the wall. Helena did the same, looking at her, terrified.

They heard the footsteps continuing. Maria's lips tightened, whitening. Footsteps. More footsteps. They looked at each other.

Then the footsteps ceased.

"Quick," Maria whispered, placing her second fur scarf on Helena's neck. She grabbed Helena's armband and tore it off in one strong movement. The dress ripped around the arm. She looked at the armband in her hand. Where should she put it? Taking it would be detrimental, leaving it behind would be stupid as well. She saw the mailboxes and shoved it into one of them. Helena looked at her, petrified. Maria breathed heavily, "Your name is Maria Bozek. Now," she tried to stabilize her breath. She put her purse on Helena's shoulder. "Now we'll go, calmly," she wetted her lips, "Roman is waiting for us at the tram station. Let's go. Calmly, we're just *regular people*."

She adjusted the fur scarf on Helena's neck.

She put Helena's arm in hers. They walked a few steps. Suddenly Helena stopped. "But…" she murmured, "If… if *I'm* Maria, then… if we get asked… then who are *you*…?"

Maria forced a smile, "Leave that to me." She pulled Helena and they began walking. They exited the narrow passage and took a sharp left, away from the group that passed moments before. They walked quickly. Maria focused on the tram station in the distance. She bit her lip and then forced herself to smile. She straightened her back, pulled her shoulders back, and nudged Helena to do the same. People passed near them. Maria told herself, we're just regular people. Just friends, going to work.

Maria tried to resist her instinct to run. It would look odd if they ran. She glanced at Helena, who looked pale as a ghost. Maria muttered from between her teeth, "Smile!"

Helena forced a smile. They walked quickly. The tram station was closer. Maria could see Roman standing there. They walked faster. Roman looked wide-eyed at Helena. Maria slowed their steps, now standing along the other few people waiting for the tram. She didn't want to look back at where they came from. Where was the tram? Each second felt like a long minute. She looked back. In the distance, she thought she saw the group of women, down the street, entering the factory. She saw the large banner of the occupying army. She looked in the horizon thinking, "*Where is the tram?!*"

Then she saw it. The tram made its way slowly through the street. Good. But then her heart stopped beating as she watched a soldier come out of the factory and run down the street, holding his rifle, and then another soldier following him, running too. She looked away. Helena did the same. The tram made its way toward the station, slowing down. The tram's doors opened. Maria nearly pushed Helena through the tram's door, quickly paying the driver for the two of them. Through the glass she saw the soldiers running toward them. She couldn't move. She forced herself to sit down, Helena joining her. She looked in the other direction, willing the tram to begin moving. She told herself, "We're just regular people… just regular people. God, please!"

Never in her life did she invoke God's name as intensely and purposefully as she did in that moment. The other people climbed into the tram, Roman among them. The driver closed the doors. Roman, standing not too far from Maria and Helena, looked in the direction where Maria refused to look. His eyes widened as he saw the soldiers approaching the intersection. But then, the soldiers turned toward the street leading to the enclosure, away from the tram. The tram began moving, gaining speed. Roman sighed a sigh of relief and nodded at Maria. She bit her lip. A tear fell down her cheek.

The three of them got off the tram near the train station. None of them dared saying a word while they were on the tram. Now Roman said only, "Follow me."

Maria and Helena followed, arm in arm.

They entered the train station and headed for the platform. Roman suddenly turned around, heading in the other direction. Maria's eyes widened as she saw two soldiers checking people's IDs. She turned around too, and Helena, startled, nearly tripped.

They walked quickly in the other direction. Roman knew the train station well. They walked down some stairs, and then back up, approaching the platform from the other entrance.

But then, just as they came up the stairs, they saw

another soldier examining people's IDs.

Maria saw Roman hesitating, and whispered to him, "Keep going." She knew turning around only a few steps from the soldier would not look good.

"Documents!" the soldier barked.

They stood before him, on the platform at the top of the stairs. Roman quickly handed the soldier his ID, and Helena, her hands trembling, found the ID in the purse Maria had given her. Maria shook her head firmly, "I don't have mine, it was stolen yesterday!"

"Stolen?!" the soldier exclaimed.

"I went to the police station and filed a report, and this morning I went to the Interior Office, but they weren't open yet!"

He looked at her, surveying her face. Her chin was raised, and she looked at him straight in the eyes. "Maybe," she muttered, "if soldiers like you were doing their jobs *properly*, people's things wouldn't be stolen like this!"

Roman's eyes widened. Helena looked down at the floor. This seemed foolish.

The soldier looked at Maria, clenching his jaw. She quickly added, "I'm certain that under *your* shift such things don't happen! But your friends *do* need to be reprimanded for allowing such—"

"Enough!" he exclaimed. He looked at Roman's ID. "Date of birth!"

Roman muttered, "September 12th, 1919."

The soldier raised the ID to his eye level, looked at Roman and at the photo in the ID. He pouted his lip, "Insufficient verifications!"

"I also have these," Roman mumbled. He handed some documents to the soldier.

The train heading out of the city approached the platform.

The soldier looked through the documents and sighed. He nodded, and handed Roman the ID and the documents. He then looked at Helena's ID.

Maria stopped her breath. "If you please, Sir, we don't want to miss the train!"

"One more word," the soldier said and stared at Maria, "and I'll throw you straight to jail. There's a death penalty for losing government documents!"

Maria stared at him, not taking her gaze off.

"Date of birth!" the soldier barked at Helena.

She smiled, "January 22nd, 1920."

He looked at the ID, raised it, looked at the photo, then at her, then back at the photo. "Insufficient verification." He said and sighed.

Helena smiled, "Of course, forgive me." She reached for her purse. She looked at the documents, hesitating. Would there be a photo of Maria there? Did Maria actually make... She fidgeted through the documents, then handing him all she had. He unfolded the papers. He looked at the name of the birth certificate, the baptism certificate, and the school's diploma. He nodded and handed Helena the

ID and the documents, "That's fine, Miss Bozek".

Helena smiled, "Thank you," she took her purse and placed the documents and the ID inside.

Maria suddenly saw the soldier's eyes widening. He looked at Helena. Maria's heart stopped beating. What did he see?

He exclaimed, "Miss Bozek!"

Maria looked at him and then caught herself. He was speaking to Helena.

The soldier barked, pointing at Helena's arm. "Why is your dress torn here?!"

"Where?" Helena asked. "Oh, this? It's just," she laughed, "that I haven't had the time yet to stitch…—"

The soldier ground his teeth and reached for the whistle around his neck. Roman thought of running away. Maria, wide-eyed, looked at Helena.

But Helena burst into loud laughter, and then said in a rather flirtatious tone, "I hope I'm not too provocatively dressed for you, Mr. Soldier, sir…?"

Roman watched the train's doors close and saw it leaving the station. They were doomed.

The soldier didn't fall into Helena's trap. "That's!" he exclaimed and pointed at her arm, "That's where the armband is worn on the…—"

Helena gasped and crossed herself, "Jesus, Mary and Joseph! Never ever!" she cried, "Don't compare me to *them*, sir!"

He looked at her face, then at the torn dress, then at her face again.

"Hans!"

They all looked over their shoulders at the other platform. An officer stood there, waving at the soldier in front of them. In front of the officer there were two old people and a child. The officer looked at the soldier, "Hans! I need you here!"

The soldier, whose name must have been Hans, now lowered the whistle, "I'll be there!" he shouted.

He looked at Helena, shaking his head. He then looked at Maria and pointed his finger at her, "You! If I see you again without documents, I'll *shoot* you then and there!"

Maria nodded and gave him a sour smile.

The soldier then hurried down the stairs heading to the other platform.

Roman looked at Helena and then at Maria, speechless. Maria began walking, "Let's go."

They went and sat at the end of the platform, waiting for the train. They saw how the officer, on the other platform, now assisted by the soldier who a moment earlier had examined their IDs, took the old man with him. The soldier, Hans, grabbed the old woman with one hand and the child with his other. The kid didn't want to go, and began screaming and crying. He fell on the floor. The soldier dragged him by the arm, as the child tried holding onto people's legs. People stepped away. None of the people in that platform said or did anything.

The screaming child disappeared into the train's offices.

Maria watched the scene, and saw how Helena gazed at the floor, not looking.

"I cannot hide another one, Roman!" the old uncle muttered.

"Uncle, it's only for one night."

"That's what you said of Rebecca, 'only for a little while', and now you're putting me in an impossible situation again!"

Maria looked at Helena, holding her hand, sitting in the living room. Roman and his uncle were whispering to each other in the kitchen.

Roman insisted, "One night, Uncle! I promise."

The older man whispered, "The neighbors in the market already noticed I'm buying too much food for one person…"

Roman said, "Uncle, please! Just for one night!"

The uncle sighed. There was a long silence. "You are tightening the rope around my neck, you childish boy. Do you know what the soldiers can do?"

"Thank you so much, Uncle…"

Roman left the kitchen. "Let's go," he said, and opened the back door.

They followed him. The uncle walked out of the kitchen, shaking his head disapprovingly.

Roman led them to the barn. They looked at the piles of hay. Roman whispered, "Sweetie? Rebecca? It's me…!"

They saw a pile of hay moving, then another, and a ragged looking young woman appeared. Maria was horrified. She looked so different from the pretty girl she remembered.

Roman and his girlfriend embraced. She exclaimed, "I missed you!" and then noticed Maria and Helena. "Who are they?"

"Friends from school," Roman said, "My friends Maria and…—"

Maria quickly interrupted, "and *Maria*. Pleased to meet you! I believe I've seen you before."

The girlfriend murmured. "Before the war…?"

Maria nodded.

Roman took Rebecca by the hand and said, "Let's give them some privacy."

They went behind one of the large piles of hay.

Helena looked around the small barn. She looked hopeless.

Maria looked at her and whispered, "I'll get you out of here. Don't worry."

Helena nodded. She said nothing, leaned on one of the hay piles, and slouched on the ground.

Maria looked at her, worried. There was something in Helena's gaze... her eyes looked... hollow.

"Eddie and Sashinka," Maria said cheerfully, "have been asking about you." She sat down on the ground, leaning against the stack of hay.

Helena said slowly, as if waking up from a dream, "Did they...?"

Maria nodded. To herself she thought, 'Where is my Helena? This person isn't my Helena!'" She shook her head. "Eddie is in the polytechnic high school, doing well, and Sashinka is going next year to *our* school!"

Helena nodded.

Maria tried smiling, "She's almost our age when we first met..."

Helena nodded her head slowly. "So long ago..."

Maria couldn't stop her tears from coming. What had happened to Helena? She shook her head. No, she needs to be the strong one. She wouldn't cry.

Roman and Rebecca were kissing in the corner of the barn. They could hear them.

Helena stared into the air, blurry eyed.

Maria looked at her, "Helena..."

Helena did not respond.

Maria shook her, "Helena! Do you hear me?!"

Helena moved her shoulder, slowly, like a child not wanting to do something. She stared into the air. Then she said slowly, "The other women... they said nothing..."

"The other women?"

"In the line... when... you took me..."

"Yes," Maria said quickly, "that was good, right?"

Helena nodded slowly. "Whenever someone... disappeared... we were happy for her ..."

Maria nodded. "Of course, Helena!"

"I don't know... what happened to Reuben..."

Maria hesitated. She didn't want to ask.

"My name... my name was on the list," she said, "Reuben, he paid someone to switch my name with his. Then they took him. And my Mother... But Solomon and Hannah hid... They are still hiding in the enclosure..." She looked at Maria in the eye, "I should try... and help them..."

Maria folded her hands together nervously, "You should help yourself first, Helena..."

Maria felt awful saying that.

Helena nodded, "Solomon is smart... he'll find a

way… But Reuben… I wonder where he is now…"

Maria said, "Shhh…" and put her arm around Helena, pulling her to her lap, "Here, rest on me, Helena…"

Helena did not resist. She laid there in Maria's arms.

Maria noticed how thin Helena was. She bit her lip. Tears began flowing down her eyes.

Helena didn't cry. She stared into the air. "I wonder… where they are… Have you ever found out where they sent my Father?"

Maria hesitated, "No dear… I haven't…"

Maria entered the house.

Her mother jumped first, then her father, then Eddie and Sasha. "Where were you?"

Maria tried smiling, "I have good news."

She locked the door behind her, and hugged her mother. She whispered, "Let's go to the kitchen."

Her mother nodded.

In the small kitchen, they had all finished their dinner. They looked at her eagerly.

Maria smiled, "She's safe."

Sasha asked, "Who? Helena?"

"Shhh…" everyone hushed her.

Mrs. Bozek clasped her hands together, "Now sit and tell us everything."

Maria took her coat off and sat near the table. Her mother served her hot potatoes. "No. So speak!"

"Roman," Maria whispered, "has an uncle, and he'll be hiding her for the night."

Mr. Bozek leaned forward, "And then?"

Maria shook her head, "I don't know."

Mrs. Bozek tut-tutted, "She's not going to hide, right? The ID you got should…"

"No, I don't want her to hide. I think the enclosure had already done some… damage… She's not well…"

Mr. Bozek stared at her, "What do you mean?"

Maria shrugged her shoulders. "She's…" her lip pouted, "She's…"

Maria began crying. Eddie put his hand on her.

"She's…" Maria shook her head, looking at them all, "She's…. so *fragile*…"

Mrs. Bozek exclaimed, "She needs to eat!"

"No," Maria said, "it's not that… not *only* that… she's… she seems…" she put her hands on her face, "broken…"

Her father shook his head. "Those bastards…"

Sasha asked, "What will you do, Maria?"

"I don't know!" Maria exclaimed, sobbing.

No one dared saying anything. Mrs. Bozek finally

said, "Well, she cannot stay there in hiding, nor can she come to the city…"

Eddie mumbled, "People will recognize her…"

Silence ensued. Maria wiped her tears.

Mrs. Bozek looked helpless. "Eat your food, Maria!"

Maria nodded, but didn't touch it. "She needs to go to a large city…"

Her father interrupted. "We need to get her to the capital."

"I thought so too," Maria said, "but… I can't go with her."

"Why not?" her mother asked.

Maria hesitated. She didn't tell them.

They all looked at her. She took a deep breath. "I… I gave her… my name…"

"You did *what?*" Mrs. Bozek cried.

"She needed," Maria said, "not only the ID, but also the other documents, you know, Mama. So, I gave her mine. I'll get new ones."

Mr. Bozek shook his head, "That's dangerous, Maria."

Maria nodded, tears flowing again, "Papa, what else could I have done? You saw how difficult it was to get the ID itself, how could I get forged documents, and how long would it have taken me…?"

Mrs. Bozek looked at her husband.

He sighed. "You did well."

Maria looked at him with her big eyes, "Yes, Papa?"

He nodded. He got up and walked the small kitchen back and forth. "Surely you cannot go with her. No two Maria Bozeks can travel together…"

Maria nodded, "And with the same date of birth."

Mrs. Bozek shook her head. "This is too dangerous. Our family is now on the line…"

Mr. Bozek said, "We need to somehow get her to the capital. Someone we trust will need to go with her. Then we need to get her a job of some kind."

Mrs. Bozek sighed and looked at her husband, "You have your friend there, old Mr. Winton…"

Maria looked at him, "Could you, Papa, write to him?"

Mr. Bozek sighed. "I will see what I can do…"

Maria looked hopeful. "Now I just need to find someone to take a couple of days off and go with her…"

Mr. Bozek said, "I wished I could, but I cannot leave work, the manager said…—"

"I can do it," Eddie said.

Everyone turned to Eddie.

He nodded.

Maria's eyes widened. "Really? Eddie?"

Eddie nodded again. Maria looked at her father,

"Papa, is that okay?"

Mr. Bozek sighed and looked at Eddie.

"I'll be fine," Eddie said, "I'll say we're brother and sister, if the soldiers…"

"Not *if*," Mr. Bozek exclaimed, "*when*! You'll be questioned several times, 'What are you doing going to the capital', 'What business do you have there…'"

Mrs. Bozek shrieked, "Can they find out that ID is fake?"

Maria shrugged her shoulders, "I hope not…"

Mrs. Bozek crossed her chest, "Jesus, Mary and Joseph!"

Silence followed.

Maria looked at Eddie. Then she looked at her mother, who shook her head. Her eyes were moist. Then Maria looked at her father, and at Sasha. She sighed, "It's what we need to do. She has no more…" she bit her lip, "She has no more family but us…"

Her father nodded. "Eddie will go with her."

Maria fell on her young brother's shoulder, "Eddinka, you'll watch her, right? And yourself, right?"

Eddie nodded.

Mr. Bozek sighed, "I'll give you a letter to Mr. Winton. Is that farm she's in safe? Where does she hide there?"

"In the barn," Maria murmured.

Mr. Bozek shook his head and looked at Eddie, "You'll need to go tomorrow."

Mrs. Bozek stood up, "I'll… prepare food for you! You make sure Helena eats, okay Eddinka?"

Eddie nodded. He looked at his big sister. "She'll be safe with me."

Standing on the crowded platform, Maria waved goodbye to Eddie and Helena.

Helena smiled through the window. She had her valise with her. And a box with potatoes, spinach, and even some meat, which Mrs. Bozek had prepared throughout the night. Eddie nodded at Maria, assuring her with his eyes that all would be okay.

Maria tried to let go. Oh, how much she would have liked to be there on the train to hold Helena's hand. But Helena did seem better this morning. A bit.

She folded her hands together, looking at poor Helena. Could the soldiers somehow find out that Helena's ID was fake? That the stamp, in fact, was imprinted in a dodgy apartment by an unknown man for an unbelievable sum? Would Helena be able to deal with soldiers questioning her on the way?

Maria looked at Eddie. Was she doing the right thing, sending him off like this? He was still a kid. Yes, he was seventeen, but he was still so young.

As the train began moving, she waved goodbye to them. They waved back, until they disappeared. The other people on the platform slowly walked away. But Maria stayed there, lingering, as if keeping her gaze on the disappearing train could somehow protect two of the most important people in her entire world.

"Dear Maria,

Please thank Eddie in my name. He's been so kind, and so mature! Staying with me for whole three days, helping me with all of the arrangements… renting a room… I'm so proud of him!

Also, please thank your dear mother for the food which reminded me of the festive times we had together. Please also thank your dear Father for writing to Mr. Winton. He was able to procure me a job at the train station, beginning tomorrow. I have no words to express my gratitude.

I feel better now. I realize I wasn't really in my right mind when we met. I am much better now. I look forward to the next time I'll see you.

Again, please thank Eddie and give him a big hug. He showed courage several times. I will tell you all when we meet again, whenever that is. Hopefully sooner than we think.

Yours,

Maria."

"Dear Maria,

I was so happy to see Eddie come back, and bringing such good news from you!

I cannot tell you how happy I was reading your letter, I read it again and again. You sound much more vital and strong. I do hope you are feeling better and better each day and that soon everything will pass, and we will be reunited in our beloved city.

I keep praying for good news about your whole family. Miracles do happen, as long as we believe in them.

Please send Mr. Winton my love, as I remember him well from his visits in my childhood.

Do write to me more, I've missed you terribly.

Yours,

Maria."

"Dear Maria,

It's been a year now, and the work at the train station has been satisfactory indeed. I am now in charge of the announcements. It's as close as you've imagined of me getting "famous". I am certainly famous among the passengers, and I can assure you that all of them listen to my words attentively. Never before have I had such large audiences!

I do miss our beloved city, though. Please walk to the city hall's fountain for me once in awhile. I remember fondly feeding the doves and pigeons there.

I went to a ballet performance a week ago. Since then I cannot stop singing.

Do tell me about your progress on your seminary about erythromycin (I hope I spelled it correctly). It sounds so exciting, what you wrote about antibiotics. Terrific!

I am more settled now here, and I enjoy the city life. There is much more I want to write to you, but it will have to wait until we meet again. Do send my love to the family. How is Sashinka doing? She must be enjoying school. Did you take her to our hiding place on the roof?

I miss you terribly. Do write to me quickly, as I anticipate your letters all the time.

Yours always,

Maria."

"Dear Maria,

Your letter brought so much joy to my heart. I cannot believe I haven't seen you for so long… When this season passes, seeing you will be the first thing I'll look forward to!

I was sorry to hear of Mr. Winton's passing. But I am happy to hear that you are well, and that your job is secure.

We are all well. Sasha is a sweetheart. She actually reminds me a lot of you. She now prefers 'Sasha' over 'Sashinka', and gives me a hard time whenever I misaddress her. She loves novels, and reads a lot. I wish you were present in her life at this crucial age, as you were in mine.

I promised her that when things change, you and I will take her to the sea.

Eddie is in his last year, doing well in school. He works a lot in the afternoons as a delivery boy. He thinks of studying engineering in university. I'm so happy for him. He has become a little man, can you believe it? He reminds me a lot of Papa.

I hope my pharmaceutical study paper won't bore you – but I thought you might enjoy the research I've done. You should go back to university when this season ends… Studying is so pleasurable…

The mail has been faulty, and I saw that your previous letter arrived two weeks later. Such things did not happen before this season. I do hope things will change soon. I pray for it each day.

My mother keeps praying and sending her love, as my father and Eddie and Sasha do too. I look forward to hearing from you as soon as possible.

Yours, Maria."

"Dear Maria,

Have you received my last two letters? I have yet to hear from you. Please respond to me, at least signaling that you are well. I get anxious not hearing from you!

Papa and Mama, Eddie and Sasha send their love. Do write to me promptly!

Yours,

Maria."

"Dear Maria,

It's been two months since I heard from you last. I wrote to Sofia, and she said she does not know where you are, and that you've been missing from the train station for some time now.

Please, I beg you! If you receive this letter, do write to me promptly. I am terribly agonized with uncertainty.

Maria."

Travelling to the capital on an overnight train, alone, Maria Bozek could not close an eye. Neither could she read or eat. She was too distraught.

When the train arrived at the capital in the morning, Maria immediately got off and took a taxi to the western Train station.

As soon as she arrived she reached for her pocket. There she had a photo of Helena. But she was too afraid to approach anyone or to show it. She had a bad feeling.

She saw a woman behind the window at the ticket counter. After hesitating for some time, she decided to ask her. She stood in line until her turn came.

"Where to?" the woman in the window asked.

"Could I," Maria whispered, "have a word with you?"

The woman raised her eyebrows, "Do I know you?"

"No, but you may know my friend, Maria Bozek. She used to work here."

The woman's eyes grew larger. "I don't know her, and you better not know her either!"

Maria sensed an alarm in the woman's voice.

There were people behind her in line. The woman behind the window exclaimed, nearly yelling, "Next please!"

Maria moved over. Now her bad feeling became a knot in her stomach.

She walked outside the station. She was determined to figure things out.

She decided to wait until that woman finished work.

Maria waited until the evening. She kept her eyes on the door near the ticket booth, afraid to go eat, even afraid to go and use the bathroom. She didn't want that lady to leave without seeing her.

When evening came the woman finally exited the booth. Maria followed her to the street.

The woman took the tram. Maria took the tram as well.

Maria knew she could not speak about Helena in the tram. She decided to wait. The woman got off at the end of the line. Maria followed her.

She kept her distance as the woman walked the small streets. Then the woman suddenly began running.

Maria ran after her. "Please," Maria called, "Please, stop!"

The woman entered one of the buildings. Maria entered the building as well. The woman stopped on the staircase, panting, looking terrified at Maria. "What do you want from me?!"

"I'm looking for my friend," Maria whispered, "I told you in the morning…"

"You're…" the woman hesitated, "you're the woman who asked about…?"

Maria nodded.

They stood there, both panting, as the woman evaluated Maria. "Are you from the *underground?* I want nothing to do with the *resistance!*"

"Me neither!" Maria exclaimed, "I just need to know where my friend is!"

The woman looked at Maria for a long moment. Finally, she nodded. "Come with me."

Maria followed the woman as she climbed the stairs to the last floor. The woman looked down at the staircase, checking no one had followed them. She opened the door, turned the light on, signaled for Maria to enter, then locked the door behind them.

The woman then approached the window. She peaked around the curtains to see if there was anyone suspicious on the street. She looked at Maria, "Are you sure you came alone?"

Maria nodded.

"How do you know Maria?" the woman asked.

"She was," Maria said and then corrected herself, "she *is* my best friend."

The woman shook her head and whispered. "I think they took her."

Maria nearly fainted, "No!"

The woman walked away. Her eyes became teary. She looked back at Maria. "There was a small party," she said, "in the office. Maria used to read the announcements…"

Maria nodded.

"And we… sang some songs. One of the guys sang some…" she sighed, "some song against the occupying army."

Maria bit her lip, "And?"

"And we all sang along. The office was locked, so we felt free. And…" she sighed, "Maria joined along with her beautiful voice. But then we heard some commotion. It turned out the microphone was on."

"No!"

The woman nodded. "The whole station heard it. Maria understood it instantly, took her purse, and ran away. The guy who led the song also disappeared.

They took him, and I think they took her."

Maria shook her head. "Did you *see* them take her?"

"No," the woman sighed, "but less than a minute later some soldiers came into the office inquiring who sang the song. When we said they were gone, they punished the whole management. I..." the woman's voice broke, "they took me to the police station. They interrogated me... for five hours...."

"I'm so sorry," Maria murmured.

The woman shook her head. "We would have heard something about Maria were she alive. I think they took her."

Maria wanted to cry. "But you didn't *see* them take her?"

The woman shook her head.

Maria sighed, "That's all I need to know. Thank you for trusting me." Maria took a deep breath and headed toward the door.

"Wait," the woman said, "if you hear anything about her, good or bad, could you let me know? You now know where I live."

Maria nodded. She exited the apartment, descending the stairs and disappearing into the night.

Maria wasn't herself anymore.

She had nightmares.

Eddie and Sasha pitied her. Her mother tried to encourage her. Her father told her to leave it to God.

But she was not willing to hear. "I let her down," she murmured. "I should have helped her get across the border, to run away. It was too dangerous for her... I should have known."

She barely ate.

She went to her old school, where Sasha was now studying, and climbed to the third floor. The window, which had once been so big, now seemed much smaller.

She climbed unto the roof. She sat there in the cold weather, crying. "Helena…" she whispered, "where are you?"

She searched her heart to see whether she could sense something. Was Helena alive? Was she dead? Was she safe?

Her heart told her nothing.

At university she couldn't concentrate. She told Roman what she had found out on her trip to the capital. He said he'd ask his contacts to see if he could find out anything.

But he came up with nothing.

Helena was gone. And Maria knew it was her own fault.

It was unfortunate, really, because the war seemed to be ending. After five years of unemployment, suffering, hunger, and terrible stories of murder and torture, it looked like an end was in sight.

The liberating allies were now attacking the occupying army fiercely.

The country was still occupied. But people understood the news reports. While the news was still filled with propaganda, people speculated that all the "realignments" and "repositioning" of the occupying army meant the approaching end of the war.

The occupying army would be defeated soon,

everybody hoped; they were now madly trying to defend the borders. Trains were used to mobilize soldiers and ammunition toward the borders. Many civilian trains stopped working. The mail, too, was extremely faulty. The occupying army was screening most letters, fearing coded and hidden intelligence of the underground resistance movement cooperating with the liberating allies.

The atmosphere in the Bozek house now changed. Mr. Bozek was hopeful. He muttered at dinner, "Soon those bastards will be gone! Out of here for good!"

But Maria could not rejoice. She felt *guilty*. She felt *helpless*. It had been eight months since Helena disappeared. Maria tried to remain hopeful, but she felt like she was simply deceiving herself.

She once thought to herself that somehow, in some way, this might be for the best. That Helena did *want* to join her parents and brothers. That this was somehow good.

But that thought depressed her even more.

Her mother begged her to eat; she had lost a lot of weight. She bought her a brand new dress, green with white lace. It was beautiful.

But Maria didn't want to wear it.

Each of the family members tried to speak to her separately. But nothing helped.

She continued to go to university, but the light was gone from her eyes. She often daydreamed. Her mind was filled with torturing thoughts. Helena shot.

Helena raped. Helena thrown somewhere in some field calling her name, "Maria!" before she died.

One evening there was a knock on the door.

Mr. Bozek answered and saw a tall man. "I'm looking for Miss Maria Bozek," he said.

"And *you* are?" Mr. Bozek barked. He didn't like the look of this man.

"I'm sorry, sir. I cannot say. I'm looking for Miss Maria Bozek."

Maria, hearing this from the kitchen, ran to the door. Her father blocked her from the door. "No!" he said, "I don't trust this man."

The tall man remained standing there. He looked at Maria coldly. "Are you Maria Bozek?"

"I am," she cried.

He nodded. "I have a letter. For you."

She cried, "From whom?"

"A woman, about your age." He looked at the street and lowered his voice, "Please spare me of saying her name out loud. I don't think it would be very wise," his eyes glared, "neither for her, nor for you."

Maria's eyes grew larger. Mr. Bozek shook his head, "It's a hoax. Where's the letter?"

The tall man clenched his jaw. "I've travelled a long distance to carry it for you. I deserve compensation. I expect two thousand for my efforts in cash."

Mr. Bozek reddened, "Two thousand for a letter!"

The man turned around.

"Wait!" Maria cried, "Papa, let me go!"

She escaped Mr. Bozek and ran to the street. Mr. Bozek remained at the door with Mrs. Bozek, Eddie and Sasha standing behind him.

Maria told the man, "Show me the letter."

The tall man looked down at her, and then at Mr. Bozek. He reached for his coat. "Put your hands behind your back Miss Bozek," he said, "I'll show it to you for one moment. Don't touch it."

Maria put her hands behind her back. Mr. Bozek took a step forward, ready to launch at the man if he tried to hurt her. The man pulled out a letter. He held it in front of Maria for a moment. She saw her name. It was Helena's handwriting.

The tall man said he'd come back the following evening at the same time. Maria tried everything she could to get the money needed, desperately. But she managed to get only half of it.

Eddie took her aside to the small backyard, away from their parents. "What are you going to do when that man comes?" he asked.

"I'm going to show him what I have, and plead…"

Eddie shook his head, "He won't accept it, he doesn't sound like…" he sighed. Suddenly Maria saw his eyes becoming moist.

"Eddie, is everything okay?"

He shrugged his shoulders, "Here's two thousand."

Maria looked at the money, shocked. "But Eddie,

where from?"

"The deliveries. It's my one year of savings."

"Eddie I can't…—"

"You must. She's my sister too."

Maria bit her lip. "I'll pay you back."

"Don't be a fool. I've been…" he hesitated, "I've been praying for Helena to return. I hope this is a sign."

Maria nodded, her chin quivering. "Eddinka, come here…"

They hugged. Maria shook her head. What a man her little brother had become!

When the tall man knocked on the door again, everyone jumped out of their seats. Helena's father opened the door, and tried a different approach. He pleaded, "We are a poor family, sir." He thanked, "We are so grateful to you for bringing us news." And he even tried flattery, "You must have gone through so much, and I can only imagine the dangers you've been through…"

But the man's face was blank. He said nothing. They looked at each other for a long moment. The man said, "You got the money?"

Maria tried to say, "All I got is one thousand, sir…—"

But the man turned around into the night.

"Wait!" Maria exclaimed.

He turned around, halfway.

With trembling hands, Maria handed him the money. He counted it. He gave her the letter and was gone.

Maria took the letter as if it was gold. She knew it was still not an indication that Helena was alive. This could be a letter she wrote in the past, possibly before she was captured.

But during the past twenty-four hours her heart felt lighter. She was hopeful. She *allowed* herself to hope.

She sat on the sofa and opened the letter. Her mother came, standing near her, wearing the kitchen apron. Sasha, too, came and sat by her, her feet on the sofa. Eddie stood near the living room's entrance in the hallway. Mr. Bozek came as well.

Maria opened the letter.

Mrs. Bozek exclaimed, "Now don't think you're just going to read it to yourself!"

"Mama," Maria exclaimed, "it's a letter to me!"

Mrs. Bozek shook her head, "It's a letter to all of us. You're a Bozek, we're all Bozeks! Read it out loud!"

Maria cracked a smile. She looked at the letter, "But, Mama, it's three pages!"

Mrs. Bozek said nothing, her eyebrows raised, and her eyes glaring at Maria.

Maria shook her head and read out loud.

"Dear Maria… first things first. That messenger carrying the letter has been very kind to carry it all the way to you. But please do not…"

Maria's speech slowed down, "…do not pay him… anything because I've paid him the best… of what I had…"

They heard the door opening. Mr. Bozek called, "Eddie!"

Eddie had run outside, screaming, "I'll catch that bastard!"

Mr. Bozek ran after him.

Maria buried her head in her hands, "Oh no… We shouldn't have paid him!"

Sasha exclaimed, "He cheated us!"

But Mrs. Bozek was not impressed by the drama. "Money is money, girls, it comes and goes. Let the men run around trying to prove they're men. We'll keep reading. Go ahead!"

Maria said "Mama!"

"Keep reading, I pray!"

Maria nodded.

> "The man promised me full secrecy, and that in case of danger the letter would be destroyed. So I feel free to write to you for the first time in two years in my own name. I'm scared to even pronounce it. I've been Maria for so long now…
>
> For the past eight months I've written you

countless of letters, but have not heard from you."

Maria gasped.

"They say the mail is faulty, but I hope at least one of the letters reached you and that you haven't worried for me throughout this whole time."

Maria began crying. Sasha put her hand on her shoulder. Mrs. Bozek bit her lip. Her eyes were moist.

Maria cleared her throat,

"I got into trouble at the train station. It's a long story. But I was caught singing a foolish song against the occupying army. We all sang in that office, but I stood near the silly microphone. When I realized it was on, I ran away, just grabbing my purse. Soldiers ran after me into the street. They must have been infuriated... But I somehow made it to the tram. It was the second time the tram has saved me; you would remember well the first time."

Sasha interrupted, "What does she refer to, Maria?"

Maria took a big breath, "Oh, it's not important."

Maria had never told them *how* she got Helena out. She thought they wouldn't have approved.

They heard steps outside. Mr. Bozek came into the house, panting, and sat down in the living room with them, "Nowhere…" he panted, "nowhere to be found…"

Eddie came in, "That bastard! He disappeared! We looked all around...!"

Maria pouted her lips, "Eddie, I promise I'll pay you back..."

Eddie shrugged. "Well, at least I got to see this old man run," he said and tapped on his father's shoulder, "He sure can run!"

Mrs. Bozek smiled and looked at her husband, "Not only running..."

Sasha exclaimed, "Can we keep reading or what?!"

Maria re-read the section that her father and Eddie missed and then continued,

> "...Soldiers ran after me into the street. They must have been infuriated. But I somehow made it to the tram..."

Maria skipped a line and then continued,

> "I knew I had to flee. I ran into my apartment, threw everything into my valise, and left the capital."

Everyone sat at the edge of their seats.

> "I took the train to another town. But I knew the occupying army would mark the name Maria Bozek as problematic... I cannot tell you how sorry I was for my stupidity. I should have never sung that song. I knew things much less serious than that had caused people to disappear. In the new town I fled to, I wrote to you, warning you... I sure hope my mistake has not caused your family any grief,

and that you weren't visited by the occupying army…"

Mrs. Bozek exclaimed, "The grace of God!"

Maria nodded. They all did.

She continued,

> "I knew I had to change my identity, and was able to arrange, with the money I saved from the train station, a fake marriage. Now my name is Maria Szymczak, and the name Bozek has been erased in my new ID. I was able to procure a new fake high school diploma and other documents."

Mrs. Bozek shook her head, "Resourceful girl."

Maria continued,

> "But I couldn't find work in that town, nor was I safe going back to the capital. Coming back to our city was not an option… So I did something that you might find foolish, but I believe it has saved me."

Sasha said, "What? What?"

Maria read, everyone listening intently,

> "With my new identity I went to the occupying army's placement office for the unemployed. I exhausted all of my money procuring a new name and documents, and knew no one in that town to help me, and was afraid of starving.
>
> So I had to put my principles aside, and went

there. They found allocation for me in a huge laundry factory. But then they told me it was in the occupying country's headquarters."

Eddie jumped, "Impossible!"

Mrs. Bozek yelled at him, "Can we just keep reading without interruptions!"

Maria kept reading, breathing heavily,

> "So I was given a train pass, and for two days I travelled to the hated country. I was put in a small apartment with twelve other women laborers, mostly local. Here I've been for the past six months. I cannot tell you of the fear I carry in my heart constantly. I fear I will somehow reveal my real identity while talking in my sleep, or somehow say something wrong…"

Maria sighed and kept reading,

> "But I do not complain. I have work and basic food, which is more than many have. I think of you everyday, wondering how your family is faring. I pray that your mother has found a good job, and that your father is still employed by the train station."

Mrs. Bozek tut-tutted, "The good girl!"

Eddie scolded her, "Mama, don't interrupt!"

Mrs. Bozek glared at him until he looked down. Maria smiled and continued,

> "I constantly think of Eddie and Sashinka (I will call her Sashinka forever, Sasha is too

formal for me!) and I hope their school is good, and that they are well.

Of course, my dearest Maria, I think of you every day. I often feel you, while I work in the factory. I imagine you encouraging me and..."

Maria began choking, but kept reading,

"...encouraging me and pushing me to keep working, even though the work is dull and physically taxing, with the huge pools of hot water and unbelievable tall piles of uniforms. And the women here are not particularly warm, to say the least. I'm here in my body. But in my mind I'm often on the beach with you, or gossiping about Alexander's new haircut, or with your family in the midnight mass..."

Maria began crying.

They all sat there silently.

Maria sniffled and continued,

"I sure hope, dearest Maria, that I have not done anything to offend you, and that the lack of correspondence is simply due to the mail discrepancies. They do say that mail to the occupied countries is very faulty, and that the intelligence and censorship barely let things through. But I've written to you so many times, and I hate to think none of the letters reached you."

Maria wiped her eyes and read,

"Recently they've been murmuring here about the end of the war coming, and the 'enemy' (the allies) attacking and penetrating the lines. I sure hope that it will happen soon, because every day without seeing you makes my heart ache.

I am afraid to ask, as I've heard of terrible stories back in the capital, but have you heard anything about my father, mother, or brothers? Reuben was indeed taken with my mother in that second transport, but Solomon and Hannah were still in the enclosure when you smuggled me out... I dread thinking of them. I try, each day, not to think of them, as it brings me unbearable sorrow. But I did want to ask... I know that you would have been the first contact for any of them, had they tried to reach me."

Maria began crying again.

Everyone looked down. Mr. Bozek wiped his tears and cleared his throat.

Maria sobbed and sobbed. Stress that had built in her for months was beginning to dissipate. Sasha rubbed her back.

They all had tears in their eyes.

Maria breathed in heavily, wiped her tears, and kept reading,

"The messenger just told me he needs to leave. I must seal this letter and give it to him. My current address is written below. I'm uncertain if mail can come through, especially from the occupied territories. But I do have hope: a friend told me that if you address me not in our living quarters, but instead send the letter to the actual *laundry factory*, then chances are high that it shall arrive. So, please, as soon as you receive this letter, let me know you and your family is safe! Address me as Maria Szymczak, at the factory's address below. I truly hope to hear from you soon! I cannot explain in words what worry and pain I have, not knowing you are all safe and sound.

Yours, always,

Maria."

Sasha gasped, "She signed with your name?"

Eddie laid back, "She must have still been afraid."

Mr. Bozek shook his head, "Poor Helena…"

Mrs. Bozek stood up in determination. "I'll prepare some food for her!"

Everyone laughed. "Mama!" Sasha said, "She's far away!"

"So what?!" Mrs. Bozek exclaimed as she entered the kitchen. "We can send food in jars… We do have some jam! And I can make fish in salt… And pickles! And some salty meat, it can last a few weeks if it's in oil… She said she doesn't have food there!"

Maria laughed and wiped her tears. "Mama, she didn't say that!"

"I listened to every word," Mrs. Bozek shouted

from the kitchen, "She said, '*basic food*,' you know what that means? They feed her…" her voice broke, "nothing but potatoes…" she began crying, "She must be starving…"

Mr. Bozek got up and walked to the kitchen.

Eddie looked at Maria, hesitating. "Can I… write to her too? Can you include a letter from me?"

Sasha jumped, "And from me too!"

Maria smiled, "Of course."

Sasha hugged her. Eddie hesitated, but then joined them too, putting his hand on his big sister.

A week before Maria's 25th birthday, the propaganda-filled radio station of the occupying army suddenly went off the air.

The occupying army in the city tried to keep a "business as usual" appearance. But everyone could sense that something was happening.

Then refugees poured in from the capital. They told of the occupying army retreating, and the liberating allies closing in. The occupying army, while retreating, burned down the capital, and blew up its bridges and many of the historic buildings. The capital was in ruins, refugees said, razed to the ground.

One evening Eddie was infuriated, cursing the occupying army during the family's dinner. The liberating allies were now advancing rapidly toward their city. Liberation felt closer than ever. But Eddie exclaimed, "People say the occupying army will do to us what they've done in the capital!"

Mr. Bozek said nothing. The atmosphere in the home was tense.

The following day Eddie disappeared. He did not come home that night, nor the following day. Mrs. Bozek was distraught, crying incessantly. Maria tried to calm her down, but to no avail. All Mrs. Bozek was saying was "Eddinka, my Eddinka…"

That night they heard heavy artillery. Guns, machine guns, tanks.

Mr. Bozek brought one of the beds from the living room into their bedroom, and he and Mrs. Bozek slept alongside Maria and Sasha, all crammed in the small room.

But they didn't really sleep. The shooting and the bombardments were unbearable.

At four o'clock in the morning a huge blast rocked the walls of the house. Sasha began crying, "Are we going to die, Papa?"

Mr. Bozek said, "It's all good signs. The liberating allies are here."

They prayed together.

That day Mr. Bozek did not go to work. No one left the house. Mr. Bozek peeked from behind the curtain. The street was empty. Not a soul was out.

They stayed home the whole day. The following day they heard some artillery again, but not as heavy. They had now nearly exhausted all the food in the house.

Mrs. Bozek wanted to go to the market, but Mr. Bozek said, "We'll manage without food. No one is going anywhere."

The day after, they heard noises of cheering in the distance. The ground shook from what sounded like marching. Mr. Bozek said, "I'll go out. Lock the door and let no one in."

The three women looked through the window. But no one was out on the snowy street.

Two hours later Mr. Bozek returned, "The liberating allies are here!"

They cried. Mrs. Bozek fell on her knees, "Thank you God! Now bring our Eddinka home!"

As if answering Mrs. Bozek's prayer, that evening Eddie came home. Never before had he been kissed as much. Mrs. Bozek kissed him and hit him alternatingly. "You fool!" she hit him, "I'm so glad you're here!" she kissed him, "I should have locked you inside," she hit him "Thank God you're not hurt!" she kissed him.

Mr. Bozek must have known something. He looked prouder than ever and said, "Tell me everything, don't spare a detail."

Eddie recounted how he knew that one of his

friends, Aleksey, was involved in the resistance movement. "But I wanted to have none of it," he said. "Until what happened in the capital. Then I was… outraged… Seeing the refugees. Papa, Mama, it was… impossible for me not to do anything, and imagine the same happening to us!"

They all listened to him attentively.

"So I came to Aleksey and said that I wanted to enlist. I wasn't the only one. There were many of us. We were trained quickly in a forest. Two days ago we were sent as the back force, covering up a front force going to the northern castle."

Mr. Bozek said, "That's where the army had all their ammunitions…!"

Eddie nodded, "So at night, we infiltrated there, and around four we lit the whole place up from several directions. We blew up their whole bunker. They planned to tear our whole city down as they were retreating. But we took them by surprise."

Mrs. Bozek shrieked, "My hero!"

"Mama," Eddie frowned, "I was at the back lines. I did nothing."

Mrs. Bozek would have none of it. "You helped the front lines. Now our city is saved!"

Eddie sighed. "It was… many were killed. On both sides. But their main reservoir of explosives was gone. Then we joined the liberating allies last night and we marched with them in the morning. The city is finally ours again."

Maria was ecstatic. They went to celebrate in the streets. It seemed as if everyone was out. After these horrific six years of occupation and unheard-of sorrows, no one had to stay inside anymore

But her joy was not complete. She had not heard back from Helena since she sent her the package, the food jars, the expensive green dress her mother got for her, and the letters from her and her siblings.

There was now no mail at all between their liberated city and the main occupying country. They were now on different sides of the conflict. She dreaded Helena's state. Would the army there do the same? Burn down factories, evidences of the war efforts?

She felt it too early to celebrate.

University resumed. Maria saw Roman, looking happier than ever, walking with his girlfriend Rebecca.

Maria was happy for them.

But she wasn't at ease.

Weeks passed.

Then one day, when Maria returned home, her mother had a big grin on her face. "You have guests," she said.

"Guests?" Maria exclaimed, "Helena?"

Mrs. Bozek shook her head, "Not Helena," and pointed at the entrance to the living room.

Maria hurried to the living room. She gasped.

The laundry factory worker, Maria Szymczak, felt the tension growing in the air. Everyone did.

One day the factory manager disappeared.

The following day three of the supervisors also disappeared.

There was unrest in the factory, as new people came to run it.

Spring came. Still there was no mail. She thought of her beloved city, so far away. She had heard that the allies conquered it.

To herself she whispered, "It's been liberated!"

But the news did not speak of the territories lost, only of the army realigning and repositioning.

Then there was a rumor about the great leader being killed.

The following day the rumor, passing like fire in the working line, was that the great leader committed suicide. But it was all speculation.

Two days later it was published that the army headquarters had been taken over by the allies.

But it took six more long days until the final news came. Everyone stopped working and listened as the factory's main radio blasted the news:

> "Today, in the early morning, our nation, through the High Command of the Army, officially surrendered to the Supreme Commander of the Allied Expeditionary Force…"

Cries of sorrow passed through the lines. Some of the women wailed. The radio continued blaring:

> "…the Army issued orders to all military, naval and air authorities and to all forces under the control of the High Command to cease active operations as of this morning. The army is obliged to hand over weapons and equipment to the local allied commanders or officers designated by Representatives of the Allied Supreme Commands…"

As the women cried for their country's loss, Helena didn't show any sorrow. She got up, walked out of the factory, went to the nearby woods, fell unto the ground and sobbed. It was over.

Maria walked into the house. Mrs. Bozek exclaimed, "Maria! Good news!"

Eddie and Sasha looked at their sister excitedly, as Mrs. Bozek handed her the short telegram.

Maria didn't even take off her coat. She turned around and ran out.

Mrs. Bozek yelled, "Where are you going?!"

"I have to let them know, Mama! They'll be so happy!!!"

The following morning Maria stood on the platform. She was waiting nervously.

It seemed like it had been forever.

She kept sitting down on the bench, then standing, then walking. Then sitting again. Then standing.

She promised herself she wouldn't cry. Today was, finally, a happy day.

It was all behind them now.

Helena's heart leapt as her city came into view.

She looked out the windows, absorbing the sights. The buildings. She was so afraid she might see ruins. But she saw none. The houses were beautiful, shining in the spring sun.

The train slowed down and the people inside stood up. The platform emerged before her, with countless people standing on it, waiting. She took her valise in her hand and straightened her dress—Maria's beautiful green dress.

The train stopped. The doors opened. She waited for a moment and then walked off.

She breathed in the familiar scents. She looked around, hoping to see Maria. Had she received her telegram? She looked at the many faces, at people greeting other people. Where was...

"Helena!" she heard her name pronounced for the first time in two years. She turned around, and before she knew it she and Maria were embracing, crying, spinning around in pure joy. The rest of the world disappeared.

They sat on the platform. They looked at each other, excited and shy, just as they were on the school's rooftop, so many years earlier, exchanging gifts after the summer break. Then they'd been separated for two months. Now it was two years, though it felt like a lifetime.

Helena had tears in her eyes. They spoke half sentences, then hugged, then spoke again, then hugged again. They cried on each other's shoulders.

"When you're ready," Maria finally said, "I have a surprise for you!"

"What is it?" Helena asked nervously.

"Solomon, he made it…—"

"Solomon?!" Helena screamed, "He is alive?!"

Maria nodded, tears in her eyes, "They came to me a few weeks ago."

"They?"

"He and Hannah."

"Oh, Maria!"

Maria laughed through her tears. "He reacted just like you when I…" she sniffled, "when I told… when I told him you were safe…"

Helena shook her head, "I knew it. I knew he'd survive!"

Maria nodded, "He was able to get your old house back, the big one, Helena, from before the war! He told me to bring you there when you came, he didn't want to leave Hannah…"

"Is she…" Helena's eyes widened, "is she injured? Sick?"

Maria shook her head, her eyes filled with tears, "No, she's pregnant, Helena. She's due to give birth any day now…"

Helena stood up, "Maria, what good news…!"

Maria nodded and stood up, "I'll go there with you. They are waiting for us."

Helena nodded, tears streaming down her cheeks. She grabbed Maria's hands, "Don't you ever leave me again, you hear me!"

Maria nodded, "I promise. Do you promise?"

Helena nodded, "I promise."

Helena Goldstein and Maria Bozek were never separated again. They remained close friend through the decades. While Helena never had children of her own, she regarded Maria's children as her own. They called her "Aunt Helena."

Helena Goldstein became a successful accountant. Among her clients was a successful pharmacy owned by Maria Bozek-Nowak.

Four decades after the war ended, Helena Goldstein passed away at the age of 66. Near her bedside stood her longtime friend, Maria

Bozek-Nowak.

Maria Bozek-Nowak dedicated her later years to educating children and teens about friendship and world peace. According to her, "The most important thing to understand is that there is no difference between people. Under our skin we're all the same. If you understand this, you will do whatever it takes to help other people when they are in need."

In 1995, Maria Bozek-Nowak was recognized by the state of Israel as Righteous Among the Nations. As of 2017, Maria Bozek-Nowak still lectures and speaks of love between the nations, now at the age of 97.

This book is dedicated to the memory of the Goldstein family members and to all of those who perished during the Holocaust.

Likewise, it is dedicated to the Bozek family, and to all of the 20,000 Righteous Among the Nations, who saved the lives of innocent people throughout the Holocaust, serving as miracle-workers in times of great darkness. Their light will shine forever.

THE END.

AFTERWORD

Following the release of *The Two Marias* I was swamped with questions from readers: Was the story true? The *whole* story? What was true and what was fiction? How did you come to hear of this story?

There were so many questions and so much interest that I decided to write this second book: *Behind the Two Marias*.

In this book I share everything about the research process: how I stumbled upon the story by mistake; how I began contacting people in Poland trying to find more about it; how I eventually found the actual Maria Bozek-Nowak, and was able to send a friend from Poland to visit her and her daughter; how I spoke with the nephew of Helena Goldstein and got a glimpse of what the real Helena was as an aunt, and more.

This book also includes 16 full-page photographs of Maria, her mother, her siblings, as well as of Helena and her brother Solomon. It offers a real encounter with the real Two Marias.

The second part of this book outlines the creative writing process. It is a commentary about the story; how I wrote it, what was important to me, how I designed the characters, what were my dilemmas in making the historic story one of fiction, etc. This second part is fascinating specifically to writers. It offers a real peek into my mind and how a book "comes to life."

These two fragments, the historic part and the creative-process part, compose the book *Behind the Two Marias*. This book is available electronically online. Following the request of the readers, in the recent printed edition of the book we have included the *Behind* book as a long appendix to the novel.

For readers interested in the historical background as well as in the artistic process, I recommend reading *Behind the Two Marias*. It is my humble attempt to answer all of the readers' questions.

Thank you for reading *The Two Marias*. I hope you enjoyed reading it just as much as I enjoyed writing it.

Jonathan Kis-Lev, Israel, August 2017

PART TWO:
BEHIND THE TWO MARIAS

INTRODUCTION

While writing my second novel, *New Day Dawning*, I noticed an intriguing footnote in one of the history books I was reading. Little did I know that that very footnote would lead me to a research spanning over a year, contacting people on three continents, piecing together *The Two Marias*.

Like *The Two Marias*, the novel I wrote beforehand, *New Day Dawning*, tells of a WWII episode: a boy finds shelter hiding with a Polish family. The story required *much* research, and forced me into a field of study I generally refrain from: *The Holocaust*.

Being Jewish, having both sides of my family, from my father's *and* my mother's side, affected by the Holocaust, caused me to hear much of it early on in life. I heard about it at home. I heard about it from my grandparents. I learned about it in school in Israel. The Holocaust was always *there*.

Over the years, like many people I know, I came to develop an *aversion* to the subject. It brought *too many* hard feelings. *Too many* raw emotions. Simply too much *pain*.

I learned not to go *there*.

In my late teens I decided to avoid books, movies, articles, and anything that had to do with the Holocaust altogether. I was simply too sensitive. In a way, I still am.

One day, in my mid-twenties, my parents wanted me to watch a documentary with them on TV. They had watched it before, they said, and wanted me to watch it as well.

I was apprehensive. "What is it about?"

My mom smiled, "It's about a Holocaust survivor who…—"

"Mom, I don't like watching this kind—"

My father interrupted, "Jon, it's not, trust me, it's not about the *Holocaust*. It's about what happens to this survivor *after* the Holocaust. You'd love it, trust me."

Somehow I was convinced to trust my parents on that.

And the documentary film, *The Final Victory*, portraying the life of Holocaust survivor Dr. Felix Zandman, left me mesmerized. His story was a story of triumph. It was not primarily a story of suffering, though suffering was in the background. It was a story of *light* coming out of *darkness*. Of the brave Polish family who risked their lives by saving this Jewish boy, and of how their light led him, in turn, to spread more light in the world.

For five years I went around with the dream of one day writing a book about that story. And this led me to writing what eventually became *New Day Dawning*. I did not know, at the time, that *The Two Marias* was just around the corner.

As part of the research for *New Day Dawning* I read *everything* I could about the Polish family who saved the Jewish boy. This family's name was *Puchalsky*. In 1987 they won recognition for their heroism by the State of Israel as *Righteous Among the Nations*.

Researching about them, I ended up reading a book by the talented authors Bill Tammeus and Rabbi Jacques Cukierkorn, called *They Were Just People: Stories of Rescue in Poland During the Holocaust*.

In this book the authors, who travelled and conducted interviews in several countries in order to write it, interviewed the daughters of the Puchalskies.

I read the interview carefully. I highlighted almost every line, as it was all quite useful for my research for *New Day Dawning*.

But as fate has it, when the chapter about the Puchalskies was over, I continued to read.

Mysteriously enough, the next chapter after the story of the Puchalskies was followed by a brief, three-and-a-half-page chapter about a woman called *Maria Bozek-Nowak*.

Instead of me telling you what I read *then*, allow me to quote the essential parts of this short story so that you can read what *I* read, and witness the actual birth of *The Two Marias*.

Note: The authors' comments are in *square parentheses*. My own comments are in square parentheses *and italicized*.

Excerpt from *They Were Just People: Stories of Rescue in Poland During the Holocaust* by Bill Tammeus and Rabbi Jacques Cukierkorn:

MARIA BOZEK-NOWAK

"It was the winter of 1942–1943, and Maria Bozek's good friend and classmate Helena Goldstein was in serious trouble. Maria knew just what she had to do for her Jewish friend. Helena, who had been confined to the Kraków Ghetto since it was created in March 1941, already had lost her father, her mother, and a brother, all of whom the Germans had deported and murdered. Now twenty-one-year-old Helena was in the ghetto alone, depressed, not eating, and frightened.

"After the second deportation," Maria told us, "I had a friend who had a Jewish girlfriend in the ghetto. Somehow he managed to get into the ghetto. So I asked him to check to see whether Helena was all right. He came to me later and said Helena was in very bad shape, physically and mentally, because her mother and older brother had been taken on the second transport. She still had one older brother living inside the ghetto with his fiancée, but they were not living with Helena. So Helena was pretty much alone. And she didn't want to eat. I decided that because Helena was alone, I needed to take her out of the ghetto.

So I contacted my friend with the Jewish girlfriend in the ghetto. We knew Helena was working outside the ghetto and thus could leave it. This was quite good. Second, we knew she needed a *Kennkarte* (or an identification paper). That meant we had to buy a false one for her […] She needed more than one document, such as a birth certificate and a baptism certificate. It was not enough to have only one *Kennkarte*. You needed as many documents as you could get to prove that you are who you are and you are not a Jew. So we bought an empty one and told Helena she needed to take pictures of herself and send them to us by this Polish boy when he came to the ghetto."

Maria was taking charge. In a pattern that was to mark her relationship with Helena until the war ended and both women had survived, Maria chose not to wait until she was asked to help. Instead, she assessed the situation and moved quickly to do what she thought was necessary, even at the risk of her own life.

"So we got this false *Kennkarte* through our friend, who had contacts and knew where to buy it. But Helena needed a new identity," Maria said.

Again, Maria did not wait but moved to find an answer. "I decided to give Helena my own name. And

I gave her some of my own documents."

[…] So Helena went through the secretive process of becoming Maria Bozek. "Helena had pictures taken and the *Kennkarte* was ready. One day before she was to escape, she smuggled out her luggage. But there was a problem of where to keep her after she escaped because she couldn't stay with my family. We were living around many railroad workers who were friends and many of them knew Helena from before the war. There was a risk that someone would tell, and it would be dangerous." Besides, having Helena around would mean there were two Maria Bozeks in the same dwelling.

This was not a problem that Maria asked Helena to solve. Again, she found a solution for her. Maria elected "to take her to the place of a Polish friend, Roman Bartel […] When Helena came out of the ghetto the next day to go to work, I was waiting for her, and I grabbed her by the arm. I took her armband [that identified her as a Jew]. It was winter, and Jews were not allowed to wear fur on their coats. So the first thing I did was to put a piece of fur on her neck so people wouldn't think she was Jewish.

"We knew that Helena could not stay in Kraków because Kraków was too small for two people with the same identity. Also, many people knew Helena. So we wrote to ask for help for Helena [*in Poland's capital, Warsaw –J. K*]."

Helena and Maria had been friends for many years. They met as young girls in school when they were assigned to sit next to one another in the classroom.

Maria's parents, Antony and Francesca Bozek, had taught her and her younger siblings, Edmund and Alexandra, to treat all people with equal respect, Maria told us.

[…] Maria told us that because many Jews in Kraków were not Orthodox and, thus, were generally quite acculturated into Polish culture, it was not unusual for non-Jews to have Jewish friends. "Even before the war, Helena took me to a concert at her synagogue for a *Kol Nidre* service [*The Jewish Day of Atonement –J.K.*] I liked it very much and I remember especially the cantors." Maria knew about anti-Semitism but said she wasn't aware of much of it among her friends.

After graduating from high school, Maria and Helena began studies […] "We were great friends. Helena was invited often to Christmas celebrations with my family, and I was invited to spend time with her Jewish family at Jewish holidays. During the first years of the war in Kraków we were helping each other. But in March 1941 the Germans established a ghetto here in Kraków. I said to Helena, 'Don't go to the ghetto. We will find a way to hide you here outside.' But Helena didn't want to leave her parents. She knew they needed to go to the ghetto. I understood this."

In June 1942 the first deportation from the Kraków Ghetto to the Belzec death camp occurred. "Helena's father was sent. At that time Germans were saying they were deporting Jews to a work camp in Ukraine. And people believed this. But my father was working on the trains as a conductor or engineer. He had a friend who worked on the deportation trains. And he learned quickly that those trains were not going to Ukraine. Rather, they were going to some forest and coming back empty. So soon everyone knew what was happening.

"And when there was a second deportation from the Kraków Ghetto, everybody knew what was going on. [The second deportation from the Kraków Ghetto to Belzec occurred in October 1942.] Not everybody wanted to believe this, but it was common knowledge. In this deportation, Helena's mother was on the list. But [...] Helena's brother decided that he would go instead of his mother. So he went. The mother was hiding in a secret place in the ghetto. The mother heard Germans in the ghetto saying this place would be made "free of Jews." So she decided that she wanted to leave, and she went from her hiding place to the transport. At this time Helena was working outside the ghetto most of the time. People doing such work were pretty much safe," at least temporarily.

So in two transports, Helena lost her father, her brother, and her mother.

Once Helena got to Warsaw, friends of Maria helped her get a job doing public address announcements in a railway station. It was a perfect fit for her because she was fluent not just in Polish but also in German. But, Maria said, one day there was a small party in the office where Helena worked. People were drinking and having a good time. Helena joined in the fun by singing, in Polish, an anti-German song. But then she realized she had left the public address microphone on, and the song was broadcast into the whole railway station. Helena had to flee. [...]

"Helena knew she had to change her identity. One way to do this was to have a false marriage so [as to] get a different name. She did this. Her new name was Maria *Szymczak*. And then she never again saw her supposed "husband." But she had no job, so she had to go to a German unemployment office, and they sent her to another city, Hirschberg, in Germany, to do forced labor."

From then until January 1945, Maria had no contact with Helena and worried constantly about where she was and what she was doing. Then she received a letter from Helena under the name Maria Szymczak that assured Maria she was all right and was working in a laundry. Once again, Maria took the initiative.

"I decided to send her some things. So my mother cooked some food and I had a nice new green beautiful dress, which wasn't easy to buy. We needed special favors to get it. But I decided to send this dress to Helena. So we sent this package. Then the Russian offensive started, and I was afraid that this package was destroyed in the bombing. We had no contact until April, but in April Helena came to Kraków wearing my green dress."

Helena elected to stay in Kraków with her one surviving brother, who also had returned to Kraków with his wife. Helena and her brother managed to get back part of the apartment in which they had lived before the war.

With the Germans defeated, Helena then had to

decide who she was going to be. She chose to return to her original first name and to give up the name Maria. But she kept her false last name, Szymczak. And she and Maria again were close friends with frequent contact. Indeed, Maria was head of a pharmacy in Kraków, and in 1981 she hired Helena as an accountant there. But one night in 1986, Maria got a call telling her to come quickly to the hospital to see her friend Helena […] "So we were together in the beginning and at the end."

We […] asked Maria why she put her own life in danger on behalf of Helena. She said, "Helena was like family. She was a friend and I wanted to help her, and there was no need for her to say anything to me about it. She was like a sister for me. I knew my life was in danger by helping Helena, but all life was in danger at this time. In the winter, if there was snow lying on the street next to your house, you could be killed for this, for not sweeping it off."

Another question we asked Maria was what people should be taught so that more of them will behave in the way she did on behalf of Helena.

"The most important thing," she said, "is to teach that there is no difference between people. Under our skin we're all the same. If you understand this, you understand that you will do whatever is possible to help other people."

Maria and her late husband, Alfonse Nowak, who died in 1987, had a son and a daughter, and Maria has two grandchildren, a boy and a girl."

The above excerpt was taken from *They Were Just People: Stories of Rescue in Poland During the Holocaust* by Bill Tammeus and Rabbi Jacques Cukierkorn, University of Missouri Press, 2009.

DIGESTING THE STORY

Wow. Still when I read the passage you have just read I get goosebumps. From the first moment I read those three-and-a-half pages I felt drawn to the story. However, being then in the midst of the research for *New Day Dawning*, I had to put the idea aside and concentrate on the investigation I had already started.

A few months later, after finishing *New Day Dawning*, I was lying in bed one night. I was contemplating which book I wanted to write next. I told my wife, Hallel, "There's this little tiny story I read about…"

"Which story?" she asked me.

"It's a story about a woman who saved her friend during the Holocaust, by giving her friend her own identity and documents…"

"Really? But wasn't that extremely dangerous then?"

I sighed, "It was…."

I then went on to tell Hallel all that I remembered from those three-and-a-half pages. Hallel was really interested in the details. I told her about how after the war, Helena was coming back to meet Maria, the friend who had saved her, and was wearing the green dress that Maria had sent her. I told her how, as teenagers, they used to celebrate the holidays together. I told her how Maria "kidnapped" Helena by tearing the Star-of-David armband from her and throwing on her a fur scarf, which the Jews were not allowed to wear. I told her how much Maria must have cared for Helena, risking her life like that....

The more I *talked* about it, the more I realized there was something here: a story I wanted to explore.

My only fear was that the story didn't have enough "meat" and that I would have to invent and fill in many details. Possibly too many details. I was also afraid that the final result wouldn't end up as a novel, but as a chapter, really, the same way it was in the book I had read, *They Were Just People*. I was afraid that it would be a small, tiny chapter, not a *novel*.

The following day I began researching. I wanted to find out everything I could about the real Maria and Helena.

It turned out that there was not much available.

I found a few pages online in Polish, and translated them using Google Translate. While the translation was raw, it still gave me bits of information that I thought important.

I then found an amazing video interview with Maria Bozek-Nowak as an older lady. It was a short, seven-minute interview. Unfortunately, it was in Polish, without subtitles.

I could not process it through Google Translate....

I had to be creative.

As an interdisciplinary artist, I do not only write, but I also paint. Four years earlier, in 2012, I had some of my paintings accepted to a large group exhibition in

Poland. It was an important exhibition, a landmark in my career as an artist, and I decided to travel from Israel to Poland for that exhibition.

I had never visited Poland before. I landed in Krakow and found the city beautiful. At the time I did not know that four years later I would write a novel about two girls living in that very same city seven decades earlier.

From Krakow I took the train to Katowice, where the exhibition was taking place. At the time I always preferred lodging with locals, rather than staying in a hotel like a tourist. This was one of the reasons why I began learning, in my early twenties, the international language Esperanto. This easy-to-learn language helped me make friends around the world, including in Poland. Prior to my trip I found, online, that a family named *Zemla* was happy to host Esperanto-speaking people in their house, and that they lived near Katowice.

When my train arrived in the city, Mr. Dariusz Zemla, the father of the Esperanto-speaking family, waited for me in the train station and greeted me warmly.

The Zemla family turned out to be the liveliest and most loving family, with four talented kids, all of whom played musical instruments and played for the family each evening. They hosted me for a week, and were the kindest of people.

In general, I found that the people in Poland were extremely nice. This eased my experience in Poland, which, being Jewish, was sometimes challenging emotionally. You can just imagine what taking the train felt like, with my thoughts constantly wandering, unwillingly, to the trains on those very routes 70 years earlier.

In the years that passed since visiting Poland in 2012 I kept in touch with the Zemla family. I even had the pleasure of hosting them in Israel, and by that paying the favor back. Dariusz and I became good Facebook friends. Therefore, when I stumbled upon the story for *The Two Marias* four years later, it was only natural for me to write to Dariusz. I asked him if he could do me a huge favor and translate the video interview for me.

Dariusz explained that they were travelling abroad, but as soon as he had a moment he would do it happily.

During this time, I also wrote to the *Yad Vashem Holocaust Museum* in Jerusalem, asking for the files about Maria Bozek-Nowak. In 1995 she was awarded the title of *Righteous Among the Nations*. I knew that the Museum conducts in-depth interviews and an investigation before granting the prestigious title. I wanted to get all they had.

After much research I also found out Maria Bozek-Nowak was associated with a History Museum in Poland. I contacted the Museum and asked them: Was Maria still alive? How could I reach her for an interview?

I was very enthusiastic about the investigation, feeling that I had stumbled upon an untold story, an undiscovered gem. Yet the world seemed less enthusiastic. The Yad Vashem Museum was taking its time to respond to me and send me the files about Maria; my friend Dariusz was still not back home to help me with the translation. And I was waiting for replies from a few other places and museums I wrote to.

THE STORY UNFOLDS

It was only when the story was starting to form in my head—the plot, the beginning and ending scenes in the train platform, the childhood scenes and the development of the friendship—that finally I received some answers. I did not know at the time how exciting this process would become. It felt like the excavation of a treasure. Little by little the story began to unfold.

First arrived a long email from my friend Dariusz:

> "Hi Jonathan,
>
> First, this story is fascinating. I feel very fortunate that I could help you. It was a very exciting work: I have watched the short seven-minute-film of the interview with Maria, with my daughter Krysia. We watched it 5 or 6 times in order to understand the whole story.
>
> Naturally, being of old age, Maria's thoughts on film wander from one to another. I tried to capture them all.
>
> Best greetings for you and your whole family.

Darek (See the text below)

If I use italics letters in this text, it means these are my words, comments, etc.

Maria Bozek-Nowak's interview text:

"My father worked for the railroad. I told him I wanted to take Helena out of the ghetto. We bought an "empty," unfilled ID (*Kennkarte*). It contained only photo of Helena, German stamps and required German signatures. It was necessary to put names and other information by oneself. *(She doesn't tell about it, but listening whole story I understood that Maria filled it with her name, so Maria gave her identity to Helena).* The photo was the most important, because there was one stamp on the photo, too.

When the *Kennkarte* was ready he *(I think – a man called Roman, but I don't understand who he was – I think a friend of Maria)* met with Helena and fixed all the details.

Helena worked at Kopernik Street. It was winter, and it was common to wear fur scurf. I supposed she would not have one in the ghetto, and it could be strange and unusual for a regular woman to walk without one. So I took fur with me for her to put on, as I wanted her to look like a "normal" Polish girl.

I went there that day and Helena came by. I

took her left arm by my right arm and I took off the *Star of David,* the Jewish symbol, which she had on her arm. I put the fur on her, and we went to Roman. I was afraid to come with her to my home. The reason of it was that railroad workers were as one big family, and my neighbours knew Helena well. Also the neighbour's children knew her, because she used to visit me often before the War and would bring sweets with her to give them. So, I was afraid somebody would recognise her.

Thanks to my Kennkarte ID, Helena found a job in Warsaw, working for the railroad. Because of her good knowledge of German, she announced trains in Polish and German in the Main Railways Station.

Each month Helena sent a letter to me, but not exactly to me... It was impossible to send letters from Helena, who at the time was known as "Maria Bozek" to another "Maria Bozek." So Helena sent letters to my father–Antoni Bozek, as if they were letters to her "real" father.

Helena was very smart. She wanted to make her story real, and make sure no one doubted her name was indeed Maria Bozek. So instead of mailing the letters herself, she would ask somebody to take the letter for her and put it in the post box. This way people would be certain that she was indeed Polish and had a

Christian family in Krakow."

END OF THE INTERVIEW.

Jonathan, I hope this translation helps you. This story is truly fascinating. I feel very fortunate that I could help you. Again, best greetings for you and your family. Dariusz."

I was thrilled to receive that bit of information from Dariusz. I thanked him heartily. I now had more pieces to the story. But I wanted to know more.

LETTERS IN POLISH

At that time, I finally received the files from the *Yad Vashem Holocaust Museum* in Jerusalem. I was disappointed to find out there were only two letters there, and that they were, too, in Polish!

I did not want to bother Dariusz again after all of the help he had given me. I decided to write instead to my Polish friend from college. From age 17 to 19 I studied in Canada at an international UN College, representing Israel. The student representing Poland was a bright girl called Agata. I had not spoken to her in years, but this gave me a good excuse to write to her.

Turns out Agata was now a lawyer, having

graduated from Oxford, practicing law in London. I wrote to her about the story and attached one of the letters, asking for her help. She promptly wrote to me:

> "Jonathan! I'd love to help! I'll translate it as soon as I can. Currently preparing an asylum case for tomorrow so forgive me for not writing more. Kisses. Agata."

I was thrilled. I did not, however, want to request Agata to translate both letters, as I thought it was much to ask. So I decided to post the other letter on Facebook and ask anyone who spoke Polish to help with the translation.

Sure enough, an hour later one of my dear friends, Kaya Tanani, tagged a friend of hers who I did not know, and asked, "*Natalia Hakenberg*, can you help him? It's for a friend!"

Natalia Hakenberg promptly wrote: "I'm translating it right now!"

I was floored.

A day later I received an email from this Natalia:

> "Hello Jonathan!
>
> Please find attached the original letter + the translation. Sorry in advance for any mistakes I made in English ;)
>
> Also, thank you for letting me help you, it was nice to read such a nice story with a positive ending :)

If you need any help with translation from Polish in the future, you can let me know :)

Greetings from Poland,

Natalia."

I was ecstatic. What moved me the most was not only Natalia's willingness to help in the future, but her writing that "it was nice to read such a nice story with a positive ending."

These words were very encouraging for me, reassuring me that the story had to be told.

I eagerly opened the attached file and read the translation. It was written as a testimony by Maria Bozek-Nowak herself, and some of the information in it was new for me.

MARIA'S TESTIMONY

"In 1941, my school friend Helena Goldstein-Szymczak had been put in the Krakow Ghetto. As long as it was possible I was in touch with her in ghetto, and later when it became impossible, I contacted her outside of the ghetto. She was working outside the ghetto among a group of other people from the ghetto.

Her father was taken in the first deportation.

After some time since the deportation, when there were no news from him, they knew the aim of these deportations was the killing of Jews.

Her mother was on the list for the second deportation, at the end of 1942. Her older brother went there instead of her mother. But at the end they took both of them. After this deportation I received a message from the ghetto that my friend was completely broken—both mentally and physically. Together with my school colleague, Roman Bartel (who later on became a doctor; unfortunately, he has passed since) we decided to get Helena out of the ghetto.

When she started working at Kopernika Street (current location of the Medical Academy), we set the date of escape from ghetto. Her brother, Solomon Goldstein-Burowski helped us with that. First, he delivered us her suitcase from ghetto. Next I took her from Kopernika Street and brought her to Roman Bartel's place [...] We gave her a *Kennkarte*. Since we bought an empty one, we filled it in with my maiden name, "Maria Bozek," and put my information in it. To make it more credible, I gave her my birth certificate from St. Salwator Church and the notarial copy of my birth certificate. I also gave her a fur collar, since it was already after Jews have been forced to give all their furs away, and for her to walk without a fur on would have been suspicious [...]

Until the year 1944 we were in regular contact, later after some break she wrote to me in in December 1945 from *Jelenia Góra*, where she has been sent to work as an Aryan.

At the beginning of January 1945, I sent her my last package. The package had been delivered to *Jelenia Góra* right before the Soviet offensive. After the war ended in the spring of 1945, she came back safe and sound.

She died of a heart attack in 1986.

Maria Bozek-Nowak."

ANOTHER TESTIMONY?

I was putting all the pieces together. I felt the story wanting to burst out of me. The same day I received the translation from Natalia, my friend from London, Agata also wrote back. From reading the translation she had sent, of the letter in the files of *Yad Vashem Holocaust Museum*, I gathered that it was a testimony of a person attesting to the *truth* of the story. I began reading the first sentence:

> "Helena Goldstein was the sister of my husband Solomon Goldstein (Jozef Burawski)."

This letter, I gathered, was therefore written by Helena's *sister-in-law*. She married Solomon Goldstein, Helena's only brother to have survived the Holocaust. But why did Solomon have another name in brackets, Jozef Burawski?

I continued reading Agata's translation:

> "They have both passed away. Throughout our 28 years of marriage I maintained a close relationship with Helena, who was a lonely person. Helena would often return to her memories of the war and strongly emphasized that she owed her life to her friend Maria Nowak nee Bozek.
>
> Maria made it possible for her to escape the ghetto, arrange her *Kennkarte* and, risking death, give her own authentic documents which she could use.
>
> In addition, Maria made it easier for her to run away to Warsaw. These facts can be confirmed also by my husband's first wife, Halina Kazawski and her son Michael Burowski, who live in Tel Aviv, Israel.
>
> (Signature) ZB, an ex-prisoner of Ptaszow Concentration Camp."

MORE QUESTIONS THAN ANSWERS

That letter gave me answers, but it also gave me more questions.

It also sent shivers down my spine to see that signature: *ZB, an ex-prisoner of Ptaszow Concentration Camp.*"

Oh man.

Now I had more questions than answers. Did Solomon and his first wife divorce? Why? Was their son, Helena's nephew, really living in Israel? Could I find him? Why did Solomon Goldstein have another name in brackets in the letter, Jozef Burawski? And what was most striking for me: why did Solomon's second wife describe Helena as a "lonely person?"

Was she *lonely*?

My heart ached.

I wanted to find out more.

Then came an email that made my heart sing.

MARIA IS ALIVE?

Among the many emails I wrote was one addressed to the *Historical Museum of the City of Krakow.* I saw Maria Bozek-Nowak's name appearing in one of their archives online, and thought that perhaps they could help me find her or her family.

The response thrilled me:

"Dear Mr. Jonathan Kis-Lev,

My name is Bartosz Heksel and I work in the Eagle Pharmacy, which is a branch of the Historical Museum of the City of Krakow, I got your e-mail from Ms. Monika Bednarek. Maria Nowak was our guest in the meeting in November 2015 and was then in a good condition, but I do not know how she feels right now. You can contact her daughter at the phone number: [phone number].

Best regards,

Bartosz Heksel"

Oh my! Oh my God! I wanted to kiss this Bartosz fellow! Here he was, telling me that Maria was ALIVE, as well as giving me her daughter's PHONE NUMBER?

Could it get any better than that?

It turns out, it could.

TALKING TO MARIA'S DAUGHTER

After reading Bartosz's email I jumped around my office. When I relaxed, I did a quick calculation, understanding that Maria Bozek-Nowak, if indeed alive, was 96 years old. I mustered up the courage and placed an overseas call to the number I was given.

A woman picked up the phone.

"Hello?"

"Yes, Hello," I said, speaking English clearly and slowly, "My name is Jonathan, I am doing a research about Maria Bozek-Nowak—"

The words spoken back excitedly were in Polish. She did not speak English. I did not speak Polish. Nevertheless, I was able to say the name "Helena Goldstein", which made her very excited. In her voice I could hear that she was pleased, and she began asking me many questions in Polish.

I tried to understand, but could decipher nothing. Nor could she understand my English. I tried speaking some Esperanto, trying to pronounce the words slowly. I then tried some of my broken Russian. Seeing that none of this worked, and not wanting to exhaust her (my understanding was that she was to be in her sixties), I simply said, "Thank you, thank you Madam!" and said, "Friend telephone, friend telephone," meaning that I would have a Polish speaking friend telephone her.

After hanging up I ran to my wife and told her, "Guess who I spoke to?"

"Who?"

"Maria Bozek Nowak's daughter!"

"No!"

"Yes!"

"What did she say?"

"I don't know!"

COULD YOU SPEAK TO HER?

I then had to figure out how I could contact Maria's daughter again. Should I have my friend Dariusz call her? No, I already asked too much of him, and he was busy with his four children. Should I try my friend Agata? She was in London saving the world. I thought of trying the new acquaintance, Natalia, but felt it was a bit presumptuous to ask, "Hey, can you call this lady for me? I have about a hundred questions I want you to ask her!"

Luckily, at that moment my mind turned to one of the nicest young women I have met.

When I was in Poland my paintings were displayed at a large gallery, and the kindest person on the staff there was a young woman called Jolanta. We to corresponded a little over email after the exhibition, but since then it had been years.

I decided to try my luck and write to her.

"Hi Jolanta,

Not sure if you'll remember me, we met during the exhibition at Szyb Wilson Gallery, and then corresponded for some time...

I've been thinking about you and how you have fared since we last wrote to each other some four years ago...

I am currently writing a book about a brave Polish lady called Maria Bozek-Nowak. I am looking for someone to help communicate with the family. This brave woman, during WWII, saved the life of her Jewish friend, Helena Goldstein (Szymcak).

I have her daughter's phone number, and I called her, but she does not seem to speak English....

I was wondering if perhaps you could help me with this? I would like to ask her some questions, as well as see if she could supply me with some photos for the book. I promise to send the family several copies of the book as a gift in return :)

If not you, Jolanta, could you direct me to someone who could serve as the liaison?

Thank you so much, I hope I'm not appearing rude to ask for that after four years, but you just came to mind being one of the nicest Polish people I know :)

Warmly,

Jonathan."

Jolanta's response was quick to come:

"Dear Jonathan,

What can I say... your email is definitely a great surprise to me :-)

I feel honored that you've asked me for help.

I have some practical questions:

1. Do you know where the lady you want me to call lives? Maybe it is better to meet her personally?

2. About the photos. If they have some photos is it enough to make some kind of high quality photocopies?
If yes please let me know what kind because I'm not really good at technical things.. :-)

Now about me. I lived for some time in the Czech Republic where I worked at some small educational theatre. Now I am back in Poland, so you are writing to me in the right time.

All the best,

Jolanta."

Yay! From Jolanta's questions about possibly visiting the family rather than speaking on the phone, I knew I had found the right person. We conversed back and forth for some time. Ten days after my first email to her she wrote to me:

"Dear Jonathan,

I spoke with Maria Bozek-Nowak's daughter, Krystyna. She was happy to hear that someone is writing a book about her mother!

In terms of photographs there are a few of them and she will have to find them.

It is a little more complicated as her mother fell down and now she is taking care of her all the time. I'll call her at the end of the week to find out about the situation.

The question is, how many pictures do you need? What kind of pictures? How can we send them to Israel (I mean, what kind of files we should send you via the Internet)?

Best wishes,

Jolanta."

I wrote to Jolanta expressing my regret and sorrow to hear of Maria's fall, and wishing her the best wishes for a quick recovery.

Now you must imagine how excited I was to be able to communicate indirectly to Maria's daughter, and through her to Maria herself!

Jolanta and I continued to correspond over many emails, me sending her many questions for her to ask Maria's daughter, Krystyna.

Finally, after Jolanta speaking on the phone several times with Krystyna, she wanted to go and visit her. I was ecstatic.

"Dear Jonathan,

Krystyna, Maria's daughter, is absolutely amazing :-) !

I love to hear her telling me her family stories – she told me that she regarded Helena Goldstein as her aunt.

I'm happy that someone else will be able to know of this story!

I will borrow a voice recorder, so I can send you her exact answers.

Probably I will meet Krystyna soon!

Oh, she told me that Helena Goldstein's nephew lives in Israel, and that he often comes to Poland! She told me he might be able to visit and join our meeting!

Unbelievable!

I'm looking forward to telling you all about it!

Jolanta."

It indeed felt unbelievable. We wrote back and forth. I was disappointed when their scheduled meeting had to be postponed. Luckily, in the meantime, I was able to get through Jolanta the email of Helena's Goldstein's nephew. Indeed, it turned out to be the same person referred to in the letter I found at the *Yad Vashem Holocaust Museum* in Jerusalem: the letter from Solomon's second wife which mentioned "Michael Burowski."

I emailed Michael, introducing myself both in English and Hebrew. He wrote to me back and said he was intrigued to hear of my interest in his family's history. He told me he was in Poland at the time. We scheduled a phone conversation. I called him at the time agreed upon and sat down with a notebook in hand.

SPEAKING TO HELENA'S NEPHEW

At first Michael sounded a little suspicious of me. Who was I, this stranger, coming to meddle in old family affairs? But by the time our conversation ended an hour later, he was thanking me profusely, saying, "You must tell this story, Jonathan!"

Michael told me that when he was very young his parents divorced and that his mother moved with him to Israel and eventually remarried. Nevertheless, over the years, they came to visit Poland. He came to know aunt Helena Goldstein, his father's sister, as a very warm person, sweet, loving, and vivacious.

"In fact," he told me, "she always hugged me, and she was very warm to me. So I called her, 'Auntie Oven' because she was warm like an oven! She liked that name and repeated it to everyone, 'I'm Auntie Oven! The child calls me Auntie Oven.'"

One question was on my mind ever since I read the testimony letter of Solomon's second wife attesting that Helena Goldstein was a "lonely person." I asked Michael whether Helena was indeed "lonely."

"Oh, no! She had a boyfriend, they were together for decades! His name was Lucjan. While they did not marry, they were still a great couple. He loved her very much. They lived together, and he was at her bedside when she died. He died a year later."

This piece of news brought tears to my eyes, and I said, "You don't know what a relief it is for me to hear that!"

I guess that knowing that Helena lost nearly everyone in the Holocaust, I was afraid she was a bitter person. But Michael reassured me, "She was very vivacious, enjoyed life. She was a tour guide—"

"Wait, I thought she was an accountant?"

"Oh no, she worked in a tourist office, toured a lot around Poland, led trips to Paris, Greece, and even to Egypt."

Again, this little detail made me tear up again. My heart, which had contracted, fearing to hear the worst, now opened up. "I'm so glad to hear that," I told him.

Michael thanked me again and his voice began cracking, "Listen," he said, and I could hear him crying, "I don't know you, but I can feel you have good intentions. This story means the world to me. I don't know how you found out about it, but it has to be told."

I promised him I'd do my best to portray the story as accurately and as best as I could.

"JONATHAN, I MET MARIA'S DAUGHTER!"

Finally, Jolanta was able to go and meet Krystyna Nowak in person. I sent her in advance a long list of questions. I wanted to know everything possible. Here are some of them:

Which feasts and holidays did Maria and Helena spend together?

What can you tell of the families?

Do you know any anecdotes from the school years?

Can you describe their characters?

Maria's brother Edmund at that time must have been at military age? Was he a teenager? What was he doing?

What was Maria's parent's reaction to her decision to help Helena and risk her life?

Can you tell of the actual "kidnapping" of Helena? How did Maria do it exactly?

Was Helena indeed wearing a green dress when coming back to Krakow?

Was it true that Helena's brother was able to procure their house back?

Who was present at Helena's death?

Was Helena Goldstein a 'lonely' person?

Was there anything in Helena's life that was giving her a sense of happiness? Was she a happy person?

Are there any personal memories that you have from Helena's later years?

Any other memories of Helena?

On the specific day of the meeting I was excited, waiting to hear from Jolanta. We agreed that the following day we would Skype and I would hear everything from her while it was still fresh.

That evening I got a lovely email from Jolanta:

"Dear Jonathan,

I'm excited to be talking to you tomorrow! I have some photos and information for you!

Krystyna Nowak was amazing, and I met her along with Michael, Helena Goldstein's nephew, as well as an older friend of Helena named Lilka Nowakowa. I felt as I was a part of the family! There is an extremely strong bond between the two families (Bozek-Nowak with Goldstein family). Every time Krystyna Nowak mentions something about Helena Goldstein, she always calls her "my auntie Helena."

In my opinion, Michael was very touched by the meeting and with my interest in the story. As I spoke with him I had a strong feeling that there is a lot he actually would like to share, but somehow it is an extremely difficult subject for him. He seemed to be very moved and breathed heavily.

I'll start tonight with translating briefly my many notes, and tomorrow we'll go over the pictures together. I have 16 photos for you!

Talk to you tomorrow!

Jolanta."

That night I had difficulty falling asleep. The whole story seemed so surreal. That me, by somehow finding a book about the Holocaust, could trace the actual woman who saved her friend's life, and somehow arrange for a friend of mine to visit her daughter's house and meet her nephew. Unbelievable.

The following day Jolanta and I had a two-hour conversation on Skype. I was so jealous of her for being able to take the time and visit Krystyna and hear the story in person. Here I was, drooling over all the facts, while being somewhat stranded in my house in Israel with my newborn baby girl, unable to just fly and pop into Krystyna Nowak's living room. But I felt that via Jolanta it was almost as if I was there myself.

Jolanta then sent me a full description of all that was discussed during that meeting. I added some of the comments that Jolanta told me about verbally. Here is the full interview. I am excited to share with you all of the information about the "real" Two Marias.

THE INTERVIEW

Here is the interview with Krystyna Nowak, Maria Bozek Nowak's sister. Michael, Helena's nephew, also contributed from his own knowledge. Interview conducted by the wonderful Jolanta Szewińska.

PART 1: BEFORE THE WAR

Which feasts and holidays did Maria and Helena spend together?

"Helena visited Maria during Christmas and Easter. Maria visited Helena at several holidays and also visited the synagogue with her. Helena's family rarely went to the synagogue, which was typical of an "assimilated" family."

Michael, Helena's nephew, intervened and explained:

"They lived according to the Jewish proverb: 'Be a Jew at home, a Pole outside the home.'"

Krystyna somewhat disagreed:

"According to my mother, Helena's family was religious, and during Passover she remembers seeing the Passover flatbread (*Matza*) on the table. But at the same time my mother also recalls seeing ham. Therefore, the family was both Jewish *and* assimilated."

What can you tell of the families?

"Helena's grandfather had an important position in the Jewish community. He was among those who took care of widows and their children.

My grandfather, Maria's father, was a railway worker. During the First World War he fought in the Austrian army, then in 1920 he fought against the Russian Bolsheviks."

Do you know of any anecdotes from the school years?

"Helena and Maria attended the *Emilia Plater Classical School for Girls*. It had a very good reputation. Pupils had to wear special uniforms, including white socks and sandals, which might have been popular in the 1920s, but after a while grew out of fashion, so the girls avoided wearing them. One specific teacher tried to enforce the sandals and socks, and an ensuing "socks-war" followed, which the students won.

In their class there were 24 girls: twelve Catholic, ten Jewish, and two Protestant. The Catholic pupils had lessons with the priest, the Jewish pupils had lessons with a visiting rabbi, and the Protestants attended religion classes at the *Saint Martin Church*. The girls used to joke that the Catholic girls were better off because the priest, Stanislaw, was very handsome, and used to ride his horse everywhere, which the girls found very attractive.

As to the rabbi, the Jewish girls complained that he gave them very low grades. The Catholic and Protestant students used to get "Excellent" in Religion Class, while the Jewish girls used to get very low grades like "Good."

This eventually led to the parents meeting the rabbi during one Parent-Teacher meeting. One of the mothers stood up and asked, "Dear rabbi, with all due respect, why do our girls receive such dreadful marks, only 'Good' and never 'Excellent' or 'Outstanding'?"

"The rabbi looked surprised and asked, "Is 'Good' *bad?*'"

(This is where Krystyna began laughing)

"That phrase, "Is 'good' bad?" became a joke in the class and in many ways became a class idiom. Helena, Maria, as well as their families used to often probe one another, "Come on, is good *bad?*" and then burst into laughter. "

Can you describe their characters?

"In school Helena was a troublemaker. Smoking was prohibited within the school premises, and Helena was caught smoking in the toilet room. Helena ran home fearing the consequences of possibly getting expelled. Maria hurried after school to Helena's home, and found Mrs. Goldstein there alone. Maria cried, 'Where is Helena?'

Mrs. Goldstein sat there in the living room, saying,

'Helena was so troubled that I decided to send her to the cinema to unwind a little. But now I'm sitting here and worrying where she is!'

Another event that the girls often recalled was at the summer before WWII broke, when all the girls from class went on a long tracking trail from *Komancza* all the way to *Pobiwan*, in what is today Ukraine."

DURING THE WAR

Maria's brother Edmund at that time must have been at military age? Was he a teenager? What was he doing?

"When the war broke Edmund was 15 years old, and Alexandra was 7 years old. Edmund, after graduating school, started to work as a hospital ward attendant."

What was Maria's parent's reaction to her decision to help Helena and risk her life?

"My grandfather simply told my mother (Maria), 'In life there are sometimes situations in which you have to behave in a way that will make you respect yourself. This is one of them.'"

Can you tell of the actual "kidnapping" of Helena? How did Maria do it exactly?

[Author's note: here you will find two differences from the plot of the book, one has to do with the timing of the 'kidnap' and the other with the location of hiding.]

"At that time Helena worked outside the ghetto. She

AFTERWORD

was cleaning office buildings at Kopernika street. With the help of Roman Bartel they agreed that Helena would come back from work near the wall. Maria pulled Helena out of the line and took her to some building gateway (a place where nobody could see them), there she took Helena's Star of David armband off and gave her some fur scurf or fur-collar. It was important as some time earlier Germans had taken off all fur lining from Jewish clothes.

Then Helena went into hiding, with Roman Bartel's help, at the attic of the Bartel family's apartment. Roman did not tell his parents, and Mrs. Bartel was surprised by the fact that her son Roman was eating more during those days.

They agreed to hide Helena at Roman Bartel's apartment and not at Maria's because Helena was liked by the children living on Maria's street, as she always had some sweets for them. That's why she could have been recognized by the children and that could have been a threat for her life.

They decided to send Helena to Warsaw because in Krakow there couldn't be two persons with the same identity. The girls dyed Helena's hair blond to make her look more Aryan."

Was Helena indeed wearing a green dress when coming back to Krakow?

"Toward the end of the war Maria worked at a shop. They paid her in vouchers. She exchanged the vouchers for green fabric so she could get a dress made. Then she sent Helena the parcel with the dress and some food. Helena got the dress, but she didn't like the color so she dyed it brown. She came back to Krakow in that very dress.

Her first steps were directed to the Bozek family. My grandmother, Franciscka, Maria's mother, upon seeing Helena, shouted, 'Hela (Polish nickname for Helena), Hela! Thank God, you are alive! Oh no, you must be starving and all I have is potatoes!'

Being extremely grateful for all of her help, Helena kissed Franciscka's hand."

AFTER THE WAR

Was it true that Helena's brother was able to procure their house back?

"No. After the war Helena lived at number 58 Slowacki Avenue, in an apartment with a kitchen and bathroom shared with the adjacent apartment, where a lady named Roza Lustgartenowa lived. Helena kept her new surname, Szymczak. In that house she eventually died."

Who was present at Helena's death?

"My mother and I were there, as Helena's boyfriend, Lucjan, called us to rush over. Helena died on June 29th 1986 at 12:00 noon after many hours of resuscitation attempts."

Was Helena Goldstein a 'lonely' person?

"Not at all. She wasn't. She shared her apartment with her boyfriend Lucjan. They were not married because

Lucjan was already married and had a family, but he lived with Helena. Helena's brother, Solomon, did not approve of Lucjan, because he was changing jobs often. But Helena loved him deeply, and in many ways she 'mothered' him. She transferred her 'maternal instinct' to him. They were very much in love, a very tender and loving couple. Lucjan died one year after Helena's death."

Was there anything in Helena's life that gave her a sense of happiness? Was she a happy person?

"Helena's life was accompanied by a mixture of different emotions. It is hard to say that she was unhappy, but it is difficult to claim as well that she was happy, mostly because of her Holocaust experience and the fact that she lost her entire family and friends except for her brother.

She smoked a lot of cigarettes and that was a kind of compensation and a way to 'run away' from difficult emotions. But she loved living in Krakow. She kept saying, 'Where else could I live in the world? Where else will I find a city with such a beautiful city square?'"

Are there any personal memories that you have from Helena's later years?

"There are many. She was always there for me, like my aunt. I remember one day when my parents, Maria and Alfonso, were sitting with Helena. Together the three of them were doing a crossword puzzled with the topic of the ancient world. They were discussing how to pronounce the word *Zeus* correctly. Maria and Helena had a classical education in Poland, while

Alfonso graduated from a German school. Therefore, they had different educational backgrounds. Helena seemingly argued with Alfonso about the exact pronunciation, when finally, Alfonso exclaimed "My dearest ladies, who can nowadays verify for sure how the ancient Greeks were speaking?!"

(With this, Krystyna began laughing.)

Any other memories of Helena?

"After the war Helena worked as an accountant at the travel agency *Orbis*. As she knew Ancient Greek and quickly learned Modern Greek, she served also as a tour guide. Her trips included Greece, Italy, Bulgaria, and other places.

During the last years of her professional career she worked halftime as an accountant at the Pharmacy managed by my mother. It was a well-known Pharmacy in Krakow that had a great variety of medicines from all over Europe.

Helena loved smoking cigarettes. According to the family one of her last words were: "This cigarette may be my last!""

This was one of the only times that Michael, Helena's nephew, intervened:

"I think that smoking was an act of compensation for her. She felt she had to hold all of her emotions and memories inside. So smoking was an escape from the traumas of the war: inhaling and then holding the emotions inside.

But you must understand, Jolanta, my aunt was very

affectionate and warm. My nickname to her was a 'Auntie-stove,' because she was always so warm. She liked that name a lot and had me repeat it often."

(Here Krystyna continued)

"To me Helena was so dear, an adopting aunt. We were very close. I could never go shopping with my mother, she did not like shopping. But Helena did. She also came with me to the dentist. I was always so terrified to go to him, but Aunt Helena came with me. She also took me a lot to the theatre, to galleries, and to some interesting lectures.

When I grew up, once each week she and I would have a "date" together in one of the evenings. We would either eat out or she would fix me a dinner. I loved when she would make me a *Matzah brei*—do you know what's *Matzah brei*?"

(I did not. This is when a long excited conversation about food sparked)

"*Matzah brei* is a Jewish dish made of the Passover flatbread, mixed with eggs. It's delicious!

Aunt Helena used to tease me about me liking all this Jewish food, and said with a twinkle in her eyes that 'there must be some Jewishness in your blood if you love all this Jewish food!'"

Helena also helped me with my doctoral thesis in chemistry, translating for me many of the English scientific publications, even though she had no clue about chemistry.

Also, you should note that Helena was very... how do

you say it… spiritual. She was not religious, but always very interested in God, and she would pose many difficult questions. She often took me to the spiritual center in Krakow, The *Seminary of Czestochowa*. There we often met with archbishop Zycinski, who became a good friend of Helena's. Knowing that Helena loved smoking, the archbishop would always offer her a good cigarette, sometimes along with wine as well. They would have conversations about God and I would be there, listening."

Actually, once after such a meeting with the archbishop, and after drinking a glass or two, Helena was so tipsy, that when we left she told me, 'Oh my, I'm so drunk, we must go home through the city square, seeing that beauty undoubtedly will make me sober!'"

(This is how our meeting ended, with much laughter and hugs. I felt a part of the family. Jolanta.)

THE PHOTOGRAPHS

We arranged all the 16 photographs in chronological order, beginning with a photo of Maria's mother, and finishing with a photo of Maria in recent years. I hope you will enjoy these photos as much as I did.

We thank the two families for their cooperation and kind permission to use the photos and present them to the readers here.

1. Franciszka Bozek, Maria's mother, Vienna, c. 1917

2. Maria Bozek (right) at her First Holy Communion,
with brother Edmund (center) and little sister Alexandra
(left), Krakow, c. 1927

3. Maria Bozek with her brother Edmund, Krakow, c.
1925

4. The only preserved picture of Helena Goldstein as a
young girl, Krakow, c. 1925

5. Helena Goldstein, picture for her High school
diploma, Krakow, 1938

6. Maria Bozek, picture for her High school diploma, Krakow, 1938

6. Maria Bozek at Roman Bartel's apartment, picture
taken by Roman Bartel, Krakow, c. 1940

8. Maria Bozek by the Vistula River, Krakow, c. 1940

9. Maria Bozek with her future husband, Alfons Brunon Nowak, at the cemetary, Krakow, c. 1945

10. Helena's only brother to survive the Holocaust,
Solomon Jozef Goldstein, Krakow, c. 1949

11. Helena Goldstein (on the right wearing a white necklace) with her sister-in-law, Zofia Burowska (Solomon Goldstein's second wife), Planty Park, Krakow, c. 1970

12. Maria's brother, Edmund Bozek, Tatra Mountains, c. 1960

13. Aleksandra Bozek, Krakow, c. 1980

15. Helena Goldstein enjoying the sun at the main
square of the Old City, Krakow, c. 1980

16. Maria Bozek Nowak c. 2000

THE WRITING PROCESS

While the previous section of the book dealt with the historical background and research, this part of the book focuses on the *artistic* and *creative* process of writing.

If the former part was for History geeks, this current part is for people who are interested in the craft of writing; I stress that because this segment isn't for everyone. On the contrary: it's for a small number of people. The reason is that it actually shows the craft and the behind the scenes elements. In many ways it can ruin the experience for the reader, as it displays the technical elements of construction. It's like an x-ray.

So feel free to not read this part of the book. Again, it's for people who are specifically interested in the creative process.

This process happened simultaneously to the research process. I wish I could tell you that all the research was done *prior* to writing. Most of it was done before writing, yes, but I simply couldn't wait until I received all the information from Jolanta and everyone else to begin constructing the actual story. I *wanted* to hold the writing of the book until I had *all* the information.

But I couldn't.

Fortuna was escaping.

FORTUNA AND THE CREATIVE PROCESS

There's an artistic method that I learned from being a painter. Once you have an idea or an inspiration, you must *act* on it. And you better do it quickly.

I tried to find everything I could about Maria and Helena myself. It wasn't much, but I had the rough story-line in mind.

This may sound a little odd for you, but I knew that my time was running out.

Allow me to explain.

In the Roman mythology there is a story about the Goddess of fortune, *Fortuna*.

In Latin, there's a famous saying:

> *"Opportunity has hair in front, but behind she is bald; if you seize her by the forelock, you may hold her, but if she manages to escape, not Jupiter himself can catch her*

again."

I first found this story when I read an interview with one of Israel's former Prime Ministers. This Prime Minister, Menachem Begin, was very doubtful about peace with Israel's Arab neighbors. He was rather militaristic.

And yet, this rather militaristic Prime Minister surprised Israel, the Arabs, and the entire world, when in 1979 he signed the peace accords with Egypt. When asked about why he did it, the late Menachem Begin said that when *Fortuna*, the Goddess of Fortune, passes by, a person must be wise and quick to grab unto her hair before she disappears. This, he said, was what he was doing.

I loved reading this story, and have often thought about it since. I love how a militaristic prime minister was able to make peace by striking while the iron was hot, by seizing the opportunity before the window was closed.

To me as an artist, *inspiration is that way.* If I want to paint something, I must act on it *fast.* Each day I postpone an idea, it is in danger of becoming more stale, less animated and vivacious. Over time it will die unless I act upon it.

I learned it the hard way, many times.

Recently, I found an echo about this phenomenon in Elizabeth Gilbert's great book about creativity, *Big Magic.* In it she writes:

> "The idea will try to wave you down [...] but when it finally realizes that you're oblivious to

its message, it will move on to someone else."[1]

I've seen this happening again and again throughout my life as an artist. And so, I knew I had to act *fast*. I kept nagging the Yad VaShem Museum, my friend Dariusz in Poland and the few other places I was waiting an answer from.

But time was running out. The idea for the book was in danger of dying. I needed to sit down with what I had, with the scenes I saw in my mind, and "drop the bucket where I was." I had to use the research available, and move to the back seat while I let the muse take over.

I sat down and wrote. Hours and hours, day and night. And before I knew it, a week later, I had the first draft of the manuscript completed.

BUT THE LENGTH!

Right from the first day I sat down to write *The Two Marias* I was in distress.

As I mentioned above, I didn't know if the story I had in my mind could fill a whole book.

My first novel, *Six Days with Gandhi,* had 70,000+ words, about 350-400 pages. That's about a good size for a novel.

Writing my following book, *New Day Dawning,* I felt like I wanted to compose in a style that would make the novel shorter, more concise, more movie-like. I was therefore proud of how I managed to shorten the lengthy story of a person's life, from teens to old age, to just a little over 50,000 words.

It felt like the right length. Not too short, not too long.

But for the story I had in my mind for *The Two Marias*, I knew it would have to be even shorter than that.

It had to be.

I thought that every scene in *The Two Marias* had to be concise, poignant, brief and powerful.

When I brought the novel to an end after a week of writing, I had to take a deep breath. The novel was short. It felt *too* short. 30,000 words.

I was terrified.

It felt like I might have done something *wrong*.

I looked at the story again. I felt that elongating it would be a *crime against humanity*... Expanding any part would harm the flow and the fast pace of the story.

But 30,000 words? That's barely a book! That's a... booklet...!

I was *terrified*. What had I done?! I wrote something that was... incomplete...

I knew that it *felt* complete to me. I knew I didn't want to extend the story into the lives of Maria and Helena after the war. It could be interesting for someone else to write. But it wasn't appealing to me. I also didn't know much about what happened after the war, apart from the fact that Helena died in 1986, that she was an Accountant, and that she worked for the Pharmacy headed by Maria.

For me, the post-war years were interesting, but not captivating. I wanted to end the book at its *peak*. At its emotional *summit*. I knew from the very beginning that the book had to *begin* and *end* in the train station.

Extending the book to include the lives of the characters after that was just not appealing *to me*. It felt like a mistake, leaving the peak behind and slowly sliding down toward an uneventful ending. I've seen novelists do it before. Have you? I wanted to avoid that trap myself.

I then thought that perhaps I should have expanded on the character's childhood. Or perhaps on the war years? Yet both these options felt unnatural.

The childhood years felt to me powerful as they were already portrayed.

And the war years – sure, I could expand. But I was afraid it would make the book darker. The book was already dark *enough*. I wanted light, hope, love – these were my main themes. Expanding on the war would have been a mistake.

So… 30,000 words?

After I finished the novel I did some research. Mostly, it stemmed out of me feeling quite… inapt.

What I found out was that, though I felt the novel inadequate, I had, in fact, stumbled by accident onto a genre I didn't know I knew.

The book didn't feel like a "novel". It was a little too short for that.

But it didn't feel like a "short story" either. I knew short stories very well from my school days. *The Two Marias* was *not* a "short story".

But it turned out that *The Two Marias* fell into the category of "*novellas.*"

NOVELLAS?

I vaguely remembered that genre from school. But not really.

Apparently, novellas are just that: something in *between* a novel and a short story.

I wasn't sure if I wanted to be included, though, in this rather odd category.

But then I found out that many of the world's greatest works of Literature are, in fact, novellas; just like *The Two Marias*, some of the world's most famous Literary Fiction pieces are under 30,000 words.

Charles Dickens' *A Christmas Carol*, John Steinbeck's *Of Mice and Men*, Franz Kafka's *The Metamorphosis*, Ernest Hemingway's *The Old Man and the Sea*, Truman Capote's *Breakfast at Tiffany's*, and Leo Tolstoy's *The Kreutzer Sonata* are just a few examples of novellas with less than 30,000 words!

But furthermore, even books that you and I could imagine as *lengthy* and *thick*, like George Orwell's

Animal Farm or Robert Louis Stevenson's *Dr. Jekyll and Mr. Hyde* are, in fact, novellas...!

The more I read about the genre, the better I began feeling. Perhaps I did the right thing? I read and liked they way publisher Blaise van Hecke put it, "A book doesn't have to be obese to be good or meaningful."[2]

I couldn't but agree. In fact, I felt that it would have been *easy* to make the book thicker. That its strength and power lay, on the contrary, in its concise and succinct nature.

Van Hecke wrote, "Size doesn't guarantee quality, and a lesser length is by no means short-changing […] There's a beauty and art-form [to novellas] which is unique."[3]

I had to agree.

I wrote *The Two Marias* in the art-form that the *story* begged for. I listened to the *story*. Let me assure you that if the characters and the story had *wanted* it, the book would have been much longer.

But I listened to the characters. I listened to the story.

And so, I had to tell myself, "Let the book be a little thin, Jonathan, that's the way it *needs* to be."

One of my great aspirations for the book was for it to be non-specific in its nature.

NON-SPECIFIC?

You see, for the book I conducted much research around the era, the war, the step-by-step mechanism applied by the Nazis. I learned much about the liberation of Poland by the Red Army. I did my best to give the book a true historic context.

Yet at the same time, I wanted for the book to be *international*. I wanted readers in China, Africa, South America, and anywhere, really, to feel *included* in the story.

I knew from my own experience as a reader that names of cities, many historical details and dates – only made me tired, personally.

But what I've done in *The Two Marias* is take it one step further.

I wanted no country to be mentioned.

Throughout the book we don't really *know* where the girls live in and where the war takes place. We don't even know which language they speak. All we know is the years, but even that is only brought to us by their *own* words, when they are *asked*. I never wrote "It was in the year of…"

This is because I wanted, as much as possible, to make the story *not* related to one place and to one time.

I wanted each reader to see *themselves* in the book. As I always do as a reader.

I even never specifically mentioned that Helena was *Jewish*, and that Maria was *Christian*. I did mention the names of the holidays, yes, but the whole theme of anti-Semitism is replaced by a more *general* xenophobia.

Jewish readers and anyone interested in the Holocaust could easily identify who and where and what and when… But for me, wanting to make the story universal, there was a danger in specifying words that bring a huge emotional response, such as "Holocaust" and "Ghetto".

Instead, there was a *war*, and *the enclosure*. Instead of Jews there was *them* vs. *us*. Instead of the Nazis there were the *soldiers*. Instead of Germany there was the *occupying army*. Instead of the Red Army and the Allies (known then as the United Nations) there were the *liberating allies*.

I know that this may have seemed rather clunky and unnatural at times. Also, I know it may upset some readers. Some may say, "Why didn't you just name things as they were?"

But to me, personally, the *benefits* of *ambiguity* were much more important. They enabled the story to be more relatable, more touching, to *everyone*. This was my ultimate goal.

With this notion in mind, I set to write the book.

But I had one big fear. It was my greatest fear. The fear that I would not be able to write the story well. After all, it was a story about two *girls*, two *women*. And (in case you haven't noticed yet) I am not a girl, nor a woman. Ouch.

BUT I'M A MALE AUTHOR

And so as I sat down to write this story, I was intimidated by it. I was afraid that I wouldn't be able to do justice to the characters. That it would feel *unnatural* to the reader, knowing that a *male* author wrote about the friendship of two *girls*.

But quite frankly, in each of my books I am intimidated about *something*. In my many non-fiction books, I feared that I would come out as too arrogant, or too ignorant, or whatever.

In *Six Days with Gandhi* I feared that the readers would sense that it is fictional work, and not *perceive* the character of Gandhi as *believable*. This led me to do crazy research, basing almost all of Gandhi's sentences on things he said in real life. Given the thousands of words spoken by Gandhi in that book, it was a gargantuan task.

In my book *New Day Dawning,* I feared that the two story lines, in two different time sequences, wouldn't work together. I therefore did much soul-searching, and learned to trust the story and let it lead me. I also learned to trust that the reader is intelligent enough to deal with two different time sequences woven together throughout the book.

In *The Two Marias* I had the fear of me being a man

and therefore inapt to write about girls. But I had to let this fear go.

"So what," I told myself, "if you're a male author? Before your sex, you are an *artist*, a *sensitive* soul. Women can write about men! And men can write about women!"

When I reached the scene of Maria having her first period, I bit my lip, and allowed the story and the characters to lead me.

They did. They led me. Maria, and Helena, and Mrs. Bozek. Each had their own story, their own outlook, their own pain, and I needed to serve them all right.

I soon learned that I could write whatever needed to be told. That I would find the words and the exact responses of each character.

And soon enough I fell in love. Both with Maria and with Helena, and quite frankly, also with the Bozeks.

And so, this book was somehow healing for me. Not only in the sense of the healing relationship between Maria and Helena, but also in a personal way, as an author. It empowered me to keep writing, and to tell stories that I feel must be told.

In the following part, the Commentary, I will take some of you into a deeper look at the book and the characters. I say "some of you" because I know that not everyone is interested in the creative process. But I am interested in it. And whenever I find interviews and in-depth recollections of writers, my heart sings with joy. I therefore wish to share with all of you creative souls out there, some of the process of writing this book. While it was written in a week, it has many parts of me that were inscribed in my three decades here on earth. I wish to chat with you, one on one, and answer some of your questions.

To the rest of you, thank you for reading all the way to here. At the end of the book you'll find a few pages mentioning my other books, some of which you may feel compelled to read. So I encourage you to have a look at them.

I wish you all love and light. May the relationship between Maria and Helena inspire us, like it inspired their families and friends, to bring light and love to others and to ourselves.

Thank you for being a part of this journey with me.

Yours,

Jonathan

COMMENTARY

One of the first things I knew about *The Two Marias* was that the book would begin and end in the train station.

I had to begin with that. I had to tell the reader – the end will be good. Hang on.

The book begins with Maria at the train station. It

ends with Maria *and* Helena at the train station. The last *sentence* of the book is Helena's, "I promise."

Maria opens, Helena closes. Who's the hero in the book? Both? For sure? We'll see.

We begin with spring, and we are told right then and there that there was a war. The war will be a shadow, cast now even on their happy childhood.

> Maria stood at the train station.
>
> It was spring, finally.
>
> The war was now over. How long she had been waiting for this moment.

We're then introduced to Maria's hands fidgeting and lip biting. These characteristics will stay with her for the whole book, even though at times she'll prove so courageous, her actions might stun us.

We then read of Helena:

> At the same time, on the train approaching the border into the country, a young woman sat watching the window.

We don't know this person's name yet. I wanted to introduce her as Maria, but that could have been a little tricky. The narrator ought to be on the reader's side, not to confuse him. So I built up a scene in which we *learn* her name was Maria.

> She sat up as the border police officers passed in the aisle. She smiled at the officer and handed him her identification papers. Before the war she knew nothing about these things. One ID was fine. But nowadays one had to

carry multiple forms of identification.

The officer looked at the photo and then at her, "Maria?"

She nodded.

"Date of birth?"

"January 22nd," she said calmly, "1920."

The emphasis on "calmly" and the importance of the identification help us see that something here is odd.

> She nodded back and put all the documents in her file, and tucked it into the front of her suitcase. These very documents saved her so many times in the past three years.
>
> But soon she wouldn't need them any more.
>
> Soon she could return to be herself. Her *real* self.

We don't know who this "real self" is. But we are then given a transition – a thought – that would lead us back to her childhood:

> And to think that she did not want to be seated next to Maria in class in the first place. How different things could have turned out.

We then find ourselves in class.

> The harsh tone of Mrs. Schlesinger startled Helena from her daydreams. "Yes, Mrs. Schlesinger!"

Helena is being seated next to Maria. Yet she wants

to be with Gisele, who she knows from elementary school. This is one of the only signs indicating to us that Gisele and Helena are part of the same *group*, the same *minority*. We will never learn that Gisele is Jewish explicitly. But we'll see several times in which it is hinted that she is.

I knew I had to "kill" some of the characters. I knew that apart from one brother, Helena's whole family would perish. But I needed to have something more. I needed to have something that would startle and move Maria into action in due time. That, unfortunately, had to be the fictional character of Gisele.

> When Mrs. Schlesinger was done, the class, now all re-seated, was quiet. Helena shook her head. Mrs. Schlesinger didn't have a clue what she was doing.

That last sentence for me is a golden one. It is pure gold. I love sometimes reading books for the second (and third??) time. This is a golden sentence for those reading it for the second time. Did Mrs. Schlesinger not have a clue of what she was doing?

Or was she actually wiser than we may think?

Then, during the break, Helena asks Gisele what she knows about the girl she was seated with.

> "Who? *Maria?*" Gisele asked, "I guess she's… well… I don't really know, I never noticed her before…"

> "Exactly," Helena sighed.

Is it only me or Helena isn't particularly kind here?

Then, there is another situation in which she is quite unkind.

> Helena noticed [Maria] always wrote the correct answers in her exercise book as if testing herself before the answer was revealed.
>
> It drove Helena crazy. One time, after the bell rang, before heading into the yard with Gisele and the others, she asked Maria, "Why don't you raise your hand?"
>
> "Excuse me?" Maria mumbled, looking down.
>
> "Mr. Kissinger asked a question, the square root question, and you knew it!"
>
> "No I... didn't..."
>
> "Liar," Helena said, "I saw you writing it in your notebook!"
>
> Maria's face reddened. No one ever called her a liar!
>
> But Helena raised her eyebrows knowingly and left the classroom.

Who is this rude Helena?

One of the key and most important things for me is to have *round characters*. This, to me, means the character must be *complex*.

I cannot stand when the villains are just villains and the saints are just saints. Life doesn't work that way. In

Six Days with Gandhi, Gandhi explains to the main character that even Hitler was once a child who wanted to be loved. It's difficult for us to accept that, but Gandhi insists.

Helena will show us her humanity soon. And Maria will show us her courage soon. Both characters will grow with us. They'll be round: light will be shed on them from different angles, in different situations. Gisele may be more flat, and so will Roman and the other minor characters. But our Helena and Maria will show us their entire soul, even the parts we less like to see, like Helena did just now, leaving Maria "frozen to her chair" and "stunned".

Later we'll learn that Helena can be that way sometimes: stating the truth blatantly, or being somewhat inappropriate. But it's this very trait that will make us fall in love with her.

As an author, I had to bring Helena and Maria closer and closer. Eventually their bond needed to be so strong, that Maria would be willing to risk her life for Helena.

I needed to create situations that would slowly and surely create this.

How could I bring the two together? "Helena was perhaps the most popular. Maria was the least." They were opposites. During breaks Maria would stay in the classroom, while Helena would be surrounded by her friends in the yard. I asked myself, how do I bring them closer?

I knew I had to create a scene in which both would be isolated: Helena from her friends and her popularity, and Maria from her books and shyness.

It was about then, after having written the first two chapters, that I began looking for a photograph for the cover of the book.

THE COVER PHOTO

I had no photographs of Maria Bozek-Nowak and Helena Goldstein. I only had two photographs I found in books of Maria Bozek-Nowak alone.

To you it may seem like it was a little early to begin looking for a cover photograph – the book wasn't even near completion. But I knew that the cover is very important. I struggled with the covers for all of my other books. It's a process.

I figured I might as well look for some inspiration. I googled photos with high resolution fitting for print, of "two girls hugging" in "black and white" around "1930".

For many minutes I kept going from one page of Google's photos results to the next. I longed to find a photograph that would show two girls in their teens, laughing or hugging or doing something together. I found a few that could work, of young women skating together, or eating ice-cream together, etc. But when I saw the photo which now adorns the cover I was swayed.

I loved it instantly.

After researching quite a bit, trying to find its backstory, I discovered that the girl on the left was Annette Kellermann, an Australian professional swimmer. I couldn't find out who was the girl on the right.

But the girls worked. They worked.

So I hope you're not upset to find out the girls in the cover are not Helena Goldstein and Maria Bozek. But—and that's a big but—that photo helped me tremendously in writing the book.

All of a sudden I knew that the girls would have to get to the beach. But there was no beach anywhere near Krakow. Everything then fell into place: summers, the rich family visits their summer house. The poor family has never been to the beach. The two girls spend their best moments, their greatest memories, on the beach. Boom. I had it.

You may call it coincidence. But for me, having been around for a few decades, I believe everything is preordained. There is a lesson or a message in everything.

I now had *visuals* for Helena and Maria. It was "clear" to me that the girl posing on the right, the dancer, was Helena. The girl on the left, somewhat more shy, was Maria.

And my "Maria" was a little fuller. My Helena was a little thinner. When I shared the photo with my parents, who were then in Thailand, backpacking in their sixties and as young as they ever were, I got some insights from them about the photo.

I asked them how old they thought the girls were. My father said, "In their twenties." My mother said, "No way, they're in their teens, look at their breasts."

I then looked, she was right. And Maria was more "developed" than Helena. Boom. I had another scene in my mind. Maria would receive her period before Helena.

Now, armed with a photo that felt to me like an intricate part of the book, I continued writing.

ISOLATING THE TWO

I was still looking for a way to "isolate" the two of them from the rest of the class. Should I create a trip of some sorts? An outdoors activity?

Then it came to me: they would be expelled from the class. Expelled?! Maria could never get "expelled"! No, Helena would somehow get her into trouble.

But how come?

Then I knew: the sea.

The same thing which will eventually become their most bonding experience, in those four days of the sea, will be the very thing that brings them together in the first place.

Boom.

"One lesson, in Literature class, Mrs.

Schlesinger asked who would like to read the poem. Helena—happy about the class finally becoming interesting—volunteered.

Mrs. Schlesinger signaled for her to stand in front of the class, and Helena jumped off her seat, grabbed the book and began reading excitedly…"

Now I had to find a poem that spoke of the sea. And I wanted it to be an authentic Polish poem.

After Googling for some time (My wife Hallel says that Google and I are best friends – can you see why?), I eventually found out about three poets called "The Three National Bards". They were a trio of great Romantic poets who influenced national consciousness in Poland in the 19th century. I searched for poems written by each of them which had to do with the sea. The best one I found was the long poem "Invocation to Poetry" by Zygmunt Krasiński (1812–1859), one of the "Three Bards".

I took the relevant lines from the poem, in their English translation by Martha Walker Cook, and planted them in Helena's mouth, as theatrically as she could be, given her young age:

""Stars circle round thy head," she raised her hand above, and then lowered it, "and at thy feet surges the sea, upon whose hurrying waves," she raised her hand again drawing a large arch, "a rainbow glides before thee, cleaving the clouds!"

Maria sat up, mesmerized. All the students

were.

"Whate'er thou look'st upon is thine!" Helena continued, "Coasts, ships, men, mountains, cities, all belong to thee!" She shouted, "Master of Heaven as earth, it seems as naught," her voice suddenly turned into a whisper, "could equal thee in glory...!"

She grinned, bowed, and went back to her seat. Everyone cheered."

The way Helena speaks of the *sea* forces Maria's shyness away, and brings her to ask Helena something for the first time:

Later when the bell rang, Maria said to Helena. "That was beautiful."

Helena, surprised by the mute friend opening her mouth, was somewhat startled. "Uh? Oh, thank you..."

"Have you..." Maria continued, as Helena's eyes grew bigger, noticing this was now the second sentence initiated by the mute, "Have you..." Maria searched for words, "You demonstrated so beautifully, Helena, the sea and the waves... Have you ever been to the sea?"

Helena bellowed, "Why of course! Every summer!" She looked at Maria, "Don't tell me you haven't...?"

Maria looked down. Helena was puzzled. What else was there to do in the summer but go to a summer house by the sea?

The sea was bringing them together. And Maria was slowly bringing Helena out of her shell. Helena grew up in a very wealthy household. I decided this early on. Why? Because of the principle of opposites.

USING CONTRAST

As an artist, I often use the power of contrast in my paintings. To show that something is extremely bright, I place it on dark background. To show that something is very red, I place it next to its complementary color, green.

Complementary colors and contrast are among the key concepts I followed in my art. All of my paintings speak in great levels of contrast, which makes everything more vivacious and powerful. This is why I love Matisse and the post-Impressionists: they were using colors freely.

When I write, I try to do the same. In "Six Days with Gandhi" I juxtapose the old and wise Gandhi with a young and inexperienced Westerner. The tension between the two creates magic. It creates interest. That's where the art lies.

A book about Gandhi and another Indian guru would not have been as interesting.

Similarly, in *The Two Marias*, I knew I had to constantly create contrast. Helena would be outspoken; Maria would be shy. Helena – rich, Maria –

poor. Helena – artistic, Maria – scientific. These tensions highlight the unique colors of each character.

The tension is important. Both character would be developed through it:

> When they were in the yard, Helena whispered [to Gisele:] "Could you believe it, Gisele? I think Maria has never been to the sea!"

> Gisele shrugged.

> "But," Helena exclaimed, "not going to the sea? What else could she do each summer?"

> Gisele smiled, "Not everyone goes to a summer house, Helena!"

> "But you do!" Helena exclaimed.

> "Yes, but not everyone." She lowered her voice, "Maria's father works for the railroad, and her mother works in some factory I hear, you see? They don't have much money…"

> Helena's eyes grew bigger, "But she's so… dignified… and smart…!"

In Helena's eyes, the eyes of a rich child, the poor cannot be dignified and smart; her contact with Maria begins to open her eyes to how people are always people, and categorizing them won't do. Later on, Maria learns the same lesson when she resists, in her own way, the xenophobia permeating through her society.

> "Well," Gisele shook her head, "that's because she's a bookworm. But," she whispered, "she's very poor. Haven't you seen how her lunch is

always only bread and a boiled egg, nothing else?"

Helena was shocked, baffled."

Now I had something to work with. Baffled Helena would ask Maria about never being to the sea. This would, in turn, lead them both to being expelled from class.

Maria glanced at [Helena's] notebook and quickly looked back at Mr. Kissinger. She gently pushed Helena's notebook away.

Helena was stunned. Did that girl just push her notebook away? Did she just refuse to talk to her? That couldn't be!

This is an important clue about Maria. While she may *seem* like she's always been quiet, week and feeble, in fact, if we look closer, the character had some strength from the very beginning. Rejecting the invitation to chat during the lesson, given by the most popular girl in class, was quite brave.

Helena] took her pen and drew a big question mark in the center of her notebook, then slid it again toward Maria.

Maria gulped. She bit her lip. She didn't want to miss a word from Mr. Kissinger's lecture. But, she had to admit, she already knew everything he was saying. He was just repeating what was in the textbook. She had read it. She knew it.

"No." she wrote on her own notebook. She

slowly moved it for Helena to see. Her heart beat fast. She felt as if she was taking part in some crime.

This was to be only the beginning of the crime. Later on Helena will further "push" Maria to become a fellow criminal as they will not return to class right away and instead spend some time together on the roof.

"SERIOUSLY?" Helena wrote in capital letters. "What do you do in the SUMMER???"

Maria bit her lip. She kept looking at Mr. Kissinger, her heart beating fast, and wrote, in her small handwriting, "babysitting". She wanted to write, "I take care of my younger brother and sister" but it would have taken too much writing.

Isn't Maria pretty smart? Calculating that it would have taken her too much writing? Do we see the seed of the woman who would, a decade later, spy and see when people got out of the enclosure, and how she could sneak one of them away?

Helena was puzzled and whispered, "Really...?"

"Helena and Maria!" Mr. Kissinger exclaimed, "To the principal's office! Right now!"

A murmur passed through the class. Maria's eyes widened. Had he just called out her name?

Mr. Kissinger wrote them a small note and handed it to Helena with gusto, "Go!"

Helena stood up, her chin held high, and walked out the class.

That's so Helena!

Maria, wide-eyed, looked at Mr. Kissinger in utter horror.

I loved writing this line. "Utter horror!" I felt the same as a student whenever such a thing would happen. In a way I'm more like Maria than like Helena.

He raised his eyebrows, "You heard me!"

Maria's legs felt heavy, her knees buckling. She got up, making her way out of the class. This had never happened to her. Never!

Now, waiting for the school's secretary, I finally had the two of them alone. That was my plot! Now, Maria weeps, thinking about her mother. We don't yet know her mother, but it's interesting that she isn't thinking of her father. This is a seed preceding Mrs. Bozek's character, which we'll get to know soon.

Maria thought of her mother. What would she think… How would she respond…?

She began weeping.

Suddenly our cool and remote Helena is forced to show some affection to the girl she until now has called "The mute":

Helena put her arm around Maria's shoulder, "Hey! Don't cry, it will be fine..."

Maria's shoulder quivered as she buried her face in her hands.

"Wait..." Helena said slowly, "is this your first time...?"

Maria nodded her head vigorously.

"Oh..." Helena said, "don't worry about it, they just write something in the book, and it's all fine, we'll be back in the class in a moment."

Maria shook her head, "I shouldn't... I shouldn't have..."

What she means to say is "I shouldn't have cooperated with you!"

Now I had to advance their relationship. This moment was crucial. I had already "invented" that they needed to "wait". In my own school there was no "waiting" – they would write down something in your record and you'd be hushed back into class. But I had worked hard to create this moment between them – the moment of isolation from the rest of the class – and I was about to use it to its maximum potential.

Helena thought of something to say to distract the poor girl from crying. "Do you," she finally said, "really babysit?"

Maria nodded and wiped her tears, "My two younger siblings..."

"No!" Helena's eyes shined, "You have two younger siblings? I always wanted to have younger siblings! Girls? Boys?"

Maria sniffled, "A boy, Eddie, and a girl, Sashinka—I mean—Sasha..."

From the excerpt I shared with you in the Afterword, from the book "They Were Just People", I knew that Maria indeed had two little siblings: Edmund and Alexandra.

When I wrote the first draft of the book, these were indeed their names. But I felt that I had to "soften" them a little. I looked for a nickname for Edmund and found Eddie. I already knew (from my Russian heritage) that the name Alexandra was often abbreviated into "Sasha". I then had the two names.

"Wow!" Helena jumped off her seat, "A boy and a girl! Wow! Which one do you like best?"

Maria tilted her head, "I don't know…"

"Sure you do!"

Maria smiled through her teary eyes.

Helena made her smile!

"I guess… Eddie can be really annoying at times. But I can speak to him… Sasha is too young, but she's as sweet as a candy!"

Helena sat down and sighed, "I wish I could have little siblings."

Maria looked at her, "You don't have any…?"

"Oh I do have two brothers, but they're older."

Speaking of contrast, this one I didn't have to create, it was given to me by the historical facts: Maria was the eldest and Helena was the youngest. This helped me to further develop the characters: Maria being overly mature and responsible, having to take care of her two younger siblings; Helena being somewhat childish and carefree, being the spoiled younger sister. Of course these are just superficial characteristics, but they are beginning points nevertheless. From there, I could create situations that would challenge these roles.

This means that I would constantly look for places in which Helena would have to step out of being the spoiled and irresponsible child and show maturity (such as in the scene where Maria has her first period). Similarly, Maria would be faced with situations in which she is forced to be less responsible and mature (such as in skipping class and deciding to join Helena on the roof).

These moments of the two characters stepping out of their comfort zone will enable us, the readers, to further understand them, and grow to like them more.

> "My eldest brother, Solomon, he has a girlfriend now, her name's Hannah!"
>
> Maria nodded.
>
> "And my other brother, Reuben, he'd do anything for me. They both spoil me to bits."
>
> "Really?" Maria whispered, "You must feel so lucky…"
>
> "Lucky? Hell no! I wish I had little ones, I would play with them, and dance with them, and sing with them…"
>
> The Principal's secretary called out their

names. She looked at them disapprovingly, "The principal is busy…"

Now comes one of my favorite of speeches. I like it both because Helena speaks without stopping, trying to exhaust the Principal's secretary and also because it shows us, for the first time, that Helena knows how to lie.

This may seem negative, but in a way, Helena will eventually be saved through her ability to lie for two years about her identity.

> Taking a big breath, Helena said excitedly: "Mrs. Burtman, I just asked Maria about the chromosome because there was something I didn't understand, you see, and I didn't want to stop Mr. Kissinger's flow, because when he begins talking he never stops, you see, and so I asked Maria and she just tried to explain to me, and when he called our names I tried to explain to him that Maria was just explaining to me about the chromosome but he would have none of it, and it's too bad, you see, because had he asked, he'd see that not everyone understands what he says, in fact…"

I don't know why, but I really like this short speech. I can just imagine Maria's response, standing there next to her, wide-eyed, listening to all these lies and fabrications.

> "Alright, alright," Mrs. Burtman sighed, and signed the slip of paper. She looked at Helena, and then at Maria, "Don't do this again! Now hurry back to class!"

In the beginning, this secretary didn't have a name at all. But I wanted to show that Helena *knew* people. Helena was a *master* of manipulating people. She would soon teach Maria (and us) a few lessons on how to talk to Maria's mother, etc.

Helena knew well that addressing a person by their *name* would make them more likely to listen. It shows both respect (by using "Mrs.") and familiarity (by using the actual name, "Burtman").

I chose the name Burtman as an homage to my own mother, who was for three decades a kindergarten teacher. Her maiden name is Burtman, and when I showed her the first draft of the book she told me, "My God! You included my name in your book! What an honor! Thank you, thank you, thank you!".

I do have a terrific mom.

> Helena grinned, "Thank you so much Mrs. Burtman, you won't regret it!"
>
> Helena grabbed Maria's hand and they ran down the hall. Then, out of sight of the principal's office, Helena began climbing the stairs to the third floor.
>
> "But..." Maria asked, bewildered, "aren't we going back to...—"
>
> Helena smiled, "No! There are only a few more minutes before the class ends, we'll go to my favorite spot..."
>
> "But," Maria gasped, looking nervously around, "I... What will Mr. Kissinger...—"

Here Helena shows us her wit again. Notice how she convinces Maria:

> "Mr. Kissinger wouldn't like us coming back now and interrupting his speech, right?"
>
> Maria stammered, "Bu... But..."
>
> "And you know," Helena continued, "how the other kids would whisper and get all excited when we come back, and Mr. Kissinger, well, this will upset him!"

Maria doesn't agree, and yet these explanations must sound a little plausible. She mumbles:

> "I... I..."
>
> "Come already!"

Notice how in the first half of the book Helena always leads. Then, in the second half of the book, it will be Maria.

> Once they reached the top floor, Helena opened a large window, stretched her leg over the ledge, and climbed on to the roof. She reached for Maria's hand.
>
> Maria pulled her hand back, "I'm not... I can't...!"
>
> "Of course you can. Give me your hand!"
>
> Maria gulped and looked at the empty hallway around her.
>
> Helena pressed, "Give me your hand!"
>
> Maria gave her hand to Helena, placed her leg

> on the ledge, and then stretched her other leg
> out. The view was frightening.

This scene was one of the earliest I envisioned. I knew that this would become their "place". Later, after the summer vacation, they both come here to exchange their gifts. A decade later, when Maria misses Helena terribly, she comes to the place in which they first bonded, and longs for her friend, alone, on that very rooftop.

> She could see the whole schoolyard below, as
> well as the street and the top of the trees. She
> gasped. The roof tile under her foot made a
> sound. She looked at Helena, "Are you sure
> it's...—"

> "Positive," Helena smiled. She squatted on the
> roof tiles and moved away from the window.
> "Here," she whispered, "if we squeeze here, no
> one can see us from the corridor!"

Helena is such a little criminal! Innocent, yes, but she definitely has some wit and *chutzpah!*

> Maria squeezed into the small place. "How did
> you find this...—"

> "In my old school," Helena said, "I knew all
> the spots. My favorite one was in the theatre's
> dressing room... Oh, it was truly magical!""

"Truly magical" is a combination of words she'll use again.

> "Maria smiled. The view was both frightening
> and exciting. A wrong move could lead them

318

rolling down. But the view was breathtaking. She had never been in such heights in her life, like this, in the open air.

"…And when this school year started," Helena continued, "the first thing I did was to look for quiet spots…"

Maria was surprised, "But I thought you always like to be around other people…"

Suddenly this gives us a glimpse into the real Helena: more complicated, more profound, less one-dimensional.

Helena shrugged, "I'd much rather be around good books. Or poems. Or plays!"

Maria's eyes widened, "I thought you only… that you only like to be with everyone around you…"

Helena shrugged her shoulders again, "Yes and no."

Maria nodded. She liked that answer. Yes and no.

They sat there quietly.

Maria wanted to ask about Helena's brothers. And which books she liked reading. And what was her favorite subject in school…. She liked it when Helena was talking. But now she was quiet.

I once read that you're truly comfortable with someone when both of you can sit quietly together, not saying anything. Helena forced on the two of them an intimate moment: silence, together.

> They looked at the view of the school and the buildings in the horizon. Each of them hugged her knees to her chest. Then Helena sighed. Maria did the same. She wanted to be as carefree as Helena.
>
> A few minutes later Helena said, "I think we should go back."
>
> Maria nodded. They made their way slowly to the window, climbed inside and closed it behind them. They hurried downstairs, and entered their class just as the bell rang.

Now, in class, we notice, for the first time, a different Maria. It's subtle, but it's there, notice the "embarrassed yet exhilarated by the attention":

> "Helena, how was it?" one of the children asked. "What did the principal say?" asked another. "Did he suspend you?"
>
> Soon a small circle formed around Helena and Maria. Helena was relating the events as Maria looked down at the floor, embarrassed yet exhilarated by the attention."

But our tendency in life is to always go to our comfort zone:

> But then she noticed the homework written on the blackboard and made her way back to the desk to write the homework down.
>
> Helena looked at her and exclaimed "Oh, stop it! Let's go out!"

Maria's eyes widened. "But, the homework...!"

Helena shook her head. She glanced over to Gisele and Isabella who were waiting near the door. She whispered into Maria's ear...

This is a sign of intimacy, whispering into each other's ears. This could have not been achieved had they not spent the few minutes on the roof together.

"It is not as if you didn't read the whole book already!"

Maria shrugged her shoulders. Helena grabbed her hand. "Come!"

Again, Helena leads the situation. But Maria is happy to be led.

In the chapter that follows we see Maria displaying kindness toward Helena:

Soon after their incident with Mr. Kissinger, there was a day when Helena was ill and did not come to school. Maria felt as if the class was dead without Helena's presence. She sent a note with Gisele, wishing Maria a quick recovery.

This would be their first note, one of many. We then learn that they slowly become closer.

During the breaks [Maria] always joined Helena and the girls. Doing her best to imitate the other girls by nodding and laughing, she hid the fact she didn't enjoy all the conversations. The ones about the boys embarrassed her. But she tried.

I now needed another opportunity for them to strengthen their relationship.

> One morning, when they were returning to class after break, Helena pulled Maria closer, "I have a ballet performance!"

In this incident Helena teaches us yet another lesson in cunning and convincing:

> "Tell your mother that you can either go for the performance *and* stay for the dinner afterwards, or that you could just come for the performance and skip the dinner."

> "I..." Maria shifted uncomfortably, "she wouldn't let me, Helena!"

> "Maria, Maria, Maria..." Helena smiled. "Trust me. Tell her the same way I've told you. Give her these two options, and she'll pick the one that is least bad for her. If you ask her if you can go or not, of course she'll say no!" Helena whispered as Mrs. Schlesinger walked into the class, "But if you ask her if you could stay for the dinner or not, she'll have to allow you to at least go to the performance!"

Oddly enough, it works:

> The following day, Maria exclaimed to Helena, "You're a magician!"

The fact that Maria then comes, in the cold weather, with her siblings, touches Helena tremendously. First, we learn that from Mrs.

Goldstein, whom we meet for the first time:

> "You must be Maria, darling. I'm Helena's mother."

> "Oh, pleased to meet you, Mrs. Goldstein!"

> "Oh, darling, you are so kind. I'm so glad you could come! Helena said she was excited about you coming!"

And after the performance, as Maria leaves, an emotional encounter explains to us that Helena was willing to skip the other girlfriends who came to see her to run to see Maria:

> "Maria!"

> Running out of the theatre came Helena, still wearing her tutu.

> "Helena!" Maria exclaimed. She stuttered, "You're… You're not dressed, you'll get sick!"

> "I just wanted," Helena said, panting, "to say hello to you all. You must be Eddie, right?"

> Eddie nodded.

> "And you," Helena said to Sasha, "must be the one and only: Princess Alexandra!"

> Sasha smiled, shyly burying her face in Maria's neck.

> Maria saw Helena shivering, "Go now, Helena!"

> "Okay," Helena said, "but I wanted to thank you so much for coming. It means the world

to me!"

Maria smiled. "Go!"

This experience at the ballet further cements their relationship. It gives us the *why* for the following emotional scene:

> Sometime before the end of the school year Maria got sick. She did not come to school, which was unlike her.

Had Maria not come to the Ballet performance, it is unlikely that Helena would have gone out of her way to go and *visit* Maria at her house. Yet the fact Maria was willing to drag her sister and brother with her to that Ballet performance, and plead to her mother beforehand to let her go, meant a lot to Helena. Which is why she, when Maria was sick,

> asked everyone but no one knew why Maria was not at school. Helena then decided that if Maria didn't come to school the following day either, she'd visit her.
>
> The following day Maria did not come. Helena, who was always rather worry-free, began to fret about it. She asked the other girls where Maria lived. No one knew the address exactly, only that she lived near the rail station heading east.
>
> Helena went to the school's secretary. "Mrs. Burtman, I have to find out Maria Bozek's address!"

We must not forget that Maria and Helena are

young, around 12 years old. Helena dares to skip school and take the tram to an area of town that she does not know, which takes some courage.

It's this courage that will eventually touch Maria's heart and move her to risk her life in order to fetch her friend from the enclosure.

This scene is very important to me. It was nerve-racking to write it. Both characters are uncomfortable: Helena being in a neighborhood she does not know, in a house she was not invited to, and meeting a mother who is not warm. Maria, of course, has to deal with her first menstruation, a rather difficult experience for her:

> She knocked on the door.
>
> There was no answer.
>
> She knocked again.
>
> Nothing.
>
> She felt aggravated. She knocked forcefully on the door, shouting, "Maria? Maria, it's me, Helena!"
>
> Maria's voice came from the other side of the door, puzzled, "*Helena…?*"
>
> "Yes! Open up!"
>
> The door was opened instantly. Maria gasped, "What on earth are you—"
>
> Helena embraced her, "I thought something had happened to you! You never missed a day, and now you missed two!"

We are not certain *why* is Maria home:

> Maria lay down on one of the three long sofas, her hand holding her belly.

Helena is now proving herself to be a girl who has never been in a poor home. She insists on going to Maria's room:

> "But why are you lying here, let's go to your room…"

> Maria tried smiling, "This… is where we sleep. That's Eddie's bed," she pointed at where Helena was sitting, "and this is my bed. And that's Sashinka's."

> "Oh," Helena said, and felt terribly stupid, "I… *knew* that…"

> She felt awkward, "I guess I meant…" she shook her head, "How are you feeling?"

This same sort of embarrassment would occur again, but in a much stronger way, in the Christmas scene later on. We often think that it's pitiful to be poor, and you're lucky if you're rich. But Helena suffers a little from having grown up in a rich household, and not necessarily knowing how to address people of lesser means in such situations as the one above.

> "I'm fine, I'm… fine…"

The situation is a little awkward, and I tried to infuse some humor.

> Helena moved and sat on Maria's bed. "Here, let me see, do you have a fever?"

Maria shook her head.

"No," Helena concluded, "you don't have a fever. Does your throat hurt? Here, open your mouth…"

Maria laughed, "I'm not going to open… *I'm fine!*"

Helena smiled. "Is it your belly?"

Maria shrugged, "I guess."

"I knew it! You ate something bad…"

"No, it's not that…"

"Then what is it?"

Maria shrugged again.

By now most readers kind of know what's going on, no?

Helena sighed. The sound of the kettle boiling broke the silence. "Well, we'll make you some tea and you'll feel just like new!"

She removed the whistling kettle from the stove and made two cups of tea. She looked around the small kitchen, crammed with the sink, an oven and a stove, and a small table with five chairs around it. She shouted, "It is certainly cozy here! What a lovely kitchen!"

Poor Helena. She is trying her best…

Maria grimaced.

Helena brought the two cups of tea, placing them on the small living room table. She noticed a blanket on the floor, covering a towel. The room looked messy. She got up and began folding some of the clothes thrown around and opened the curtains.

Maria sighed.

When Helena came to the blanket thrown on the floor, Maria grabbed to it, "No, please don't…"

Now, here I skipped what Helena "saw". I thought it would be more appropriate to jump into the conclusion she came to. I had to somehow make her *understand* what was going on without the shy Maria *telling* her.

Poor Maria didn't even tell her mother, and was forced to deal with the situation the best way she knew how to, with a towel. Upon the knocking on the door she threw the towel on the floor and put the blanket over it. But now her "secret" was revealed.

Helena saw the towel underneath it, "Oh my God!" she exclaimed, "Dearest Maria!"

Maria covered her face with her hands.

"Dearest Maria!" Helena exclaimed, "You're a woman now! Congratulations!" she jumped around the room, "I can't believe it, I'm so happy for you!"

The contrast here is rather funny: Maria, who is dying from shame of what's happening to her body, and Helena, who is "longing" for the time she gets her first period:

Maria's face reddened, "Shhh…" she whispered, "you want to shout it to the whole street?!"

"Why not! What a blessing! You are now a w-o-m-a-n!" Helena collapsed dramatically onto the bed, "My mother would be so *happy* for you! What a celebration!"

Maria stared at her. Was Helena *out of her mind?* What was there to *celebrate?*

"Tell me tell me," Helena begged, "how does it *feel…?*"

Maria sighed, "It… hurts… my belly…"

"Of course!" Helena exclaimed, "That's because one day you could have a *baby*, and now your cycle is… um… disappointed for not having a baby, so it goes away!" Helena sat up and sipped her tea, as joyful as ever.

Maria looked at her, puzzled.

Now we need to find out more of how "severe" the situation is for Maria.

Helena looked at her face, "Your mother told you about the whole…"

Maria shook her head.

Helena's eyes grew larger, "Didn't your mother…"

Maria shrugged.

"What?!" Helena exclaimed, spilling some of the tea, "Are you telling me your mother didn't tell you what was *going on?* Wait," she hesitated, "Maria, does she... know...?"

Maria shrugged, "She thinks I have just some tummy ache..."

"This is..." Helena jumped up, "ex... exasperating!"

While it is exasperating for Helena, many women can relate to Maria's situation: a tough mother, Maria being her first daughter, and she simply does not know *how* to talk about these things.

While we may be judgmental about Mrs. Bozek, we must put ourselves in her shoes, and we'll find out that the education that she received was in fact worse.

Helena then gives Maria a "speech. As this scene is very delicate and rather sensitive, a little bit of humor is good for us readers:

> She stood up, mimicking her own mother, "I guess I must tell you what every woman should know."

> Maria buried her face in her hands, "No, please don't!"

> "Now-now," Helena said, trying to remember her mother's words, "there's nothing to be *ashamed* of. This means that your body has *ripened* and is ready for the *art of reproduction*...! Which only means that for *now*, for many years, until you are an old woman, you'll be... um... *visited* by this... a... splendid visitor! Sometimes it will hurt..." she nodded, reciting

her mother's explanation, "but you will get used to it! It is a blessing from God, as it means that you have finally come of age!"

Maria blushed and shook her head disapprovingly, her eyes closed.

"Now," Helena said, "we'll have to tell your mother, and make sure she gets you some menstrual apron, or one of those pads, you know…"

"I'm…" Maria whispered, "I'm not going to wear *that!*"

"Sure you will! What are you going to do, sit around the house once every month for the rest of your *life?*"

Maria shrugged and covered her face in her hands again, "I don't know!"

Here comes the real liberation for poor Maria. Perhaps Helena arrived there just to share this little bit of information:

"Well, Gisele already got hers, and so did Isabella!"

Maria peered between her fingers, "Impossible!"

Helena smiled and nodded.

Maria's eyes widened in surprise, "Gisele?! Isabella?!"

We must remember that Maria has no friends, really. It may sound strange, but put yourself in her shoes: she's the first born to a mother who wasn't the best teacher when it came to social skills, as we'll soon learn. Also, each day Maria *has* to come back home and be with her young siblings, so she never really *has* time for friends.

So for Maria, hearing that she is not "alone" and that it is a perfectly healthy thing, is nothing less than liberating.

> "Helena nodded, "I've been praying to get mine soon, but the doctor has said it will take more time…"
>
> "You… spoke about it with your doctor?"
>
> "Yes, she's a *wonderful* doctor. My mother took me to her. And she said that it will take some time. Look," Helena whispered, "you already have some real breasts budding, and I don't even…—"
>
> Maria now covered her face in her pillow.

I just love Helena's response:

> Helena reached over and pulled it away, "Now-now we must be able to talk about this like ladies!"
>
> Maria reddened, "I can't… believe… we're *talking* about *this!*"
>
> "Well believe it! Sooner or later we'll *have* to! You've seen the funny little hairs on under Roman's nose, and the voice change of Alexander… We have our share too!"

A little side note: this is the first time we meet

Roman and Alexander. Both will be instrumental. While you may remember why Roman is instrumental, Alexander is infamously instrumental as well: he'll demonstrate to us later on how warped and sick the society has become during the war. Later in the book he'd meet Maria and ask her, "Are you still a friend of Helena? Well, it's not very *wise*, you know…"

So both characters will be important for the progress of the plot.

Now we come to the moment that helps us better understand Maria and really *feel* for her:

> At that moment the door opened. A rough woman's voice was heard, "Why isn't the door locked! Maria, I told you a thousand times…"
>
> "Mama," Maria exclaimed, "I have a guest!"
>
> A tough-looking woman appeared through the small corridor and looked at Helena. "Who are you?!"

Helena may be the complete opposite of Mrs. Bozek:

> Helena reached her hand cordially, "Helena Goldstein, Madam!" she bowed, "And you must be Mrs. Bozek. I'm most honored to meet you!"
>
> The woman looked at her suspiciously, "You're the dancer."

It's sounds almost like a curse, doesn't it? "You're that 'dancer' that convinced my eldest daughter to run around town going to some 'ballet' in the evening?!"

> Helena looked at Maria and grinned, "Aspiring dancer, Madam. *And* actress, and singer too!"
>
> Mrs. Bozek muttered something under her breath.

Now, for me Mrs. Bozek is one of the most important characters in the book. In fact, I may very well declare that she's the third most important character. She will transform before our eyes. We dislike her in the beginning, but by the end of the book we want to hug her.

That, to me, is the power of good literature, which I aspire to write: to transform the reader's heart, to make the reader less judgmental and more loving to *all* people. If we knew what Mrs. Bozek has been through in her life, or how good she really is in her heart, we wouldn't hurry to judge her, like we most likely did in this part.

> She looked at Maria, "How is your tummy? Could you collect Sasha from the kindergarten?"
>
> Maria tried to say something, but her voice broke.
>
> Helena jumped, sensing the complicated situation, "I…"
>
> Maria and her mother both stared at Helena. She took the plunge and said, "Congratulations, Mrs. Bozek!"

Wow. If that's not courage, what is? Helena, being in this house for barely an hour, now tries to really help—no, *save*—her friend:

> She reached and shook the mother's hands firmly, "I believe that your daughter has received it."

> "Received what?"

> Maria mumbled, "*Oh God…*"

> "Well," Helena said, "Mrs. Bozek," she exclaimed, "she has received it. It-it. *It!*"

> Mrs. Bozek's eyes suddenly widened. "Oh!"

> Helena smiled at her, her big smile, anticipating.

Let's not judge poor Mrs. Bozek, who is so terrified of her daughter growing and becoming a woman. She would rather have only boys than have to deal with situations such as this. Mind you, no one had ever taught *her* those things. She had to learn by herself how to be a woman in the world.

> "Oh," Mrs. Bozek said again and frowned, "well… That's quite *early…*"

> "No it isn't!" Helena said and sat down,

I just love how brazen (and somewhat rude) Helena could be sometimes.

> "A few girls in our class have already received it… My mother keeps waiting for me to receive it, Mrs. Bozek…—"

> "Does she?" Mrs. Bozek said, looking at her daughter, and sighed.

What will she do now? How will Mrs. Bozek deal with the uncomfortable situation? In the future we'll learn that she either cooks or cleans. Now she chooses to clean:

> She eyed around the room and began folding the few clothes.

But in her heart, she longs to *know* how to deal with the situation. A sentence we might have overlooked in the first reading is quite important:

> "Well," she groaned, "what else would she say, that mother of yours?"

(I know, I know you haven't missed it, but some did!)

> "Well," Helena said, looking puzzled at Mrs. Bozek and Maria, who was hiding her face in her hands, "she'd say... *'Congratulations'* and she'd get me the needed... *equipment*... to... *deal* with... the *situation*..."

> Mrs. Bozek groaned, "I see," and quickly disappeared into the kitchen.

This is not the first time that rough Mrs. Bozek will make the genteel Helena feel terribly uncomfortable. But, over time this will equip Helena for her life in knowing how to deal with certain people, and will force her to develop a thicker skin. Which may be unfortunate. But that's what the characters have led me to.

> Helena leaned toward Maria and whispered, "*Should I go...?*"

Maria's eyes widened, "No! Please don't! I'm so glad you are here!"

They heard Mrs. Bozek's voice from the kitchen, "Well," she shouted and paused, "I had better go and collect Sasha before I am too late." She passed by the living room, "Do lock the door, Maria, I beg you!"

"I will, Mama," Maria murmured.

The door closed.

Helena motioned to Maria to keep lying down. She hurried to the door and locked it. She sighed to herself. Wow, what a mother. She didn't say a thing!

When she entered the living room again she put on a big smile,

This does show us how tactful Helena really is. She didn't tell poor Maria, "Your mother is so… not nice!"

"Well, we *must* celebrate, Maria!"

Maria sighed. "Right now I can't imagine doing anything…""

In fact, Helena, who not many pages ago called Maria "the mute" and provoked her to raise her hand in class, now shows us her kind side:

Helena wanted to say something to cheer her friend up. "Well, you were certainly missed yesterday in school, as well as today."

Maria snorted, "No one probably noticed I…—"

"Of course everyone noticed!"

"You are very kind to me, Helena."

"Well," Helena searched for words, "Mr. Kissinger looked for your approving eyes… And he stared at me with constant disappointment!"

Maria laughed, "I don't give him 'approving eyes'…"

"Of course you do," Helena laughed, "you are the only one actually *listening* to him. He speaks to you and to you only!"

"No he doesn't! Roman listens as well!"

"Well, maybe Roman too, but that's it!"

Mr. Kissinger is the biology teacher. In the future, Roman will take Maria into the Biology building in University, where he'll have the key to one of the labs. These little things may not seem important to you, but to me, as the author, those little, tiny things, make the book seem *real* and *believable*.

Now they grow silent.

Silence ensued. This was a little odd. Sure, they were friends. But they weren't *good* friends. Helena tried to think, what would she speak about with Gisele?"

You see, this silence is different than the one on the rooftop, which was one Helena chose. Now it is forced upon them by the awkward situation.

She knew the answer. Gisele was mostly into

talking about boys. But Maria always seemed so... shy, about this kind of things.

Finally, Maria spoke. "What... what did you study, with Mrs. Schlesinger?"

"Right!" Helena jumped up, "We learned 'Captain, O Captain.' Do you want me to recite it to you?"

I know that you couldn't care less, but I care: the poem here speaks of a captain, and a boat. Again, the theme of the *sea* bonds the two girls together.

Now, I think it's unlikely that the poem "O Captain! My Captain!" would have been taught in 1930's Poland; though it was written sixty years before, it is an *American* poem, by Walt Whitman, about the death of American president Abraham Lincoln.

In the 1930's, the era of nationalism, it is unlikely that an American poet would have been taught in Poland. And yet, I took the liberty, as the author, to include it. Why?

Well, apart from the fact it speaks of the sea, this poem speaks of a great friendship that was ended. The captain dying is a traumatic experience for the poet.

Also, many poems are not meant to be dramatized. I mean, this poem has a very *dramatic* feel to it, and Helena could use this drama. I wanted her to demonstrate to us two key characteristics that she would need later on: memorization and dramatic abilities. In a second we'll discuss *why* this was important to me:

Maria smiled and nodded.

"O Captain!" Helena exclaimed, "My Captain! Our fearful trip is done, the ship has weather'd every rack, the prize we sought is won… The port is near," she put her hand to her ear, "…the bells I hear, the people all exulting, while follow eyes the steady keel, the vessel grim and daring…"

She grabbed to her chest, "But O heart! Heart! Heart!"

Maria laughed, "Three 'hearts'?!"

Helena nodded excitedly, "But O heart! Heart! Heart! O the bleeding drops of red, where on the deck my Captain lies," she fell down on the sofa, "Fallen… cold… and dead."

Maria clapped, "Terrific!"

Helena smiled, "Then there's more, something about 'Rise up' and 'hear the bells', but I don't remember it…"

"But you memorized the whole first stanza!"

"Yeah," Helena shrugged, "I also memorized the end, 'From fearful trip the victor ship comes in with object won; Exult O shores, and ring O bells! But I," Helena got up again, "with mournful tread… Walk the deck my Captain lies… fallen… cold… and dead…"

"Bravo!" Maria laughed.

Helena demonstrates to us that she can both *memorize* and *act*.

In one of the most dramatic scenes in the book, she is asked to do both.

Having then just escaped the enclosure, Helena is in a bad emotional and mental state. Yet, when she is confronted by the soldier at the train station, who asks her, Roman and Maria for their IDs, she shows us that even though she is in a bad emotional state, she still remembers her best friend's birthday:

> "Date of birth!" the soldier barked at Helena.
>
> She smiled, "January 22nd, 1920.""

And she also shows us her uncanny acting abilities, that may well have saved her life:

> "The soldier barked, pointing at Helena's arm, "Why is your dress torn here?!"
>
> "Where?" Helena asked, "Oh, this? It's just," she laughed, "that I haven't had the time yet to stitch…—"
>
> The soldier's grinded his teeth and reached for the whistle around his neck. Roman thought of running away. Maria looked, wide-eyed, at Helena.
>
> But Helena burst into laud laughter,

(Which does require great acting abilities)

> and then said in a rather flirtatious tone, "I hope I'm not too provocatively dressed for you, Mr. soldier, Sir…?"

This slows down the soldier a little bit, but still,

> The soldier didn't fall into Helena's trap.

> "That's!" he exclaimed and pointed at her arm, "That's where the armband is worn on the...—"
>
> Helena gasped and crossed herself, "Jesus, Mary and Joseph! Never, ever!" she cried, "Don't compare me to *them*, Sir!""

Here she knows how to imitate her Christian friends. While she had most likely never crossed herself before, here she does it without a problem.

> "[The soldier] looked at her face, then at the torn dress, then at her face again.

At that moment the other officer calls the soldier, and Helena is saved. But her *acting* abilities as well as the fact she has memorized such details, that may seem trivial to you and me, but under pressure may not be as easily accessible in our minds, such as the birthday and the way a Catholics cross themselves.

The scene of Maria receiving her first period leads us to their first time together outside of school, when Helena offers to take Maria shopping with her mother.

> A few days later, during Mrs. Kissinger's class, Helena wrote to Maria in her notebook: "I want to take you out on Sunday."
>
> She gently rotated her notebook for Maria to see.
>
> Maria wrote back in her own notebook, "Can't." She pushed her notebook toward Helena but then quickly took it back and

wrote: "Sorry."

Helena drew her usual large question mark, drawing and thickening its curved line several times.

[…] Maria wrote in her small handwriting, "Will be with my family. Sorry…"

Helena wrote, "You need to…" and then drew balloons and fireworks. "My mom said she'll take us both shopping!"

Maria pursed her lip and sighed. It sounded so good.

Helena wrote, "Sunday! Surely you don't have to babysit on *SUNDAYS!*"

"No," Maria wrote, "but my mother won't like it…"

Helena demonstrates to us then again her understanding of people.

Helena had anticipated this. She appreciated Maria's honesty. "Tell her," she wrote, while nodding a little too enthusiastically at Mr. Kissinger's speech about Plasma and red blood cells, "that you have to HELP me with the MATH EXAM next Tuesday."

Maria read and gulped.

"Either that," Helena wrote, "or you could come and sleep over at my house on Monday. This way she will let you go."

Somehow, this works, and

343

That Sunday Helena's mother took them both shopping.

Now, notice what Mrs. Goldstein is buying for her daughter's friend. And think of how, years later, when Mrs. Goldstein has already been killed in the gas chambers, her daughter's friend's mother (that is, Mrs. Bozek), pays back for this act, unknowingly:

> Maria tried to resist Mrs. Goldstein's offer to buy her a dress. But Mrs. Goldstein said plainly, "Don't insult me, young lady! When someone offers to give you something nice you simply say, 'Thank you very much.' And that's it."
>
> Maria nodded, her heart pounding, "Thank you very much Mrs. Goldstein."
>
> "You are most welcome!" Mrs. Goldstein said cheerfully.
>
> The dress looked stunning and was incomparable to anything Maria had ever worn. It was expensive, too. Helena smiled at her. "It complements your eyes, Maria!"

Some thirteen years later everything will be upside down. Helena will be the poor one, not Maria. And Helena's mother will be "unavailable" just like Maria's mother was "unavailable" for her daughter all these years before. The dress Mrs. Bozek will buy to cheer her own daughter up, will serve as a gift for Helena herself.

These moments of completion, showing of some divine order, are what I live for as an artist. The notion that what we give to others will come back to us is proven through this symbolic act of dress swapping, which Mrs. Bozek didn't even intend to do.

But the book shows it as a divine event, even though many readers don't notice. We often don't notice the great miracles in life. But they are there, always.

In that scene there is also another hint of the future:

They then proceeded to a local pharmacy.

Later on, Maria will choose to become a pharmacist. As an author, I could have skipped this scene, easily leaving Maria and Helena outside the pharmacy. But I wanted the readers to have this tiny little line implanted in their subconciousness:

Maria loved seeing all the bottles and jars spread across the counter.

Again, to me those little things are very important. Maria then sees a man behind the counter, and is embarrassed about the whole situation. This whole scene may be one of a few seeds planted in her heart, that eventually led her to the pharmaceutical profession.

But when she heard Mrs. Goldstein asking the man there for a menstrual apron and twenty pads, she immediately pulled Helena out of the store. Helena exclaimed to her mother, "We'll wait for you outside, Mama!"

"Good, I'll be there in a moment."

Outside, Maria covered her face in her hands,

"Oh dear, this is so embarrassing!"

"No it isn't, Maria!"

Mrs. Goldstein exited the pharmacy smiling and handed Maria the bag.

Maria whispered, "Thank you, Mrs. Goldstein, very much."

Mrs. Goldstein smiled. Helena jumped, "Soon will be my turn, right mama?"

"Everything in its due time, darling."

I knew I had to eventually take the two to the beach; knew that they would have so much fun together. I also discerned that these very memories would one day help Helena emotionally through the war.

But I also thought it was implausible for Maria to leave her family for several days. Her mother wouldn't let her. Also, Helena's parents may find it odd.

I knew I had to wait one more year. I had to let the relationship ripen.

I knew that if I built up their shared experiences, they would slowly become best friends. And then it *would* be plausible for Maria to come and spend some days with Helena in her family's summer house.

Now I was working toward that goal. First, during the first summer, they would correspond. Then, they would have to visit each other for holidays. Then, and only once they have bonded, and the families have met one another, Maria could join Helena and see the sea for the first time.

So I had all this in my mind as I reached the end of the first school year together. Remember, at the beginning of this very school year, they did not known one another, nor had any particular interest in one another. At least not Helena in Maria.

But things have slowly changed. And now the summer, though they will be apart, will actually bring them closer together:

> As the school year came to a close, Helena made Maria promise to write to her at the Goldstein family's summer house. She also made Gisele and the others agree to do the same.

> But Helena was surprised a few days after they arrived at the summer house, when the family's servant handed her father his letters and then said, "And this, young Miss Goldstein, is for you."

Now, I'm not sure if you remember the joy of receiving a letter addressed to *you* for the first time. I don't remember that moment *specifically,* but I do remember the excitement I had each time I received letters in my childhood.

> Her eyes grew wide as she received the letter in her hands. She recognized Maria's handwriting. "Oh my!" she exclaimed, "I received a letter! I received a *letter!*" She ran to the balcony, "Solomon! Reuben! I received a letter!"

> "Who from?" Reuben shouted at her as she

ran back into the house.

"My friend Maria!"

Lying on her bed, she carefully opened the letter.

Notice the subtle short sentence following, explaining to us something important:

Whilst she had wished for Gisele and Isabella and Sofia to have written, it was Maria who had sent the first letter.

Gisele, Sofia, Isabella and the others were also invited to write. But none of them did. Maria was the first to write, and, if you ask me, also the only one. The others were too busy having fun. Maria, taking care of her young siblings, truly missed that girl she sat next to for the whole school year. She simply *had* to write to her.

Again, this is a seminal moment. It is similar to the time that Helena came to Maria's house when Maria received her period. Or like the time when Maria dragged her siblings to the Ballet performance. Each of these events was yet another brick, laying down the house of their friendship. Had Maria not written to Helena, Helena would have *not* written to Maria.

By writing to Helena, Maria began elevating their relationship *above* the ones that Helena had with Gisele and the others. How do I know that? Later on, in the first day of school, Helena would prefer spending the midday break in between classes on the roof with Maria, exchanging gifts. Also, she would bring nothing to Gisele and the others.

And so, the "elevation" of their friendship from just another one of Helena's friends, into Helena's best friend, happened in many ways due to the courage of Maria to write:

> "Dearest Helena,
>
> It's been three days since the beginning of the summer break, and I think of you often. Yesterday I sang to Sashinka and Eddie the song you taught me about the Queen of the Night… It was great. I couldn't quite sing it like you, but we had lots of fun in the living room, while I dressed up in black, trying to hit those soprano notes of yours…"

Maria is generally a shy girl. And yet, something from Helena's dramatic character rubs on her as well. She might have even missed Helena so much, that it led her to sing to her young siblings.

> "The city feels empty. Especially without you. I think of you and your brothers having fun at the sea, and, while I refrain from being jealous, I must admit that I wish I could be with you and see the sea as well…"

This is yet another clue of what will eventually take place, the time on the beach they will spend together.

> "Sashinka prepared some food with me today in the kitchen, and we had lots of fun. Eddie is with his new Karl May book,

You will notice that I rarely incorporate names of authors. In the actual book (not in the commentary) I did not write the names of the poets who wrote the two pieces Helena read out loud. I generally refrain from loading the manuscript with details that I find irrelevant.

But Karl May is important to me for some reason.

As part of the research that I've done for another child who grew up in this time in Central Europe, for my book *New Day Dawning*, I found out that Karl May was quite a sensation at the time.

My main character in *New Day Dawning* loved Karl May's books. Interestingly enough, and somewhat appallingly, when I conducted research for *Six Days with Gandhi* about Adolf Hitler, I was bewildered to read that Hitler, too, as a boy, loved Karl May's books.

This bit of information was interesting to me.

Late on in the book Eddie would have a chance to become rather pro-Nazi. At the table, there will be a scene that is very important to me:

> Eddie, who was usually quiet by the dinner table, said, "But there is *some* truth to it, isn't there? What about that corrupt minister? He was one of *them.*"
>
> Mr. Bozek suddenly slammed his fist on the table. They were all startled. "I will not," he muttered through his teeth, "let you... speak this way... in my household!"
>
> [...]
>
> Eddie sighed, "But they found..."
>
> "I'll have none of it!"

Through Eddie we will learn of the pervasive state of the society at the time. But due to his overall upbringing, he will eventually walk away from his anti-Jewish views, and dare to risk his life to help Helena reach the capital.

So this little bit information, for me, as the author, was important, knowing these were the same books that Hitler read early in his life, and later on even printed many copies of them and sent to his soldiers at the front.

Maria's letter reveals the hints for that:

> "[Eddie is] reading and pretending to be an American cowboy. He's so funny...

She then continues in a motherly tone toward Helena,

> Promise me you'll look into the math assignment early on, and not leave it for the end of the summer. I found that for me, bit by bit every day is the best. Don't put it off!

> Tell me everything about the sea, shore, and the sand... In fact, everything else too!

> I Hope I wrote well (surely not as artistically as you!).

> Fondly yours,

> Maria Bozek."

I love the following description of Helena's reaction, as it reminds me a little of myself as a child:

> Helena stood up, then sat down, then lay down

and smiled. She read the letter again, lavishing each word. This letter was for *her*. For her *only!*
"

Then Helena

[...] quickly pulled out her notebook from the desk's drawer and sat back on the bed. She turned to the middle pages, where she could pull out some papers without damaging the notebook. She wrote:

"Dearest Maria!"

She then embellished the writing with her cursive twirls, adding a few stars next to the line,

"It was such a pleasant surprise to receive your kind letter. I feel glad to hear you like The Queen of the Night. I'm sure Mozart would have been most pleased to hear it!"

The Queen of the Night is a character in Mozart's opera The Magic Flute; it depicts a fit of vengeful rage in which the Queen of the Night places a knife into the hand of her daughter. Her aria is one of the most famous of all Opera: memorable, fast paced and menacingly grandiose. It is extremely difficult to sing.

Mind you, I don't sing it very well either. I do hope to do so one day, after enough training! My singing teacher said that one famous singer, when she finished that whole aria of ten minutes, collapsed on stage! And she also said that Mozart had designed it that way! To "pull out your soul!"

> I disagree though, dearest Maria. I think he designed it to evoke emotion. If that requires writing the most complicated of arias, then he was willing to do so. But not to make the singer faint! If anything, he might have wanted the audience to faint!"

I really like this first letter. But as I was writing it, Helena told me it was stupid and not good at all, so I did what she told me:

> Helena looked at the letter. She frowned. It was so boring.
>
> She decided to start anew. She pulled out another paper from the notebook.
>
> "Dearest Maria,"
>
> This time she didn't invest as much time in the twirls. She felt a little guilty about that.

Again, in order to write Helena and Maria's characters in a believable way, I had to pull myself back to my own childhood. I was the kid not pleased enough of with his letter, and would then discard it to start anew.

As the author, I had to think of all these little things, such as pulling the paper from the middle of the notebook so it wouldn't get damaged, or putting a letter I wrote aside, or embellishing the title but feeling guilty it's not embellished enough. These little details may seem silly, but in fact they are exactly what makes the work more believable and relatable. They are crucial.

"[...] then she concentrated and wrote:

"Your letter finds me well."

Good. She liked the sound of it. She went on.

"It was splendid to read of your adventures with Sashinka and Eddie. You have such a lovely family. The fact that you could sing to them is incredible. Whenever I sing to Reuben or Solomon, they most often roll their eyes.

Solomon thinks of Hannah all the time.

And Reuben, too, I bet you, is thinking of some girl as well. I've seen how eager he was to go to the beach and look at all the women there. I told him he should close his mouth so that he won't drool all over. But he didn't like my comment!'"

Trying to put myself in Helena's shoes, these things were important: Solomon and Hannah, Reuben and his attitude toward other girls.

Helena smiled and sighed. She continued writing.

"I like it here. I especially like that my father is around more. Back in the city he is busy all the time. Here he reads the newspaper. Sure, don't be mistaken, he did bring with him quite a few folders from the office. But he's also available. Somewhat."

Notice the "somewhat". While Mr. Goldstein is generally a kind person, we never hear of him much. Mr. Bozek is more present: he plays the guitar during

Christmas, he balances his wife's fits, he is simply more present. Mr. Goldstein is more reticent and remote.

"My mother is the happiest. And so am I."

I like this sentence too. No two people can be the happiest. The very ending of "-est" means that someone will be the first, then the second, etc. But young Helena doesn't care about these little nuances.

> Helena wanted to write more. But she didn't know what to write. This was odd. In the books, whenever she read about such correspondence between friends, she thought that had *she* been partaking in such correspondence, she would fill pages and pages.
>
> She thought of writing about a boy she saw on the beach, who reminded her of Alexander.
>
> But it wasn't proper. Not for a letter at least. Besides, Maria wasn't that kind of girl.
>
> She thought of writing about a novel she was reading. But she thought that would be boring.
>
> She thought of writing about how much she missed everyone in class. But the truth was that she didn't *really* miss anyone. Not yet. She might, later on in the summer.
>
> And so, she spent the two further days trying to figure out what to write. This became her obsession. She even skipped lunch one day, trying to think of what to write in her room.

Poor Helena. I feel for her. For adults this may seem a trivial thing, but remember, this was the first letter she had ever received. She wanted to respond perfectly.

But it paralyzed her.

> Two days later her mother said finally, "Helena darling, just send the letter as it is. Don't worry about it any more."
>
> "But Mama, it's only one page!"
>
> "Better short and concise than long and melodramatic, darling."

You might have noticed that Mrs. Goldstein is the only one in the whole book to say "darling" all the time. These little continuity details make the character more recognizable.

> Helena grimaced. This task had become overly difficult.

Here I planted something that you might have noticed, because it's almost too obvious:

> Had she needed to write a long fairy tale about two siblings separated in some mysterious circumstances, she would have completed it in a couple of hours! But this whole *letter thing* was not as easy as she had expected.

This plants the seed for the "separation" of two "siblings" in "mysterious circumstances". Which is basically what this whole book is about :) it's a little wink from the author.

> Finally, she took the piece of paper, which had

accompanied her to the beach, every meal and even to bed, and wrote on it,

"P.S.

I searched for what else to write. I wish I knew what to add! But I see that each day makes the letter older and also further away from you,

I just love that sentence, "older and further away from you." So poetic!

[...] So I will let the letter go as it is. This does NOT show of my utter appreciation for your kindness to have addressed me here. Please do so again as soon as you receive this letter! I hope that by then I will know what to write to you next time!

Until then, faithfully yours,

Helena Goldstein."

She added her swirly new signature, one on which she had worked for hours and hours during Mr. Kissinger's lessons.

Notice the last sentence, so endearing:

It was perfect. Almost.

The following chapter we find ourselves in Maria's shoes.

Maria waited to open the letter until the evening. She wanted to have time alone, and she wanted to read it when she could concentrate and able to respond right away.

> She sat in the kitchen and excitedly opened the precious letter.

This is so calculated of her. Completely the opposite of Helena, who just ran with the letter and read it then and there.

> "Dearest Maria,"

> She loved seeing Helena's handwriting. It had been ten days since the end of the school year, and there were still fifty-two days ahead.

> She had always loved school, as she loved learning. But now she also missed school for other reasons, such as seeing her neighbor's beautiful handwriting as she was practicing her twirling signature again and again in her notebook.

> She smiled to herself and looked at the signature. She didn't want to hurry.

"She didn't want to hurry" – again, a sign of maturity. We'll see a few of those.

> She saw it was only one page, and wanted to linger on each word. She remembered how she had once asked Helena, "How many times do you intend to write that signature of yours?"

> Helena was not taken aback. "Why, until it's perfect, of course!"

I love the following sentence by Helena, which reminds me of myself a little:

> "I'll have to sign it thousands of times, you understand? So I must practice!"

Maria loved that answer. It was so Helena.

As she loved the twirling and the little stars next to her own name. "Dear Maria." The way Helena wrote her name made her feel special.

"Your letter finds me well.

It was splendid to read of your adventures with Sashinka and Eddie. You have such a lovely family. The fact that you could sing to them is incredible. Whenever I sing to Reuben or Solomon, they most often roll their eyes."

Maria laughed quietly, wishing not to wake her siblings. From her parents' bedroom she heard her father snoring. This was now time for *herself* to read this letter, this treat she'd been awaiting the whole day.

Maria carries the burden of the world on her shoulders. In that way, she is extremely mature for her age. One may say, too mature.

She read the last sentence again, enjoying every word.

"…whenever I sing to Reuben or Solomon, they most often roll their eyes.

Solomon all the time thinks of Hannah.

And Reuben, too, I bet you, is thinking of some girl as well. I've seen how eager he was to go to the beach and look at all the women there. I told him he should close his mouth so that he won't drool all over. But he didn't like my comment!"

As the author, I hesitated whether to include this letter for the *second* time. But it was important for me to have the reader now read it all from *Maria's* perspective, for the little moments such as these:

> Maria shook her head, "Helena, Helena…!"

Or for moments such as these:

> […] Maria touched the paper with her finger, over the small stars separating the next paragraph.
>
> "P.S.
> I searched for what else to write. I wish I knew what to add! […]
>
> Maria bit her lip. This was wonderful. Just wonderful! She took her paper out and her favorite pen. It was now late already, but this was important.

Notice what happens to her, as she gets distracted. So human, so real:

> She wanted to write back. Now.
>
> But instead she found herself copying Helena's beautiful signature. Again, and again. Trying, unsuccessfully, to get that twirling going, especially around the "H" and the "G". She sighed. She knew she needed to begin writing soon.

We then find ourselves again with Helena:

> "I received another letter! I received another letter!"

Everyone was amused.

It is never *explicitly* told that Helena is rich. But through descriptions such as the following, we learn that:

> Helena ran around the house, told her brothers, the servant downstairs and the maids upstairs.

This is important. Remember the development of the characters: eventually this child, who was born into great wealth, will have nothing except one small valise. Everything will be taken from her. This is important, and makes what happens later on even more dramatic. Imagine I made Helena poor in the first place. Then the moving into a smaller apartment, and later on moving into the ghetto, would have not meant as much.

> She thought of running to the beach and screaming it out loud. But... that, she knew, would be a waste of time.

> So she ran into her room, slammed the door,

Unlike Maria, she intentionally makes noise:

> indicating she had some *real* work to do. Staring and sighing at the math assignment could wait.

> She lay on her stomach on the bed, and eagerly opened the letter.

> "Dearest Helena,

> I just now read your letter [...]

Maria wishes to respond promptly. She plans the following day in advance:

> [...] and I intend on going first thing tomorrow, with Eddie and Sashinka to the post office. They will enjoy it.
>
> It's been now ten days since the beginning of the summer break, and I dread thinking of the rest. This break is too long. I wish they would divide it into smaller pauses throughout the year. Also, this would be so much better for the students, as the flow of our education would not stop so abruptly."

Helena shook her head. This was so typical of Maria. "The flow of our education." *Maria, Maria!*

> "The city feels a little dull. I realize many people have gone out of town for the summer. Father spoke of busy days at the train station, but now it has eased.

Maria is a grown up. Even too much of a grown up. She is like a little mother. I could have said something about it, as the narrator. "Poor Maria had to take care of her little siblings and do grocery shopping." But instead, I let her share these moments subtly. We learn of her day without noticing that we are told those little things:

> At the post office there is nowadays no line anymore. Nor there is a line at the grocery store. Also, the vendors seem less enthusiastic to work. It's a pity. Everything happens so

slowly.

Sashinka is excited about being the eldest in kindergarten next year. I promised to sew her a bag, embroidered with her initials.

This is a hint of the meaningful present that Maria will give Helena at the end of the summer.

I hope this will keep me busy for several days. But I desperately think of what to do.

I did take out some books from the library. I was the only one in the Youth section, can you imagine?"

Helena laughed and exclaimed at the letter, "Of course, Maria!"

"Eddie finished his Karl May book, which makes me happy. We'll borrow a new book for him soon, maybe tomorrow. In the meantime, all he talks about is Indian chiefs and cowboys, and speaks in tongues and explains it is Indian... he can be so funny...

These words "so funny..." are Maria's. Also, in her last letter, she wrote the same about Eddie. Again, these tiny things are important, and I did my best to capture each characters' specific vocabulary, such as Helena saying "Truly magical" and "Oh my!"

Maria's letter continues,

Do tell me about the sea, and the waves, and the sound of the seagulls. I would love to explore the sea life, see sea stars and seahorses... Do you notice the tides? Does it really change according to the moon? Tell me, please, do not spare your thoughts.

Then the letter ends the same way as Maria's other letter:

> Yours fondly,
>
> Maria Bozek.
>
> P.S.
>
> What do you think of my new signature? Not as beautiful as yours, but I like it better than my old one!"

> Helena turned over onto her back and smiled. What a beautiful letter! She took it again and looked at it. Two full pages. She must be able to respond with *at least* that length. She looked at the small handwriting and at the funny-looking signature. "Oh, Maria!" she laughed.

Though I wanted to possibly continue with their correspondence, wondering how Helena's second letter to Maria would look like (More than two pages? Would she tell about the sea life?) – I had to move on. The story had a certain pace, and I had to let it lead me, now straight to the end of summer and the beginning of the school year:

> Helena had never before wanted to return to school as much as she did that year.

> "I have a surprise for you!" she whispered into Maria's ear as they hugged when seeing each other for the first time after the long summer.

"And I for you!" Maria whispered back, her eyes shining.

During the long break between classes they ran up to the third floor and quietly climbed out the window onto the roof, each holding a small bag in her hand.

Helena looked at the view. "It's so good to be here again!"

Maria nodded. There was so much she wanted to say.

"I've missed the city," Helena continued, "and I even missed the school!"

And I will add, "And I even missed sitting next to you!"

Maria smiled.

"Here," Helena said and handed Maria a small brown bag, "I got these for you. But…"

Helena, who understands people well, suddenly realizes the implications of her not bringing a gift to the other girls.

She hesitated, "please don't tell Gisele or Isabella or anyone because I didn't—"

"I promise."

This is the first "I promise".

The second "I promise" will be a year later, when they finish their four days on the beach together.

The last "I promise" will end the book.

In a way, the first and second moments of "I promise" are only preludes. When we see those words in the very last scene, there is a feeling of completion. Though they'll be 25 and have been through so much, the little girls in them will come out again to end the book with "I promise".

So, for now, we're planting the seeds for that final moment.

> Helena then took the brown bag back, "Guess what it is!"
>
> Maria shrugged her shoulders, "I don't know."
>
> "Guess!"
>
> Maria searched for the right guess.
>
> Helena pressed, "Just guess!"
>
> "Helena! I don't know!"
>
> Helena shook the bag in front of Maria's face. It sounded like small stones.
>
> Still, Maria wouldn't guess.
>
> Helena shook her head and handed Maria the bag, "So open it!"
>
> Maria opened the small bag and exclaimed "Helena!"
>
> Seashells in various golden colors filled the bag. She touched them, caressing the different shapes and sizes. She held them to her nose. "They smell like the sea!"

Sweet Maria. She has never been to the sea. This means a lot for her.

> Helena laughed, "Of course they do!"

> Maria inspected them, turning each one, looking at it from every angle. "Wow, Helena, it's *exactly*… it means so *much* to me…"

> "Did you see the small bag inside?"

> "Small bag?"

We also see her the motif of surprise. In that last scene on the train platform, Maria will say:

> "When you're ready, I have a surprise for you!"

> "What is it?" Helena asked nervously.

> "Solomon, he made it…—"

> "Solomon?!" Helena screamed, "He is alive?!"

All these elements of surprise, of "I promise" are here to prepare us, subconsciously, for a feeling of completion in the last chapter.

> Inside the brown bag there was a tiny paper bag.

> Helena's smile grew bigger, "Open it!"

> Maria opened it. It was a fossil of a…

In moments such as these, I always try not to reveal to the reader the surprise before the character experiences it. I try to create a little bit of a suspense that way:

> "No!"

"Yes!"

"No! Is this the tail of a… *seahorse?*"

"Yes Maria! Reuben found it! He said it must be from a tiny seahorse."

"Oh Helena!" Maria said and embraced Helena. "This is…"

"Magical, right?"

"Yes!"

Helena smiled. The schoolyard was busy with people. Gisele and the others would be wondering where she was.

As I mentioned, this little indication lets us know that Helena's preferences have begun to change. When we meet them again at the end of High school, we will hear of them being referred to as "Helena and Maria" together. Here is the beginning of the shift, as Helena *chooses* to spend time with the less popular girl, who she really likes.

Maria bit her lip. She had also brought Helena a present, but it was nothing like… She sighed, "Helena, I'm afraid this does not match your generous gift…"

Isn't that feeling accurate? Feeling like your gift is not adequate when compared to another?

Helena tut-tutted, "Don't be silly!"

Maria handed the small brown bag to Helena.

Helena opened it. Inside she saw a small handmade purse. "Oh my!" she exclaimed,

"It's beautiful! And it has my initials!"

Maria looked down, "I tried to make it so as to capture your swirling signature…"

"I love it! This is so much better than my gift!"

Maria shook her head, "Yours is much better.

Oh, this is so endearing, and so child-like:

All I did was to sew this together…—"

"Yeah, but you *made* it, Maria, I just *found* these…"

Helena hugged Maria. "Thank you so much!"

The school bell rang.

They made their way carefully back to the window and climbed inside, closing it behind them and running to class. Each girl hid her precious bag in her hand, protecting it.

I just love this scene. It's one of my favorites: the thoughtful gifts, the excitement of being back to school, going together to their hiding place. I love it! And I love how they both go back to class, "her precious bag in her hand, protecting it."

Now I had to show that this was more meaningful than we might imagine.

Here's how I did it:

She was 25-years-old now. But she looked older. She'd been through so much these past few years. The war. Escaping.

The train, now in her beloved homeland, made

its way through fields and forests. The announcements in the train were now made in her own language. She missed her language.

We are thrown into the future. Let's call it the "present". In many ways, the whole book can be looked at as memories. Memories thought of by Helena and Maria, as they both anticipate their meeting after the war.

This "present" time was what we opened with, and what we close with.

But this "present" time appears also in two other times throughout the book. This is the first, and soon we'll get to the second.

Why was it so important for me to throw back this "present" time? This was the "frame" of the story. Why did I have to remind us that we began here, and here we will end?

I guess it was important for me to show how this little relationship, and these little moments, would later play out in our character's life.

Entering for a moment into this "present" time, I say here, "This is important". Those little things, that may seem meaningless, are important.

In a way I say, "Don't be mistaken. This is not a story about two little girls and their silliness. This is about love that grows and expands and reaches beyond the years, reaches beyond conflicts, reaches beyond religions and backgrounds."

She sighed. Somehow she felt safer now, in her

own country.

She opened her valise, which held her only possessions in this world: some clothes, a few letters, a journal and the little, old, time-worn brown bag...

Remember: Helena would move so many times: from her large house, to a smaller apartment, then to an apartment inside the ghetto. Then she'd smuggle her "valuables" with a "boy" a few days before she is kidnapped by Maria. Then she goes with this valise to the "capital" (which is Warsaw).

She is then no longer H.G. She is no longer Helena Goldstein. She is now Maria. But she still carries that one little thing with her. Why?

> She reached and brought out the old, time-worn brown bag. It had been folded and unfolded over hundreds of times over the years.

> She had thought of getting rid of it. It was too revealing of her true identity. It could have proved disastrous. It could have cost her her life.

> But she had kept it.

Why? Why? Why?!

> Carefully opening the brown bag, she took out the tiny purse.

> She had not allowed herself to cry for so many years. But now her eyes stung and the tears filled them as her fingers caressed the

embroidered letters.

"H. G."

I don't know about you. But reading this now for the second (or twentieth) time, it really touches my heart.

People in the Holocaust clung to pictures of their beloveds. They clung to little things that reminded them of love, of better days, of hope.

To me, this little purse she had received at age 13 was one of those things that kept her going; this is the meaning of love. This is the meaning of true friendship. This friendship helped Helena survive the war.

In those moments that bring us back to the "future" time, I tried to show just how important Maria was for Helena.

This is one of the main reasons why I included that scene. Later on in the book we return to Helena on the train, but then the role of that appearance will be different, and will reassure the readers.

Now I was intending to create more and more bonding scenes. I was curious to see how this relationship would mature how the characters would respond to certain situations.

> Not long after the school year began, Helena invited Maria to come to the synagogue with her. "It's a special day for us, I think you'd like it."

Maria asked her parents. Whilst her mother did not want her gone for too long, her father insisted that she should go.

Mr. Bozek must have understood the importance of developing the wings of his daughter, and also saw some benefits in her visiting a Jewish family and learning a different heritage.

This should not be taken lightly. My own mother, having read the manuscript, said, "The four parents were brave. Things like this didn't take place in my childhood."

My mother was born in the former Soviet Union in the 1950's, three decades after Maria and Helena were born. If this didn't happen in her times, we can conclude how brave and daring the girl's parents were, on both sides.

> Helena was in heaven when she heard the good news. "We'll have so much fun together! It's always so boring for me alone…"

> Maria was excited. "Do I need to bring anything?"

> "No, just come dressed in white."

> "In white?"

> Helena nodded.

Each year, around the beginning of the school year, we Jews celebrate the Day of Atonement. We dress in white and go to the synagogue, fast, and pray. Even families who are less traditional often go to the synagogue on that one day even if it's the only time they visit the synagogue in the whole year.

> As they approached the building, Maria was amazed to see everyone was wearing white: men, women and even the children.
>
> They climbed the stairs following Mrs. Goldstein to the second floor of the large synagogue.

The tradition separates men from women, with women often being given the "balcony". This is where they go.

> Helena whispered to Maria, "We call it the Day of Atonement. And we need to atone and ask for forgiveness for our sins, I think...."

The subtle "I think" shows us that Helena's family is not very traditional.

> They sat down in the wooden benches, looking at the grandeur below. Maria liked the stained glass windows. The place looked like a church, but... whiter. Especially with all the people wearing white.
>
> Helena whispered to her, "It goes on like this for hours, sitting, standing, it can be very boring..."
>
> But Maria found none of it boring. The men downstairs were moving and nodding their heads incessantly. And many women upstairs, around Maria, did so as well. She watched with fascination how the women were moving their lip rapidly, as if under a trance.

Notice how it's way more interesting to describe the situation from the eyes of an outsider. In this scene we see things from Maria's perspective.

In the following scene, Christmas, Helena will be the outsider. Next, during the Jewish Passover at the Goldstein's, Maria will be the main character.

> But what moved her most of all was when people began crying, really crying, when the lead man (Helena called him the 'cantor') started singing with a deep voice, looking up to the ceiling, and the entire synagogue shook with the power of his voice.

This scene, in which the cantor sings the prayer that Jews identify as *"Kol Nidre"* is very much based on the *real* Maria Bozek-Nowak's recollection:

> "Even before the war, Helena took me to a concert at her synagogue for a *Kol Nidre* service. I liked it very much and I remember especially the cantors."

It was a pleasure for me to revive that scene and make it come to life:

> Even Helena's mother had tears in her eyes.

> Maria couldn't stop herself from asking Helena, whispering ever so quietly, "What is he *saying?*"

While her family has invested much in her education, singing, ballet, etc., they have not bothered to give her much religious education. As Maria Bozek-Nowak noted, many of the Jews in Krakow were "not

Orthodox" and were quite "acculturated into Polish culture".

This makes us understand why Helena doesn't really know much:

> Helena grimaced, "I'm not quite sure... I'm not sure anyone here understands really..."

The following sentence will help us comprehend this society a little more. It's subtle, though.

> The following day, Helena did not attend school. It was a day of fasting for her. Nearly half the class did not come to school that day. And a few teachers were missing too.

This extremely subtle hint shows that many in Maria's school were Jews. I read somewhere during my research that about half of Maria's friends were Jews.

Then the story continues:

> But the day after, the whole class was back, and life continued as usual.

Here I tried to paint a picture of the day to day life in the school, in a brief paragraph, summarizing several months:

> Mr. Kissinger spoke monotonously while most students didn't follow. Mrs. Schlesinger was in love with the current poet they were studying. And the new History teacher spoke about the Great War with fervor.

Notice the "Great War". Again, this is a hint of the shadow that is coming. Up until WWII the First World War was never called "the first". It was called "The

Great War." This reminds us of what is looming in the distance.

Now we are coming to one of the most important scenes which, I must admit, took some work and sweat to create:

THE CHRISTMAS DINNER

We begin this chapter by creating the atmosphere:

> Winter approached, and the streets were decorated for Christmas. In the schoolyard Roman boasted to the girls about how he and his father had gone to the forest and cut down a *huge* tree to place in their house for the Holidays.

> When he was gone, Helena lamented to Gisele, "I wish we could celebrate Christmas as well."

> Maria, sitting next to them, reading a book, tilted her head and listened.

> Gisele shrugged, "But they don't get to light the candelabrum and eat our great food…"

> "Yeah, I know," Helena lamented, "but, you know, Christmas is so festive…."

Here is the seed for what will happen next:

> Maria's eyes widened. She thought it was impossible for someone not to celebrate Christmas. It was the best thing about Winter!

Up until now Helena was usually the initiator. "Come to my Ballet", "Write to me!" or "Come to synagogue with me." But now Maria is taking the wheel:

> Two days later, during History lesson, she wrote down: "Do you want to come and celebrate Christmas at my house?"

> Helena squinted at the note, her eyes growing large with disbelief. She quickly wrote "Really???"

> Maria smiled and wrote, "YES!"

> Helena's eyes glittered. "But," she wrote, "your parents...???"

For the editors of the book those three question marks were a pain. But I tried to stay loyal to what I thought Helena would write. She would use three question marks.

> "My mother invited you" Maria wrote.

> "That can't be!!!" Helena answered.

> Maria smiled and wrote, "But it's true!"

> Helena grinned too. She couldn't believe it.

In the book I try not to waste a line. This scene established the background. Now, without further ado, I jump straight into Christmas Eve:

> Maria ran to the door, "I'll get it!"

Some have told me that my writing is rather movie-like. I can understand why. There is quite a bit of dialogue, and very little description. I like the story line to be the main thing, rather than descriptions or beautiful prose. This is why I always jump to the most essential moments. Without having this tiny scene above, of Maria inviting Helena, we would have been lost but, having established the Who and what and why, we can now plunge straight into the important evening:

Mrs. Bozek hurried to walk to the door from the kitchen, and shouted at her husband sitting in the living room, "Come now!"

Maria opened the door and exclaimed, "Helena!"

Helena stood at the door, wearing her new fur coat and carrying a suitcase. Mr. Goldstein was standing behind her in the snowy street.

Eddie and Sashinka hassled to join and hid behind their parents.

Mrs. Bozek quickly said, "Well, come in already Helena, don't stand there outside!"

The girl walked in.

Mr. Goldstein raised his hand, "Thank you. Merry Christmas!"

Maria's father upturned his hand as well, "Happy holidays!"

Mr. Goldstein is very kind to wish the family "Merry Christmas" even though he is not Christian.

Likewise, Mr. Bozek is quite aware of the situation, and he says kindly, "Happy holidays!" He knows that Jews don't celebrate Christmas. But he is not all too aware of their holidays, which is a pity for him. This is why he hopes his daughter will know more than him in the future.

Mr. Bozek shows us the kinder side of the Bozeks:

> "Why don't you come in for a moment, have something warm to drink? Make a toast?"

> Mr. Goldstein waved his hand, pointing in the direction of the tram. "My wife…"

> Mr. Bozek gestured, 'Of course!' and nodded his head.

> Mr. Goldstein bowed his hat and walked away.

> Mr. Bozek closed the door and headed back to the living room. Mrs. Bozek was already back in the kitchen.

This scene portrays Mrs. Bozek in a rather negative light at times. But again, we must not judge her, as she is very stressed preparing dinner.

Also, I often like to present negative features of a character and by the end of the book show the extremely positive; In *The Two Marias* that character is definitely Mrs. Bozek. You will love her at the end, but now, at the beginning stages of the book, she appears to be rather vulgar and impolite.

> Helena and Maria began jumping in each other's arms. "I can't believe I'm here!"

> "I can't believe you're here!"

> "Girls," Mrs. Bozek shouted, "enough with that. Maria, take Helena's coat already!"

"Yes, Mama!"

Helena whispered, "It's okay," and took her coat off, placing it on the hanger.

Maria whispered, "What's with the suitcase?"

Helena's eyes glittered, "Well, my night clothes and all, but also," she whispered, "presents for Eddie and Sashinka!"

Maria shook her head, "You shouldn't have!"

"I wanted to!"

Eddie and Sashinka were now in the living room, playing. Helena entered the living room and gasped, "Wow! What a beautiful tree! And what a huge table! Where are the beds?"

Maria's mother came out of the kitchen, beaming. "Beautiful, right?"

Even Mrs. Bozek wishes to receive some compliments.

Helena nodded, and Eddie and Sashinka hurried to show her the decorations they had made for the tree.

Helena smiled, "Wow, you made that, Eddie? The star?"

Maria smiled at her.

Helena then looked at the large table with chairs and plates already set up. A white tablecloth covered the table, but there seemed to be hay all around.

I must admit that for this scene I did some extensive research. The Christmas Eve vigil supper in Poland is called *Wigilia,* and it is held on December 24th. Often hay is placed under the tablecloth or in each of the four corners of the room to symbolize the fact that Jesus was born in a manger.

> They must still need to do some final cleaning, she thought.

And so, this is a prelude to what happens at the beginning of the meal, when Helena "cleans" a little hay from under the tablecloth.

> Maria looked at her with joy and whispered, "The table – it's made of two beds put together!"

My own grandfather lived in a very small one-bedroom apartment which served as bedroom, living room, etc. When we celebrated holidays with him, the table took up the whole room.

In the Bozek family, the small living room has three beds. I thought of what they would have to do, and then envisioned Mr. Bozek, who has good hands (unlike Mr. Goldstein who is an Accountant), putting together two beds on top of one another, securing them, and finally putting a wide board on top of them, to serve as a table. I liked that idea, as it was inventive and resourceful.

> "No!" Helena motioned with her mouth.

> "Yes! My father put a big wooden board on the two beds, see?" She moved the large tablecloth.

"Brilliant!" Helena whispered. She smiled at Mr. Bozek, who was reading the newspaper.

Mrs. Bozek shouted from the kitchen, "Maria, I need you!"

Maria walked to the kitchen, and Helena followed her, saying, "I can help too!"

Mrs. Bozek waved her hand, "You are our guest. Now go to the living room and leave us alone, I need to concentrate!"

Poor Mrs. Bozek. Poor Helena. This hints of what is to come.

Maria smiled at Helena. Helena smiled back and went to the living room to play with the younger children.

Now, theoretically, to such a dinner, more people would attend, such as the siblings of Maria's parents. But I had to simplify things.

Simplification is often important; as long as it does not make the scene empty or unbelievable, it helps to place the attention on what is *important*. I constantly try to *advance* the plot. And having more family members would have not done it. So I only brought in the grandparents.

A few minutes later the grandparents arrived. Helena was introduced to them.

We know that Helena has two older brothers, while Maria is the eldest. This means that, most likely, Mrs. Bozek is younger than Mrs. Goldstein. Therefore, her parents are also younger.

They were Mrs. Bozek's parents, and were much younger than Helena's grandparents.

They sat in the living room and the grandfather began having a long conversation with Mr. Bozek; the two laughed together amiably.

Mr. Bozek's own father, who will soon come, is older and feeble. Therefore, Mr. Bozek finds good company in his father in law.

The grandmother tried to help in the kitchen but was soon shooed away by Mrs. Bozek, "Mother, don't disturb me," she exclaimed.

This helps us realize that Mrs. Bozek isn't just rude toward Helena, but also toward anyone else who crosses her path, including her own mother.

The grandmother then came to the living room and played for a while with the grandchildren.

All these little details are scanned by the reader quickly. But they did take some time to form and to be written in a way that would flow. The more characters there are, the more I find it challenging to convey the scene in a reliable way. I want to say what each character thinks and feels, but that *slows* down the pace of the scene, which is dangerous. So... it's a little complicated for me as an author....

Soon, the doorbell rang again. This time it was Mr. Bozek's parents. They looked much older. Helena thought that, in fact, the grandfather looked quite ancient.

Mr. Bozek is much older than his wife. I imagine that he is in his fifties, while his wife is in her thirties. This explains the difference in age of their parents.

> The small living room was packed. Helena tried to fit in, but really hoped Maria would come out of the kitchen.

I know how awkward these situations are. Remember, she is only 13-years-old.

> Eddie was running to the window every minute or so, exclaiming, "I don't see it yet, Papa! I don't see it yet!"

The meal only begins upon the appearance of the first star in the sky.

> Mr. Bozek kept talking with his father in law. The other grandfather soon fell asleep on his wife's shoulder.

> Then, Eddie exclaimed from near the window, "I see it, Papa! The first star!"

> Mr. Bozek walked to the window. "Indeed."

I like the visual aspect of the following sentence, as super-woman comes out of the kitchen:

> As if waiting for that moment, Mrs. Bozek ran out of the kitchen, snatching off her apron, "Very good. Now sit down everybody! I don't want the food to get cold!"

> Everyone sat down quickly.

"Quickly" – as in, everyone is afraid of Mrs. Bozek.

> Silence ensued.

Now, according to the Wiglia, the eldest man is supposed to bless.

> Mrs. Bozek elbowed her husband, who coughed, "Papa!"
>
> The old and feeble grandfather seemed to be awoken from a daze, "Yes?"
>
> "The prayer, Papa!"
>
> "Why, of course," said the puzzled grandfather, and the children burst into laughter. Mrs. Bozek silenced them at once.

Now, remember, Helena is Jewish. In Judaism, while we bless for the food etc., we do not tend to hold hands together; this feels very foreign to us. I remember the first few times I ever ate with Christian friends – it was nice, but also quite... *different*.

> The old grandfather joined his hands with his wife and the other grandfather, and soon everyone was holding hands. Helena held Maria and Eddie's hands. She found it quite weird. They each held their hands very tightly.
>
> The old grandfather said a prayer, and they all said "Amen" and crossed themselves. Helena did not, hoping no one had noticed.

But Helena definitely *looked* and *learned*.

> Then Eddie exclaimed with excitement, "The Christmas wafer!"

In the Wiglia, there is an important role to the Christmas wafer (opłatek). It symbolizes bread. After the prayer, usually done by the man of the house, the opŁatek is broken and pieces are given to everyone in the table. From there, everyone breaks off a piece of their opŁatek, and shares it with everyone else, wishing luck and joy in the upcoming year, for Christ has been born.

> The old grandfather took the large piece of unleavened wafer at the center of the table, and broke it into two pieces. He looked at his wife and said, "Merry Christmas!"
>
> He then turned to the other grandfather and said, "Merry Christmas." He handed them the broken pieces of wafer, and soon they began passing and breaking the wafers to others, blessing everyone with Merry Christmas and other wishes.

Maria is sitting next to Helena. We already know it. How? We know that Helena held the hands of Maria and Eddie. This little detail is important, because soon Eddie, sitting next to Helena, will notice her cleaning the hay.

But now Maria, passing the piece of wafer to Helena, hesitates. She knows that Helena does not celebrate Christmas. Nevertheless, she wishes to treat her as one of the family. This is how it looks:

> Maria handed her a small piece of wafer and smiled, shyly, "Merry Christmas Helena!"
>
> Helena smiled, "Merry Christmas Maria!"
>
> Helena also received a small piece from Eddie, and to her surprise everyone kept chopping their pieces of wafer and passing from one to

the other, exclaiming "Good year!" and "Health and prosperity".

Then everyone ate their wafers and crumbs. Helena thought it was so peculiar!

Maria's mother left the table, and Maria hurried to follow her.

Now comes the moment I was waiting for. I needed to highlight that Helena was an outsider. While it is not fun for us to read of her embarrassment, it *does* serve the plot, building up to her discomfort, that will eventually result in her crying in the bathroom.

Notice how subtly I try to describe what she's doing:

> Helena noticed there was something tilting the plate under her plate—no, under the tablecloth—and quietly sneaked her hand below the tablecloth to remove some... hay?

Unfortunately, someone notices. An adult would have said nothing. This is why I seated her next to Eddie:

> "Father," Eddie said, "she's removing the hay!"

> Helena's face reddened at once. Was she not supposed to...—

> Maria, serving the first bowls of red beetroot soup, smiled and whispered, "It's the tradition, to place hay under the table and under the tablecloth."

What will Helena say?

Often, in my childhood, rather than admitting that I didn't know something, I would say, "Oh, of course" and even, "I knew that!"

Didn't you?

> Helena mumbled, "Of... of course..." She was determined not to move or do anything else that would attract attention.

One may think: but Helena likes attention!

Well, Helena likes attention when she is in *control*. Here she is not in control at all.

> But the old grandmother smiled at her from across the table,

Don't we know how it is when adults try to "help" and instead make things worse? All Helena wanted is for people to carry on, and stop looking at her!

> "It's to remember that Jesus was born and put in a *manger*, you see?"

> Helena mumbled, "Of course..."

But there is someone sensitive at the dinner table:

> Luckily, Maria's father changed the subject, "Tell us, Eddie, what have you been studying in school..."

> When the soup was served, Maria sat down and noticed Helena's red face. She smiled, "Is everything okay?"

> Helena whispered, placing her hands on her hot cheeks, "Why? Do I look redder than the soup?"

> Maria grinned and said reassuringly, "It's so great to have you here!"

As a side note I will say that my own grandmother used to make this red-purple beetroot soup. I ate it a lot as a child.

> The evening continued with more and more food. The tiny kitchen kept producing dishes heaped with

I sometimes *love* scenes with descriptions of food. Now it's serving the plot, and helps us feel like we are actually a part of the table.

> ...rollmops, cabbage rolls, cooked mushrooms, dumplings filled with cheese and potatoes, stewed sauerkraut, many kinds of salads, and many kinds of fish.

How does it serve the plot, to have all these dishes mentioned?

> Mrs. Bozek looked at Helena, "There is no meat here, only fish, so eat!"

> Helena looked at her, puzzled.

It turns out that Mrs. Bozek, who we may have judged as ignorant and impolite, actually cares about a Jewish person coming to her meal.

She doesn't know much about Jews. But she does know that there are things they don't eat, and she has to find out what and how and all the details.

Which does show her in a good light. She cared.

Nevertheless, while her husband has some tact, she

does not, and she exclaims at the table:

> "I went to the market," Mrs. Bozek said, "and asked what you *cannot* eat, but I understood fish always works, right?"

Fish is "kosher" and is allowed for Jews to eat. The evening of Wiglia (this may surprise you) is what's called a "Black Fast", meaning that most Polish people abstain from eating meat on this day.

> Helena nodded.

> "Well, eat everything then!"

The following is also a tradition: 12 dishes, all of which you must eat:

> Maria, feeling a little guilty, whispered to Helena, "It's our tradition, that you have to eat all twelve dishes."

> Hearing her, Mr. Bozek added,

(Trying to be kind to Helena)

> "Because of the twelve months of the year. It's for you to have a good year!"

But Mrs. Tactless intervenes:

> "Fool," Mrs. Bozek retorted, "it's because of the twelve *apostles!*"

> "Well I heard it was the twelve months of the year!"

Maria senses a little tension, and her parents fighting is the *last* thing she wants her friend Helena to see, so she immediately intervenes

"Who," Maria jumped, "who... wants *kompot?*"

I tried to refrain from foreign words, but "kompot" tends to be quite well known. Regardless, in less than one sentence it is explained:

> Everyone wanted, and so Maria hurried to go and fetch the pitchers of the sweet beverage from the kitchen. Helena, seeing that Mrs. Bozek was sitting, got up to help Maria, and looked at Mrs. Bozek worriedly, fearing she would scold her. But she was busy eating and talking to the grandmother.

Finally, Maria and Helena are alone.

> In the small kitchen, Maria smiled at Helena, "Is everything okay?"
>
> Helena, still red and quite embarrassed, said a little too eagerly, "Yes! It's so... *lively!*"
>
> Maria smiled, took one pitcher and pointed at a second, and Helena carried it and followed her to the living room.
>
> They poured kompot for everyone. When Helena poured some kompot for Mrs. Bozek, she was surprised to see Maria's mother looking at her and nodding, "You're a good girl, Helena."

Here comes an important sentence creating some suspense:

> This made Helena feel much better. But it would not to last for long.

By now we are midway through the meal; as an

author, I want to keep the reader always on edge, and by now I'm afraid that the reader may start feeling "full" of all the food and "traditions" and wonder where is this all going and what need is there to hear all these details.

This is why I "intervene" and add that while it was a nice comment from Mrs. Bozek and it made Helena feel better, "it would not to last for long."

This gives the reader energy to push on. That's the power of suspense. Later on in the book I'll use it a lot. Not because I like suspense (I avoid suspense novels), but because it serves the advancement of the plot.

> After all the poppy seed cakes were eaten, the dried apples and plums were finished, and all the small sweets were tasted, Helena helped Mrs. Bozek and Maria take the dishes to the kitchen. All the while Eddie kept nagging, "Now, Papa? *Now?*"

> Mr. Bozek did not respond, and kept talking to his father-in-law. Eventually he said to Eddie, "When your mama says!"

> When the table was finally clean Mrs. Bozek said, "We can now move to the tree."

> Eddie and Sashinka cheered. Everyone carried their chairs, and Mr. Bozek, with the help of his father-in-law, pushed the table-made-of-beds to the corner of the room.

> Helena hurried to her suitcase. She opened it and excitedly took the two large packages out.

> She placed them under the tree along with the other presents, and asked Maria, who came and sat down, "Is it okay where I put them?"

> Maria smiled and nodded.

> The old grandfather once again fell asleep on the old grandmother's shoulder. Eddie and Sashinka were ecstatic.

In a moment will notice something tiny, but important, about Maria's parents. Helena's own parents may seem to us "civil", but also rather cold. Her father rarely speaks to her, as he is always busy with his work, and even when he is in their summer vacation, he reads the newspapers all the time.

Unlike them, the Bozeks are warm. Later on, Mrs. Bozek will even make a sexual comment, saying that her husband is good "not only in running…"

Mrs. Goldstein would never call her husband "fool", like Mrs. Bozek did earlier in the meal, but the Bozeks are nonetheless more warm. This is why Mr. Bozek will allow himself to massage his wife's shoulders in a second. She worked to prepare the meal, and he wants to show her his appreciation. But Helena finds it a little embarrassing, as if she is not supposed to see this act for grown ups only:

> Mrs. Bozek sat near the tree, and Mr. Bozek stood behind her, massaging her shoulders. This was a little embarrassing for Helena to watch.

> Mrs. Bozek then cleared her throat, "First, Sashinka will open her present."

Little Sasha eagerly took her gift from under the tree, and tore the wrapping paper apart.

I had intended for this scene to take place the following morning, but then I read that in Poland, at least back then, gifts were opened during the evening celebrations.

Maria smiled at Helena.

Sashinka discovered a white dress, perfect for her size. "Mama, Papa!" She exclaimed.

Ever the parent,

Maria said to her, "Now kiss Mama and Papa!"

Sasha kissed them.

I knew that having more gifts would slow down the scene and postpone the moment of drama I'm building up for, so I followed the logic that since they are all rather poor, the family gives one gift together. I also think that Mrs. Bozek would not want to spoil the children with too many gifts. This is why I made the gift also come from the grandparents:

Mrs. Bozek said, "It's from your grandparents too, go kiss them too!"

After Sashinka finished the round of kisses, Eddie shouted, "Now it's my turn!"

Mrs. Bozek said, "Now you Eddie."

Is it clear by now that Mrs. Bozek wears the pants in the family? She's the boss. Earlier Mr. Bozek said, "When your mama says…" and now Eddie waits for his mother's approval.

This is important because when she gets up and leaves for the kitchen, it means that the "head" of the household has disapproved of Helena's gifts. But now back to Eddie:

> He opened his gift. It was a small train, made out of wood, painted in red.

Do you see why the description of the train is important? "Small train, made out of wood" ... I researched and found out that at the time there were already more expensive trains made of metals.

> He thanked his parents and kissed them, and then kissed the grandparents.

Notice how he did not exclaim anything, nor showed great enthusiasm.

> Then came Maria's turn. She opened her package. "New notebooks!" she exclaimed.

> Helena smiled. She was a little disappointed for Maria.

> "Look inside," Mrs. Bozek said proudly, "with a set of pens! Like those you like!"

> "Mama! Thank you!" Maria kissed her mother, "Papa!" she kissed him as well. She went around and kissed the four grandparents. She then said excitedly, "But... there are two more packages! Let's guess who they are for?"

> Sasha and Eddie began screaming, "Me! Me!"

> Maria looked at Helena, who whispered,

Why does she whisper? Well, even to begin with

she is not very comfortable about this situation. Now allow me to step back and let you read the whole scene in one flow; notice how I build the tension, up until Helena runs away to the bathroom:

> [Helena whispered:] "The red for Sasha, the blue for Eddie."
>
> "Go ahead Sashinka," Maria said and pointed at the large red gift.
>
> Sashinka opened it eagerly. It was a beautiful doll, with a dress and brown hair plaited into braids. Sashinka couldn't hold her excitement, "Is this for me? Really? Really?!"
>
> She jumped around and ran with the doll. Maria laughed, "Now kiss Helena!"
>
> Helena leaned down as Sashinka kissed her shyly. Helena looked at Mrs. Bozek, who did not seem overly pleased for some reason.
>
> Then Eddie exclaimed, "My turn, my turn!"
>
> He waited for his mother's nodding approval, and then opened the large package. "Wow!!!" he screamed. "A train! A mechanical train!"
>
> Helena smiled. Then, her smile disappeared instantly as Eddie screamed, "This is so much better than the wooden one!"
>
> Mrs. Bozek got up at once, "Come, Maria! We need to clean the dishes!"
>
> It all happened very fast. Maria gave Helena a sorry look, and she was gone. There was a long silence in the living room, as if Helena had

done something awful. The only one speaking was Eddie, who was running the train around, looking at its intricate wheels, rocking levers and the various springs.

Mr. Bozek was the first to speak. "Well! Let's... sing a little!" He got up and brought out a guitar. He began singing, and the grandparents joined him.

Helena knew the song, and in different circumstances would have begun singing with her beautiful soprano. But now she stared down at the floor and tried to smile at the excited two kids with their gifts.

She wanted so badly to go and see Maria in the kitchen, help her, speak to her, hear from her that it was just her imagination and that she hadn't done something unforgivable....

But Maria was gone. Mr. Bozek tried cheering the atmosphere, but Helena felt stupid. Stupid, stupid, stupid! She shouldn't have brought such expensive gifts! Tears welled in her eyes, and she got up and ran to the back door. She exited the house and entered the small bathroom hut in the backyard.

Oh my God. This scene is so difficult for me. Why did I even write it?

Why?

I guess because I wanted to further bond the girls. Friendship is formed not only in the good and cheerful moments. In fact, one may say that it is formed in the difficult moments; this is one of those.

The editors of the book begged me to get rid of the three "Stupid, stupid, stupid!"

But this is what Helena thought to herself. I had to be loyal to her inner dialogue.

We then see how this low point actually brings Maria and Helena closer to each other:

> She stood there, in the cold and smelly toilet, for what seemed like forever, cursing herself, crying, wanting to go home so badly.
>
> "Helena? Helena is everything okay?"
>
> Helena heard Maria's voice, wiped her tears and shouted over the door of the bathroom hut, "Sure…"
>
> "Helena, did you *cry?*"
>
> "No…!"
>
> "Helena, open the door for me!"
>
> Helena opened the door. Maria looked at her face. She stretched her hands to hug her, "Come here!"
>
> Helena hugged her. "I feel like a *fool*; I didn't mean to…"
>
> "Enough with that, all is well! Did you see how Eddie liked your gift—"
>
> "But your mama…"
>
> "My mother can sometimes be… You'll see, tomorrow she'll be hailing your generous

gifts…!"

"No, she won't!"

Maria grabbed Helena's arms, "Listen to me, Helena! You are *so* kind, you've been *so* kind, you should be *proud* of yourself for being so… *generous*…! Helena!"

Helena sniffled and nodded.

Now we'll see Maria taking charge, in a similar way to how she'll take charge in the future, during the war:

> "Now," Maria said, "in a moment we'll go inside where it's warm, and you'll join us for the singing… I want the little ones to hear you sing! And then we'll go to the midnight mass. Have you ever gone to the midnight Mass?"
>
> Helena shook her head 'no' and wiped her cheeks again.
>
> Maria smiled, "You'll *love* it!" She hugged Helena again, "I am so happy you are here!"
>
> "You *are?*" Helena murmured, "Didn't I embarrass you…?"
>
> From inside the house they heard the singing. Maria said, "Of course not! And I'm so happy you are here with us! Now come, let's go inside."
>
> Helena nodded. All she wanted was to go *home*. But she was a big girl now. What would Reuben and Solomon say if she suddenly returned home?

'No', she thought to herself. She was strong. She would stay.

She would even have fun.

Maria looked at her. "Ready?"

Helena nodded.

They walked inside.

I'm not sure why this scene is so important to me. But it is. Helena, in most of her social encounters, is always strong, leading, powerful, opinionated, laughing. But this scene reverses it all; it shows us an intimate portrayal of Helena. She may seem powerful and as if she couldn't care less. But that's not the truth.

The truth is that she is like every other child: sensitive, caring about how she looks, caring of what others think of her.

And in this scene we saw her vulnerable face. And it didn't scare us. All it did was to make us feel closer to her. We like her even more now. And we care for her.

We also appreciate Maria's handling of the situation, the best she could, in a sensitive, loving way: hugging, reassuring Helena.

I don't know why, but this part always makes me a little emotional. I remember the feeling of being at other kid's houses when I was young. Each house had its own rules and codes of conduct, and as a sensitive child I always wanted to fit in. But sometimes it was difficult.

Helena only wanted to be nice and kind. She was

excited about coming to Christmas. I can just imagine how she went with her mother shopping, thinking exactly of what would make Eddie and Sashinka happy. She bought the best, most expensive and most beautiful doll for Sashinka; she expected Mrs. Bozek to be as thrilled as the girl.

And she thought Eddie would love having a fancy train. She got the best one.

But then it all collapsed. Poor girl. How could she, being only 13, have thought of the socio-economic tension, and of not giving something that would be more expensive than the parents could afford? She couldn't have foreseen it. And Mrs. Goldstein had never been to the house. She did not know where they lived and how their house looked. She, too, wanted to give generously, from all that they had.

Neither do I judge Mrs. Bozek. She felt embarrassed. Sashinka couldn't believe that doll was for her. "Is this for me? Really? Really?!"

Mrs. Bozek must have felt inadequate.

I can clearly recall an event in my childhood. I went to visit a friend; as a child, I did not know that Tal was rich. And I did not know that my parents, having five kids and struggling to make ends meet, were not.

I loved everything in Tal's house. Especially the computer. But not only that: also the large fridge, and the room with all the toys...

When I came back home I raved to my mother

about it all. I nagged her to get us a better computer (ours barely worked), and I spoke excitedly about their other things.

This must have touched a sensitive spot, as my mother snapped at me, "Then go ahead and move with them, okay?!"

The reason I remember this incident is that it was a little traumatic. I felt is if my mother didn't want me, and was willing to give me up just like that.

But I also sensed her to be unhinged by my words.

Nowadays I understand what she must have felt. She always wanted us kids to spend time with more educated families. But this often involved us coming back and lamenting and criticizing our household for not being enough of this or that.

So I have much empathy for my mother, as well as for Mrs. Bozek. This was too much for her. First Sashinka being more excited about that doll than about the dress she bought, and then Eddie exclaiming that the mechanical train was better?

Good thing she didn't slap him then and there. Her rushing into the kitchen was the best that she could do in that moment.

Poor Mrs. Bozek, poor Helena, and poor everyone. But this did help all of them grow. As the story unfolds, Mrs. Bozek will learn to show love to her daughter's friend, even though she was of a different breed, one that often made her feel inferior. And Helena will learn to feel love for the rough woman, who taught her to be a little more socially aware, and understand complex situations that have to do with people that come from less affluent backgrounds.

With that scene bringing them closer, I could see how soon it would be more natural for the Goldstein family to invite Maria to join them in their summer house.

But I still needed one more scene to help cement their friendship.

> Spring came. And in Helena's house everyone was preparing for the big Passover dinner.
>
> Helena made sure that everyone in the household wouldn't say or do anything embarrassing during the big dinner. She was so excited about Maria coming and sleeping over for the first time. But she was also nervous.
>
> Memories from her uncomfortable stay at Maria's during Christmas made her extra cautious about Maria's visit. Helena knew that her uncle, Bernie, could be rather foolish and inappropriate, and so she asked her mother to speak to him in advance.

I had to have this character thrown in. Everyone was already too polite in the Goldstein family. I needed to have an "incident", a sort of "chagrin", and this is why I made uncle Bernie.

Later on in the story, uncle Bernie will be portrayed as both "smart" and "ruthless". Smart for exiting the country given the Nazi-occupation and, while I don't judge him, to some ruthless for leaving his parents behind. This will be in a rather loaded scene later on.

But for now, all is cheerful.

Almost. There will be a shadow coming in a few paragraphs.

> She wanted no embarrassments. No chagrins. No exasperating moments. She wanted Maria to feel like a part of the family. Welcomed.

We then jump straight into dinner.

Now, a small note: as an author, I had to avoid the danger of the dinners sounding too similar; that could have been boring. So this scene is much shorter, and it is rather bare. Only what had to stay stayed, and much was omitted:

> Maria fit in perfectly. She was pleasant, cordial, and smiled politely to everyone: Maria's parents, two brothers, four grandparents, uncle and aunt and two cousins.

> Everyone seemed to like her. Helena was so pleased. As the long and arduous ceremony continued, she prayed that it would soon finish without any incidents.

> But then it came.

> Helena watched it happen. She saw uncle Bernie as he looked at Maria a little too intently.

We are now with a Jewish family, celebrating Passover, which is one of the most important Holidays. Over the years in Europe there have been several blood libels, according to which, Jews "kidnap"

Christian children and "drink their blood." This has been an often-repeated story about the Jewish Passover.

Bernie, who is absolutely tactless, drops a bomb:

> He snorted at her loudly, "Aren't you *afraid*, little girl, that we will all *cook* you tonight and drink your *blood?*"

> Mrs. Goldstein exclaimed, "Bernie!"

> His wife, aunt Goldie, buried her face in her hands, "Bernie!"

> Helena was *mortified*.

I just love how Maria responds. Is it only me or has she grown up a little over the year and a half since we met her as the "mute"?

> But Maria didn't miss a bit, "No, Sir. And Helena had already warned me about you!"

> Everyone laughed, and Helena, who had caught her breath, now exhaled deeply. Mrs. Goldstein said, "Well done, Helena, for warning Maria. And well done, Maria, for listening. My brother Bernie can be rather nonsensical!"

> Uncle Bernie smiled lovingly and nodded.

> This was not it, though.

This is yet another sentence creating suspense. In fact, what was about to happen proved not to be *that* bad. But suspense is sometimes needed, especially if that is what the character *feels*. And in our case, Helena *felt* fear that somehow things would go wrong.

> When the ceremony was about to end, Helena's grandfather stood and began an emotional speech, which Helena found quite embarrassing, about the "enemies of the people", and how in each generation someone comes to "kill us all".

This, to an extent, is part of the Passover Haggadah.

Now, we must realize where we are chronologically. The two girls were born in 1920. They are now 13, which means we are in 1933. It is spring. Hitler's "rise" can be considered to have ended in March 1933, after the Reichstag adopted the Enabling Act of 1933 in that month.

This was ideal for me, as I looked for a way to cast a shadow, foretelling the future.

> He exclaimed, "And now we should not be afraid of this lunatic…!"

> Maria looked at Helena and whispered, "Who is he talking about?"

Wanting the book to be universal, and not focus *specifically* in WWII, but also in wars and xenophobia around the world, I did not mention Hitler's name.

> Helena shrugged and whispered, "I think he's talking about this nationalist fella who was just elected somewhere… My father and brothers have been arguing about him… but I'm not sure…"

> The grandfather continued for what seemed like eternity to Helena, passionately talking with his hoarse voice about how "this *lunatic* won't succeed where *Pharaoh* failed!" and how all will be well, "...as long as we put the *family* above all!"

Here I have to make a side note, and I hope I won't cry.

You see, this grandfather, along with most of the family, perished. (That's a softer word for brutally killed).

I believe that many people in the Holocaust could have survived had they *not* put the family above all. I learned that in my research for *New Day Dawning*, reading of how Felix Zandman's father refused to escape with his wife and children if that required leaving his parents behind.

This subject is a little too raw for me to speak about.

But I guess this grandfather, with his hoarse voice, expressed what many Jews felt: "We will not leave our families." Even in Maria Bozek-Nowak's testimony, we learn that it was Helena's commitment to her family that stopped her from escaping in the first place:

> "I said to Helena, 'Don't go to the ghetto. We will find a way to hide you here outside.' But Helena didn't want to leave her parents. She knew they needed to go to the ghetto. I understood this."

In fact, it was only when both her parents and one of her siblings were *gone* that Helena was willing to escape the ghetto.

I'm breathing in. This is an emotional issue for me.

But going back to the commentary, I'll just say that this little speech moved me. Putting the family above all. Later on Mr. Goldstein will say the same.

But now we are in 1933. No one envisions what is going to happen. And Mrs. Goldstein wants for the long speech to end, so that people can finally eat.

> Mrs. Goldstein hurried to use his dramatic pause and chimed, "Well said, Dad, they tried to kill us, we survived, now let's eat!"

This is one of my favorite sentences in the whole book.

My editors advised me to change it, but I stuck to it as it is. If you Google the words "They tried to kill us", Google's auto-complete feature will offer you the entire sentence, "They tried to kill us we survived let's eat."

For Jews, this is a little bit of a joke. What's Passover about? "Pharaoh tried to kill us, we survived, let's eat!"

What's Hanukkah about? "Antiochus tried to kill us, we survived, let's eat!"

What's Purim about? "Haman tried to kill us, we survived, let's eat!"

So this very phrase, coming from Mrs. Goldstein's mouth, feels almost sacred to me. It captures the

Jewish spirit of always getting up and beginning anew. I love it.

> Everyone clapped as the grandfather finally sat down. Helena whispered, "Phew! What a speech!"
>
> Maria smiled. She actually enjoyed the passionate speech. She whispered to Helena, "My grandpa, had he needed to give this speech, would have probably fallen asleep in the middle!"
>
> They smiled at each other.

Notice I didn't elaborate on which foods they ate, though the table was not less packed and interesting than during Christmas dinner, because I knew that it was not important now. Back *then* it was important because of the "kosher" thing and Mrs. Bozek's comments. Now it was not. We could jump to the moment that Maria is "accepted" by the family.

I love this little scene:

> Maria loved all the various foods. But more so, she loved how after the dinner they were all looking for the hidden flatbread, which the grandmother hid somewhere around the house.

In Judaism we call it "Afikoman." I wouldn't have mentioned the actual name had Helena not yelled it out loud in a moment:

> Helena and Maria looked for it like mad, and so did Reuben and Solomon and the two

cousins.

From the library, Maria called to Helena, who was searching the pantry, "Helena, is it wrapped in a white towel?"

"Yes! Did you…?"

Maria came with the towel wrapped flatbread, "I'm not sure…?"

"Everyone!" Helena jumped, "Maria found the hidden Afikoman!" Helena ran to the living room where everyone was resting after the meal, "Maria found the Afikoman!"

I almost felt uncomfortable calling it "Afikoman" and not "hidden flatbread". But that's exactly what Helena would have announced. So I guess I'm okay with many readers not knowing what's going on…

The grandfather leaned forward and exclaimed, "Very well!"

Maria looked at everyone staring at her.

Helena clapped her hands, "You get to ask for a *prize!*"

Maria reddened, "A prize? I don't…"

Everyone looked at her.

Maria looked down, "I don't…" she shrugged her shoulders, "Just *being* here is a prize…"

Everyone clapped, "Well said."

The grandmother exclaimed, "Helena! What a good friend you've got!"

Helena beamed.

This is important. This paves the way to the Goldsteins inviting Maria to the summer house, and, inevitably, paying for the train back and forth, the bathing suit, etc.

Now, we must remember that Maria is *Christian*. She is the only Christian present.

Yet her extremely polite conduct makes everyone feel like Helena has picked a friend carefully. This is important. This builds upon the real Maria Bozek-Nowak's testimony:

> "We were great friends. Helena was invited often to Christmas celebrations with my family, and I was invited to spend time with this Jewish family at Jewish holidays."

While Maria was up until now liked by Helena, now she is liked by the entire family.

> Helena's grandfather said, "But that won't do. You need to choose something, anything!"

> Mrs. Goldstein hurried to say, "Leave her alone. It's okay, darling," she said to Maria, "you can decide later. Now, everyone, let's sing some of the oldies… Bernie…?"

One bit of information that we finally never got was what did Maria eventually ask?

I'm not quite sure, personally. But I have a hunch that Helena used this "prize" as an excuse to invite Maria to spend time in the summer with her, in the family's summerhouse.

One last thing. Let's call what I'm about to say a "Treaty About Reticence".

There were many little parts that I thought of including. In the Polish Christmas, the family leaves an empty chair near the table, symbolizing that if anyone comes and knocks on the door, there is room for them.

In Passover, the Jews leave one chair empty for Prophet Elijah. I loved the similarity between the Christian and Jewish tradition of that empty chair; and I wanted badly to include it in. This might seem to you a little extreme, being so frugal about my words.

But I believe that an author must treat each word as if it was expensive; he must be careful not to overload the story with details, and trust the reader to fill them in. Paulo Coelho, one of my favorite authors, said:

> "Trust your reader, don't try to describe things. Give a hint and they will fulfill this hint with their own imagination."

I think this is some of the best advice I ever received when it comes to art in general, and to writing in particular.

If you knew how many details I had in my brain that I had to push aside; how many descriptions I wanted to share that I moved away, you'd appreciate the frugality and the economy with which the words were written.

I think it's easy to write thick. It's easy to make a long book or a film. But the brilliance that I strive for is in creating a "wow" while using less, not more.

Now comes the most seminal scene, which adorns the cover of the book. The one Helena would constantly look back to, and be supported by the memory of:

> It took three weeks of pleading.
>
> "But mama!" Maria cried, "It's not charity!"
>
> "Even if it's not, I'm not going to let you go away for a whole week! What will I do with Eddie and Sashinka?"

I just love opening scenes like that. I trust the reader to be okay with being plunged into the scene. Sure, it takes a moment to understand what's going on, but at least there is something going on!

Now there's a little bit of an homage:

> "Mrs. Szymborska said she'd help with them!"

You know how much I try to avoid mentioning names. But here, I knew that Maria was mentioning a name. Simply saying, "The neighbor said she'd help with them!" wouldn't do it.

Looking a Polish name, I thought of my favorite Polish poet, Wisława Szymborska; throwing her name into the manuscript made me smile.

> "Well, you know what I think of Mrs. Szymborska!"
>
> "Mom," Maria cried, "I really want to go, I've never been to the sea!"

Now, through the dialogue, we understand what's going on.

Of course, I could have written a paragraph saying, "After Passover, Helena began thinking of inviting Maria to the summerhouse. Maria had never been to the sea, and Helena thought this could be magnificent for her. She also thought it could be so fun for the two of them! But would Mrs. Bozek allow Maria to leave? Helena began…"

But this would have slowed me down. I don't want to be slowed down. You see, I threw you into the scene, and you began swimming easily. Sometimes we don't need all the explanations.

I just love the following response of Mrs. Bozek. This is so *her*:

> "So what?! I've never been either, and do you see me crying?"

At school, Helena gave Maria *all* the methods. Whenever Maria gave up, Helena came up with a new plan. Maria would memorize it, but she didn't have much faith in any of Helena's weird ideas.

"Mama," Maria tried again, "I promised Helena I'd help her with the *summer math assignment*. Last year she couldn't do it, and she asked me to—"

"Isn't her father an accountant? He can help her!"

"But we also told Mr. Kissinger we'd do the summer biology experiment at the sea, with barnacles and seaweed. He already approved the experiment for us!"

"Oh leave me alone Maria will you!"

Here's a quick anecdote on punctuation. Grammatically, I should have written:

"Oh, leave me alone, Maria, will you?"

But when we compare it to the sentence I finally used we see that sometimes mechanically correct means less powerful result, as I much prefer the:

"Oh leave me alone Maria will you!"

I learned this from Stephen King's "On Writing". At one point he explains that there is no comma in a specific sentence "because I want you to hear it coming out all in one breath, without a pause." [4]

So no, no commas. Also, since it is a question ("will you") we expect seeing a question mark. But you and I know that Mrs. Bozek isn't *asking*. She's *commanding*. Therefore, though it's "incorrect", sometimes it serves the story to forget all that nonsense we learned in school and to write like a virgin, fresh, not intimidated by the editor.

Let's continue.

> Helena kept searching for more ideas. Finally, she decided to involve her mother.

> Mrs. Goldstein came one day to pick Helena up from Maria's. "Mrs. Bozek," she said in the living room, "can I have a moment with you?"

> "I'm here, am I not?" Mrs. Bozek said.

This is such a typical Mrs. Bozek response. Sometimes I tried really hard to think what she would say, how she would react.

> Mrs. Goldstein smiled to Helena, who, along with Maria, took Eddie and Sasha to play outside.

How can they play outside? Oh, right, we are now after spring, toward summer.

> Helena's heart beat fast. "You'll see," she told Maria outside, as they were throwing the ball among the four of them, "my mother will make it happen."

What was said in the house between Mrs. Goldstein and Mrs. Bozek? I guess that had I *wanted* it, we could have found out. But sometimes I like to leave a little bit of mystery unsolved. Instead of being in the room with them, we are taken outside with the children. What was said? We will never know.

Out of fun, I shared this with my wife, Hallel. We then both tried to guess what was said there. We guessed that Mrs. Goldstein said something about Helena *needing* Maria there. Or perhaps saying something about how *good* this would be for *Maria*.

Whatever she said, it worked.

> Thirty minutes later Mrs. Goldstein came out the house, smiling. "She'll think of it," she said to Helena. "Now say goodbye to Maria and the kids and let's hurry, we don't want to be late to the Ballet."

From this little scene we also understood that Helena and Maria visited each other not only in the holidays, but also in their day-to-day lives.

I love how the following section opens:

> It was unclear what was said in the living room, but, miraculously enough, it worked. On July first, boarding the train for the full-day journey toward the country's seaside, was was —in addition to the usual yearly quintet of Mr. and Mrs. Goldstein and their three children— also the daughter's best friend: Maria Bozek.

I'm not sure why, but I like this rather antiquated introduction: the quintet, and "the daughter's best friend."

Through this we learn that by now, at the end of their second year together, they are number one for each other. We haven't heard of Gisele or Isabella for a while now. That's it. It's cemented.

We already know that Mr. Bozek works for the railroad company, through Gisele's words early on, the day Helena found out that Maria had never been to the sea; soon this information will be important, as he will be able to find out a bit of intelligence that other people are not privy to: the destiny of the Jews of the first transport.

So, since we are now in the train station, I figured it was a good time to bring him to say hello:

> Maria's father, who worked at the Train Station, climbed on the train to bid them all farewell, wearing his engineer's uniform. Mr.

Goldstein reassured him, "Don't worry, Mr. Bozek, Maria will be safe with us."

"It's not me who's worried, it's her mother. As for me," Mr. Bozek said and winked at Maria, "I'm just jealous!"

Maria laughed.

Can you notice how Maria feels more and more comfortable? Remember she is now with Helena's two brothers, sitting in the train. In the past she would have "bit her lip and looked down" or something along these lines. But she is a little more sparkly, a little more like Helena.

And Helena, in her childish naiveté, says:

> "Perhaps next time the whole family could come?"

This costs money. And Mr. Bozek is not self-employed or the owner of his own accounting firm. He cannot miss days at work so easily. But Helena doesn't know that, and beautifully offers this invitation. Mr. Bozek, being the tactful man he is,

> Mr. Bozek smiled, "Whatever God wills." He looked at Mr. and Mrs. Goldstein and tipped his hat at them, "Have a pleasant journey!"

> He then got off the train, and tapped the train's conductor on the back, "Take care of them, my daughter is there!"

> Maria looked eagerly through the window. "I can't believe we'll spend four full days together!"

From this we learn that Mrs. Bozek negotiated the "one week" proposal down to "four days".

> Helena jumped, "Right?! Oh I have to take you to the deserted house on the hilltop, if it's still there. Oh, and to the ice-cream parlor, you'll love it…"
>
> "But we must leave time for the biology assignment," Maria added.
>
> "Right." Helena smiled. "Plenty of time!"

The following paragraphs may be my favorite in the whole book.

> It's hard to point out a person's happiest moments in life; most of the moments blend together. But those four days on the beach were, for both Maria and Helena, some of the most memorable moments in their lifetime. For many years later the two would remember how Mrs. Goldstein bought them both matching bathing suits and Helena cheered ("Don't you just love the belt, Maria?"); how they ran up the hill to the deserted house and hid and scared one another (given Helena's many times there with her brothers, she was already a pro); how they ate ice-cream trying *all* the different flavors (until they got sick); how they sunbathed on the beach for hours (and Helena cursed each cloud that hid the sun); how Maria tried learning a few ballet moves from Helena (without much success, but with tons of laughter); how they gossiped on the beach about Reuben and Solomon ("I can't

believe you think Reuben is handsome!"); how they giggled into the night, chattering about Alexander, Roman, and the other boys in class (rating them according to new categories they came up with); how they took pictures with Reuben's new camera and made funny poses (which Helena masterfully directed) and how they took the biology sampling of barnacles' level of acidity in the tide pools (that is, *Maria* took the sampling while Helena mostly chattered).

When the four days were over, they cried in each other's arms at the train station.

The above paragraph was the longest of the whole book (by far).

I wanted to give a feeling of condensed time, one thing leading to another. A bit like someone talking without gasping for air in between sentences.

Mind you, my editors were not impressed.

But I was.

> Solomon was with them, taking the trip back in order to help in his father's accounting firm for a few weeks, or, according to Helena, to spend time with his darling Hannah. He was also to escort young Maria to the doorstep of her house, as Mrs. Goldstein promised Mrs. Bozek.
>
> Helena cried to Maria, "Promise you'll write to me as soon as you enter your house!"

"I promise. Promise you'll look into the math assignment, a little each day!"

"I promise."

Here we have the second "I promise". The last one will come at the end of the book. It will then feel a little bit familiar to us. And this feeling of familiarity is important for me as it brings a sense of coming back home, a sense of closure of a journey.

They hugged and whispered, "Friends forever."

"Forever!"

Solomon coughed. "Shall we?"

Helena nodded.

Maria climbed with him unto the train, "I'll write as soon as I get home! Please thank your parents again!"

Helena exclaimed, "I will! Have a pleasant journey!"

Helena walked on the platform, following them as they took their seats. They waved goodbye to each other on both sides of the window. The conductor blew the whistle. The doors closed.

Helena motioned with her lips, "I'll miss you!"

"I'll miss you too!"

Oh, this is so endearing for me. Soon the train will move. And not only will we say goodbye to the summer, but also (and that, the reader does not know)

– to this age. Next time we meet them, it will be some five years later.

> The train began moving. They waved to each other. Helena kept waving on the platform as the train left, leaving a trail of smoke above the platform as it slowly disappeared in the horizon.

The next chapter begins:

> The years passed.
>
> An older Maria and an older Helena now sat at the front of the class.
>
> Over the years their friendship had only grown stronger.
>
> Maria often spent holiday evenings with Helena's family, learning of their intricate traditions, deeds, and unique humor. Helena, too, didn't miss an opportunity to be with the Bozeks. She developed thick skin with Mrs. Bozek, learning that ultimately the matron only had good intentions. When they held hands before each meal, she prayed with them too. When they crossed their chests, she looked down and waited for them to finish.

Again, this is a preparation for one of the most suspenseful scenes, when she suddenly crosses herself in front of the soldier, in such a believable way, that it may have saved her life.

> But apart from such minute differences, they

were like sisters.

This is the first time I refer to them as "sisters". But time has passed.

> They had their ups and downs, too, like sisters.

> Helena was very much interested in the boys of the class, while Maria was always more reticent about the subject. Helena sometimes scolded Maria, explaining to her that life "Isn't all about books and exams!"

When the story initially developed in my head, I kept wanting to "insert" some episode in which the two are fighting because of a boy; perhaps a boy that Maria would love, but who would choose Helena instead.

But as the book unfolded, these scenes never made the cut.

I had to move on. I had to continue with the story. In my mind, Helena was on the train heading home, and Maria was on the platform, waiting for her. I knew I had to be short, brief, and let the events carry me forward.

Notice the subtle changes in their characters. Helena just scolded Maria, but...

> But Maria didn't spare Helena from her reprimands either, explaining to her, as if to a child, that she must "invest time in studying", and that "grades do matter!"

> Peculiarly enough, they slowly became more similar. Helena began to find some pleasure in

numbers, especially when it came to money.

This was a little frightening for me to write, because of the stigma about Jews loving money (in an unhealthy way).

But I knew that the real Helena Goldstein would eventually become an Accountant.

And in my mind's eye, she *did* in fact like money.

One of my editors suggested changing it to "finances". But I stuck with money. It was the "truth" of the character; and I tried to stick to it.

> Maria began to enjoy social circumstances. She was still very quiet, but some of the freedom that she learned from Helena began showing up in her.

> The other students referred to them as "Helena and Maria." Helena's name did come *first*, but Maria's name was never forgotten. They were invited together to parties. They were always seated together when going to a café or a performance.

Can you sense how rapidly we move through the years?

> They sometimes even completed each other's sentences, bursting into laughter and leaving everyone else a little envious of their close bond.

Now I needed a transition to explain what was happening around them:

> However, while their relationship seemed

unbreakable, the safe world around them began to crack.

Here I am trying my best to explain, without mentioning names, how Germany took over Poland:

> The army recruited many young men, trying to prepare for a severe blow from the growing army-nation across the borders.

> But the military, as much as it tried, soon lost to a brutal attack. Now, the new occupying army was beginning to change things.

> It started with laws that at first seem trivial, such as not allowing people of a certain heritage to wear fur, for example.

Can you see the hint? This prepares us for the escape scene.

> Then, large businesses, some of which were owned by members of Helena's extended family, were confiscated and nationalized.

In "extended family" I may mean "the Jewish people."

> Helena and Maria were not too worried. They were excited to finish school and begin University together, making sure they were both going to the same place. They fretted for months about what to study.

Here we will see how Helena has begun changing. This will give us a hint of what's going on in the country.

This is a little sad, as the war killed the dreams of

many. Helena represents here a whole generation of people who were affected very negatively by the war, even if they weren't persecuted:

> Helena thought of following the footsteps of her brothers.
>
> "But Helena," Maria retorted, "*Accounting?* Seriously? I cannot see you possibly…—"
>
> "Look," Helena sighed, "it's a good profession. It's a *stable* profession…"
>
> "You sound just like Mr. Goldstein!"
>
> Helena tried to smile, "Well, I guess, there's acting in it *too*, you see? With large clients one must know how to present and convince… And being a *woman* accountant is quite a big thing, Maria, there aren't many, and I can change that…"
>
> Maria sighed. "I'm not sure you'll be happy…"
>
> "Well," Helena said, calculating her words, "it is a *needed* profession. And now with the *war* and with things changing like that…"
>
> Maria understood that reasoning. The Goldsteins had now moved from their large house into a smaller apartment, trying to save their money and assets as much as possible. She could understand Helena, to an extent.

This bit of information is delivered to us just like that, by the way, without dedicating too much attention to it. The Goldsteins were forced to move to a smaller apartment.

"And you?" Helena asked, "Are you sure about Pharmaceutical sciences?"

Maria's eyes glowed, "It's the closest thing to being a doctor, you know, and I hope to help people that way…"

Helena smiled, "One day you'll invent the cure for some big disease, and you'll be world famous!"

Maria laughed, "If anyone will be famous out of the two of us, it'll be you!"

Without wasting time, we're now jumping to University. Notice the fast pace; more descriptions would slow things down.

The atmosphere at University was different than in High school. Sure, it was larger. But that was not it. There were some people who were adamant that Helena and people of her heritage should not be admitted into Universities.

Instead of telling about it, I now "show" it:

Maria argued with one of the new friends on campus, "Of course they should be admitted! And to *all* universities!"

"Are you a one of *them* or what?" the friend retorted, "Besides, there isn't enough place in all of the academies for all of those who seek higher education, so it's only reasonable…"

Maria tried arguing, but she slowly saw how the army's radio, the pamphlets and the posters were being successful in changing people's thoughts.

This is sad for me to write. But I tried to convey the changing atmosphere.

> People changed. Even people from her old class.

> One day she met her old friend Alexander on the street. She hadn't seen him for over a year. They spoke for several minutes. He then asked, "Are you still a friend of Helena?"

> "Of course! Why shouldn't I be?"

> Alexander looked around. "Well, it's not very *wise*, you know…"

Now we're going into the Bozeks. Many scenes in this part of the book will happen at their house.

> At home, Maria shared her frustration with her parents and siblings. Eddie was now in high school, and Sasha was soon finishing Elementary school. Maria complained all the time, "I just can't understand people's idiocy!"

> But things were tense at home as well. Her mother was now laid off from her work in the factory, as the occupying army was bringing its "own" people, and unemployment among factory workers was high due to the occupation of this new workforce. The occupying country's economy was booming, but Maria's beloved country was now carrying the burden.

> Her mother ceaselessly looked for employment, but to no avail. In the meantime, she was cleaning houses when she could, although the demand for cleaning ladies and maids was not high.
>
> They were all now dependent on Maria's father's income. The occupying army had fired many of the train's workers. There was the danger of Mr. Bozek being fired as well.

Enough with descriptions and backgrounds. We long for a scene. Finally, it begins:

> At the dinner table, Maria was exasperated. "I just can't stand seeing how people fall into this talk of hatred…"
>
> Eddie, who was usually quiet by the dinner table, said, "But there is *some* truth to it, isn't there?

Eddie is young, around seventeen. This is a very impressionable age, so naturally he is influenced by what's going on.

> [Eddie continues] What about that corrupt Minister? He was one of *them.*"
>
> Mr. Bozek suddenly slammed his fist on the table. They were all startled. "I will not," he muttered through his teeth, "let you… speak this way… in my household!"
>
> Eddie looked down.
>
> Mrs. Bozek went to the stove to get more potatoes.

Can you sense the tension? Not only is the father upset, but things are different. Also, notice the mentioning of "potatoes", signifying that food is limited; no mention of "meat" or "fish".

> "Father," said Maria, "there's no need to—"

> "What do you even know, Eddie," Mr. Bozek stood up, pushing his plate, "what do you even know about that Minister, huh? Don't believe everything you hear, son. I think it was set up!"

> Eddie sighed, "But Father, they found…"

This is important. Eddie is brainwashed.

Why is this so important?

Because we, as readers, long to see characters transform. We long for the characters to be two things: continual and changing.

Continual is rather obvious. When we see characters changing too fast, we feel like the character isn't well written, isn't believable.

But it's also boring when a character is rigid. The best moments of any drama are when a character changes.

We love to see Mrs. Bozek shifting from a harsh mother to a loving one.

And Eddie, too, will change. This makes the storyline more interesting.

Mr. Bozek, who we knew as a rather mild man, now shouts:

> "I'll have none of it!"

"Now-now," Mrs. Bozek said, "we should all finish eating. Sashinka, how was school? You had an exam, didn't you?"

"Yes, Mama. It went well."

"Good," Mrs. Bozek said and tried to smile.

Silence ensued. All eyes were fixed on the plates.

It was a short scene, but through it we get a sense of the times.

We'll now have a look at the following scene, which will be the last one we'll examine together in this commentary.

In the novel this is the time things get worse. Instead of writing about the process of how the Jews were moved into the ghetto, I had to create a scene to describe it happening:

One morning, as Maria left the house to University, she saw large posters stuck to walls everywhere. Reading them, her heart sank.

She hurried to the Accounting studies Faculty to find Helena. But she wasn't there. No one had seen her.

Maria, uncharacteristically, decided to skip University, and took the tram to the Goldstein's apartment.

As she climbed the stairs, she heard noise behind the door. They were talking and arguing. She rang the bell.

Silence ensued inside.

This shows us the time. Bell ringing, and the people becoming quiet. Suspense.

"It's me!" Maria called, "Maria, for Helena!"

"Maria!" Mrs. Goldstein opened the door.

Maria looked at them. Helena was there, along with Mr. Goldstein, Reuben, Solomon, and Solomon's fiancée, Hannah. Helena came over and hugged her. Her eyes were worried.

"Have you all," Maria asked, "seen the signs?"

I like the word "signs" because it has double meaning. Not only "the posters", but also "the direction" of things.

They nodded.

Helena sighed and walked over to the sofa. Maria followed her and sat down next to her, holding her hand.

Mr. Goldstein looked tired. Maria realized how old he had become.

Maria and Helena are now in University, most likely in their second or third year. The time is March 1941, and the ghetto is created. Mr. Goldstein has had the most difficult three years, seeing his business shrinking, his large family struggling, his house replaced by a small apartment. Sure he looks older. Much older.

The scene we were just thrown in is a very dramatic

one.

> He looked at Mrs. Goldstein. "I'm not leaving my parents! If your brother wants to go, let him go."

> Mrs. Goldstein fidgeted with her hands.

Do we remember Mrs. Goldstein ever fidgeting with her hands?! Things have changed. She is not as confident as she was before.

> "Bernie says nothing good will come out of it. And that the war won't be over any time soon. The occupying army, he said, is only advancing..."

> Maria murmured, "My father says the same."

Maria seems more confident than before, interrupting Mrs. Goldstein's speech.

> Everyone looked at her. She nodded, "He's been saying how the army is only sending more and more soldiers and equipment on the tracks all the time, advancing East and South."

> Mr. Goldstein sighed. "This too shall pass."

> Maria looked worriedly at Helena, whose eyes looked somewhat hollow. "You all," Maria said slowly, "should not move into the enclosure. I don't feel good about it."

> Solomon walked around the room. "Me neither. Father, it's insane! Now this enclosure, then what?"

Here's a hint to Solomon's character; he

understands what's going on. This makes his survival more understandable.

> Mr. Goldstein sighed. "Bernie says he's unable to procure any permits for my parents or," his voice grew stronger as he looked at Mrs. Goldstein, "or for your parents. I'm not leaving *anyone* behind! We are together in this!"

This was one of the most heartbreaking sentences in the book. It was difficult for me to write.

> Solomon stormed out of the room; Hannah got up and joined him.

Let us finish the commentary with this last sentence. Rarely do I use rhetorical questions in my writing, but this moment was one in which I felt it was necessary. It really puts us in the shoes of the characters, which is ultimately the goal of a good novel; to step into someone else's story.

> Maria realized she had walked into a sensitive situation. What would she have done had she been in their position?

FINAL WORDS

Wow. If you made it all the way here, then you and I have spent some time together! Most people do not show such great interest in the behind the scenes process of writing. I am honored that you chose to spend this time with me and to peek into my mind. As an author, my mind is often hot with ideas, scenes and plots. This was an opportunity for you to become as intimate as possible with my creative process. But there was also another opportunity here.

This was an opportunity for me, personally, to invite you in. I thank you for giving me this opportunity. Writing about the research and the writing process was also revealing for me personally. So again, thank you for serving as my conversation partner.

I hope to see you in one of my other novels, and hopefully even in person one day. Thank you for supporting my writing, for posting online reviews and for lending the book to friends and family. It is an honor for me to be able to partake in the ancient and noble art of storytelling.

Please do feel free to contact me, now that we've spent so much time together. I'm always available at kislevtv@gmail.com

Yours, Jonathan Kis-Lev

ACKNOWLEDGEMENTS

I would like to express my gratitude to the many people who saw me through this book; to all those who provided support, talked things over, read, wrote, offered comments, allowed me to quote their remarks and assisted in the editing, proofreading and design: Tania von-Ljeshk for the editing and the support; Doug Ellis Photography for making me look good (; Slava "Inkjet" Noh for the cover design; Jolanta Szewińska, Michael Burowski, Kristina Nowak, Agata Patyna, Natalia Hakenberg and Dariusz Zemła for your wonderful translations from Polish; Bill Tammeus and Rabbi Jacques Cukierkorn for your wonderful work in *They Were Just People: Stories of Rescue in Poland During the Holocaust;* Susan Leibtag for the encouragement; Marianne Azizi for your brilliant suggestions; Alissa Bickar for your encouragement and corrections; Debra Tischler for your compliments and thoughts; Jenny Hamby for reading and commenting; Kaya Tanani for always shining your light, Amy Kilgore for being there for me through the valley. This book could have not come to life without you.

I would like to thank my parents, Betty and Isaac, for

their love and constant encouragement over the years. This book is a tribute to the education you have given me.

I would like to thank my family: Steve, for believing in me; Romi for your love; Yoav, for your praise; Moria, for your wisdom; Elinoy, for your encouragement; Yanush, for your brotherhood in all times; Ilana and Shlomo Harel who were like second parents to me; Rachel and Michael Cherkis and the whole loving Cherkis family. Tal, Shirya and Moshe Bar-Ness; Samantha Silverman and Cyndi Silverman – I am blessed to call you all family.

I would like to thank my teachers: Geoffrey and Lilian Tindyebwa for countless of hours of listening and support; Peter and Alison Gardner for believing in me and encouraging me along the way. Louise Guenther for whispering courage to my ear. To all of those who left their mark of love on my soul: Edna Ziv-Av, Rachel Abramovitch, Rina Baruch, Cynthia Mackenzie, Daniela Kraemer; Sherry and Bryan Crowther, Gita Baikovitz, Michal Pinkwasser, Shifra Milshtein, and Arthur Kogan.

I would like to thank my mentors: Jack Canfield, for showing me a new kind of manhood; Shuli Ziv, for always telling the truth; Carol Kline, for your unconditional love; Ilan Hasson for bringing light in dark times; Avi Ben-Simhon for believing in me early on; Dudu Gerstein for encouraging me along the way with a knowing smile; Uvik Pundak, for always being there for me. To all of the inspiring figures in my life: Dr. Deb Sandella, Dr. Khursheed Sethna, Dr. Holly King, Alissa Bickar, Bryan Mannion, Gloria Belendez

Ramirez, Lotte Vesterli, Ather Alibahi, Rina Hafiz and Amy Cady

I would like to thank my heroes inspiring me from afar: Iyanla Vanzant for finding peace from broken pieces; Oprah Winfrey for always sharing what you know for sure; Joel Osteen for the inspiration; Les Brown for shooting for the moon; T. D. Jakes for showing perseverance; Elizabeth Gilbert for never ceasing; Glennon Doyle Melton for being a true warrior; Lizzie Velásquez for your beauty; Nick Vujicic for your devotion; Tyler Oakley for your authenticity; Sidney Poitier for teaching me to say 'no'; Neil Strauss for constantly seeking the Truth; and Whitney Thore for standing against shaming and also for doing *it* whichever way (;

To my inspiring peace warriors: Jean and Dr. Reed Holmes for adopting me into your nest while I was still a little chick; Sami Al Jundi and Jen Marlowe for the great inspiration and for bringing sunlight into my life!; Ian Knowles for teaching me how to walk my talk; Andrea Kross and the Kross family; Sarah Stooß and the Stooß family; Dina and Oded Gilad; Debbie Rimon Ansbacher; Lee Rimon and Yitshak De Lange, Riman Barakat, Cara Bereck, Michelle Gordon, Atheer Elobadi, Karym Barhum, Tom and Hind, Max Budovitch, Micah Hendler, Eliyahu Mcclean, Mark Gopin, Amer and Asmaa Merza, Tarek Kandakji, Adi Yekutieli, Adaya Utnik, Alisa Rubin Peled, Peter Berkowitz, Elliot Jager, Chaya Esther Pomeranz, David Keller, Anita Haviv-Horiner, Oded Rose, Idrees Mawassi, Dalia Bassa, Rutie Atzmon, Ronny Edry, Anat Marnin, Muhammad Elbou, Dana Wegman,

Omer Golan, Vardi Kahana, Rakefet Enoch, Avi Deul, Robi Damelin, Khalil Bader, Eyal Naveh, Uri Ayalon, Yael Ben-Horin Naot, Yosef Avi Yair Engel, Noa Karmon, Sivan Shani and Anchinalo Salomon and all the members of the President Young Leaders' Forum – you inspire me!

To all of my Pearson friends and UWC friends – I feel honored to call you my family.

To all of my Esperanto family – to mia E-o familio! Mi amas vin!

To my friends: Sharona Kramer and the Kramer family, Daniel Prag and the Prag family, Hila Bakman and the Bakman family, Netta Granit-Ohayon and the Granit family, Edna Zamir, Hani Oren June Moore, Judy Martorelli, Salah Assanoussi, Mimi Green, Divya Lalchandani, Tara Sirianni, Michelle Tessaro, Julia Darmon Abikzer, Pat Newman, Aleta and Faith Kelly, Ileana and Andrea Tarkan, Sari Cortes, Vanessa VandeNes-Parrish, Lisa Purcell-Rorick, Michael Mann, Jennifer Zorrilla, Yinon Tsarum, Judith and Stephan Beiner, Clifton McCracken, Bobbi and Yaki Vendriger, Gaby and Dr. Jacob Reiss, Abigail and Dan Chill, Ileana Bejarano, Saba Misaghian, Jana Morehouse, Carmen Braden, Amanda Leigh, Samuel Thrope, Amir Djalovski, Dvir Pariente, Chen Arad, Natan Voitenkov, Niki Kotsenko, Itai Froumin, Gadi BenMark, Uri Shafir, Kay Wilson, Daniel Beaudoin, Your constant encouragement is water to my inner garden. Thank you!

Last and not least: I beg forgiveness of all those who have been with me over the course of the years and whose names I have failed to mention.

Above all I want to thank my wife, Hallel, who supported and encouraged me in this magical journey. I love you!

OTHER JONATHAN KIS-LEV BOOKS

Readers have asked me to include a section at the end of the book and speak of my other books. This section is therefore dedicated to all of you.

I've always loved writing, since childhood. Writing as well as reading (can you guess I was a real nerd?). For me, books were a way to expand my world. To travel. To "wake up". In the little village I grew up in books were all I had. Television was okay. But books – they were magnificent…!

I therefore always wanted to be a writer. In my early twenties I won an encouraging prize from an Israeli magazine called *Bamahane* for a short story I wrote. Yet it was only in my late 20s that I felt inclined to write a whole book: I realized back then that many lessons which helped me in my life came from my own tradition, from Judaism, from the holidays, from customs and sayings, from my parent's and grandparent's wisdom.

I therefore sat down and wrote for over a year a book which I called "Chutzpah: Success Secrets from My Jewish Upbringing". This book is filled with stories, anecdotes and lessons from Judaism. I believe that it helps explain why the Jews, who comprise only a half of one percent of the world's population, receive some 20 percent of the Nobel Prizes. It has nothing to do with genes, but with a way of thinking about service, and purpose, and calling... It's a very personal book, I share much about my grandfather, what I learned in my Bar Mitzvah ceremony, what are the key lessons imparted to children in each holiday and how, in my opinion, they shape the children into adults who want to contribute to the world. The book is filled with many photos as well, covering 3000 years of Jewish thought – but doing so in a simple and captivating way. I'd love for you to read it.

I then proceeded to write a book about pain and loss and hope in the Middle East. Ever since age eleven I participated in numerous peace programs between Israelis and Palestinians. These personal encounters not only won me Arab friends but also taught me quite a few valuable lessons about peacemaking. It's an emotional book, which I guarantee will not only move you, but also make you *hopeful*. It portrays the movement for peace in both sides of the conflict, a movement about which you rarely hear in the news... This book is called "My Quest for Peace: One Israeli's Journey from Hatred to Peacemaking" and I'm super proud of it.

One of the key ways for me to work for peace has been my art. Since my early 20s I have been fortunate enough to be able to make a living from my art, painting large canvases and selling them in galleries around the world. Many artists have asked me over the years how I was able to achieve that level of success with my art. Between you and me – it wasn't really my talent. There are artists who are *way* better than I am. It was instead a set of *values* which I adopted from several older artist mentors I found. These values and valuable lessons made me successful in a field which most people affiliate with starving and suffering and being poor. Right?

Over the years, I shared these valuable lessons with many artists – not only with painters, but also with musicians, writers, and anyone interested. This led me to writing my third book, which I called "Masterwork: A Guide to All Artists on Turning from Amateurs into Masters". It's a beautiful book, filled with inspiring quotes by the history's greatest artists. I speak a lot in that book about the importance of finding a mentor and how to find one, of how originality isn't important but authenticity is *crucial*, and why the old myth of money spoiling the quality of art simply has to be thrown out the window. Many artists have reported to me that this book was a *game changer* for them, and I'm honored each time I hear that. "Masterwork" is an ideal gift to anyone you know who is into the arts or wishes to take their hobby to the next level.

My fourth book was not really a book. It was a journal. As part of my daily habits, I tried for many years to write five things each day for which I was grateful. This led me to design a journal that I would love to write in myself: each page has a date written on top. Five small lines are laid out for you to just jot down five things for which you're grateful. But the cream on the cake is a small picture frame for you to doodle in for few seconds. Those few seconds of doodling give a rather fun thing to do at the end of the day. At the bottom of the page I put an inspiring quote by people such as Gandhi or Oprah Winfrey or Eleanor Roosevelt - different quotes each day. For me, it's the perfect way to close the day before going to bed.

I called this journal "Gratitude Doodle: The One Minute a Day that Can Change Your Life." In it, there are a few chapters about the importance of gratitude, and an explanation as to how to use the journal to get the most out of it. I'm proud to say that there are whole families using it, each person in the family having their own copy. My wife Hallel and I also write in ours daily. It's a neat thing. It's one of the best ways I know to turn your life around and become more positive and grateful for all the good we forget to notice.

Another key way with which I bring joy to my life is affirmations. While for most of my adult life I doubted the benefits of reading out loud positive phrases, in recent years I nevertheless found that it... *works!* I compiled over two hundred of my favorite empowering affirmations, and designed a book that is the most aesthetically pleasing book I could have ever envisioned. Each affirmation is given its own unique botanical illustration (gorgeous!). Flowers, plants, and even birds and butterflies fill each page, and it's impossible to not feel tranquil when you read it.

This book is called "Better Thoughts, Better Life: Super Powerful Affirmations to Snap You Out of the Funk in Two Minutes or Less." In it I also thoroughly explain about how to rewire our minds. Research shows that most of our thoughts are negative. A trained mind can *shift* that. I am working on it myself, and I'm glad to report that due to using affirmations, my negative inner-chatter has dramatically subsided. I look at this book, "Better Thoughts, Better Life" as the best gift you can give *yourself*. It's simple, but true: when you improve your thoughts, you improve your life. That's what "Better Thoughts, Better Life" is all about.

I followed that book with one about choosing happiness. Over the years I learned that in each and every moment I have a choice. A simple choice: I can either focus on what doesn't work, or on what brings me pleasure in that moment. It's a simple exercise that can be overlooked due to its simplicity. But it is as powerful as gravity. Every other moment during the day I shift my thoughts from negative to positive ones. This enables me to be happier, as well as makes me more motivated to achieve more in life. It's really powerful. I wrote a small book about this habit and how to acquire it, and called it "Every Other Moment: A Manual on Choosing Happiness". I love it. It's a great reminder about the power we have at each given moment to change our lives for the better.

Being a rather positive guy, over the years I encouraged many friends around me to go for their dreams, to get that ideal job, to ask for a raise, to create a side business. I noticed how many of my women friends had a harder time boasting about their abilities than my friends who are men. This puzzled me for a long time, and it wasn't until five years ago, when I found myself with a highly capable woman as my partner, that I began questioning why that is. Why is that that women tend to be smarter than men (there's research to back this up) but at the same time don't toot their horns nearly as much? Why don't women negotiate their salaries like men do? And why do women attribute their success to luck while men attribute their success to their own doing?

This led me into writing a very emotional guide for

women called "Brag Woman Brag!" This book is my gift to my wife, my mother, my daughter, my sisters, and all of my friends who happen to be women. I quote many researches showing how there is a negative bias toward girls who lead. Boys who lead are called 'strong', while girls who lead are called 'bossy'. I take the reader through a very profound emotional journey to rediscover their power. It's my gift to women. And even the most skeptic of females, who have disliked the title, the cover, and the whole idea, write to me back saying "Wow." I cried reading some of the emails from readers of "Brag Woman Brag", simply because this book hits a nerve. I hope that in a few years the subject becomes irrelevant. But for now, it is one of the most significant topics each woman (and man) should explore. It's important for us ALL to own our power.

All of these books are available both electronically, as well as in print. You can find them easily online. Thank you for your support and interest!

Jonathan.

CONTACT

The author can be reached via e-mail at
s@kis-lev.com

Or on Facebook, Twitter and Instagram as:
KislevTV

ABOUT THE AUTHOR

Jonathan Kis-Lev is an Israeli peace activist, artist, a television personality and an author.

As a peace activist, Jonathan has been involved with several peace organizations in the Holy Land, beginning from age 11. In 2014 he co-founded the Hallelujah Dialogue Group in Jerusalem, along with Palestinian peace activist Riman Barakat.

As an artist, Kis-Lev developed his own unique style, dubbed as "Naïve Art". His paintings were shown in exhibitions around the world, most notably in Europe, Canada, and the United States. Kis-Lev also acted in numerous Israeli television shows, and co-hosted Israel's Balbalev Talk Show for teens.

As an author, Kis-Lev won the 2007 Bamahane Magazine Award for Short Story. He since then published five books: "Chutzpah: Success Secrets From My Jewish Upbringing"; "My Quest For Peace: One Israeli's Journey From Hatred To Peacemaking"; "Masterwork: A Guide To All Artists On Turning From Amateurs To Masters"; "Gratitude Doodle: The One Minute A Day That Can Change Your Life"; and "Better Thoughts Better Life: Super Powerful Affirmations To Snap You Out Of The Funk In Two Minutes Or Less".

Jonathan lives in Israel's Galilee, with his wife Hallel and their daughter Sarah. This is his eleventh book.

NOTES

[1] Elizabeth Gilbert: When a magical idea comes knocking, you have three options, The Irish Times, January 7, 2016

[2] Blaise van Hecke, *The Great Novella Search*, Busybird, Busybird Publishing, Jun 7, 2013

[3] Ibid.

[4] Steven King, *On Writing: A Memoir of the Craft*, Charles Scribner's Sons, 2000, p. 127

Made in the USA
San Bernardino, CA
20 June 2018